MORNA'S LEGACY CHRISTMAS NOVELLA COLLECTION

BETHANY CLAIRE

Editor for A Conall Christmas: Dee Pace
Editor for A McMillan Christmas & Morna's Magic & Mistletoe: Dj Hendrickson

Available in eBook, Paperback & Hardback

eBook ISBN: 978-1-947731-55-4
Paperback ISBN: 978-1-947731-57-8
Hardback ISBN: 978-1-947731-56-1

http://www.bethanyclaire.com

PREFACE

WHAT YOU NEED TO KNOW: A BRIEF INTRODUCTION TO THIS COLLECTION

Dear Readers,

Christmas is my favorite time of year, so it only seemed natural that Christmas stories would work their way into Morna's world. While these novellas are complete stories, they are a part of a larger series. In order to make sure that you get maximum enjoyment out of these books, I wanted to give you a brief introduction to each story. Don't worry though, I won't give any spoilers in case you want to go back and read the books surrounding these novellas after you finish.

A Conall Christmas:

This story is all about Adelle, the mother of the heroine in my first book, *Love Beyond Time*. She's a modern lady in every way—a blunt, young-at-heart Mom who would do anything for her daughter's happiness—even travel through time to live hundreds of years in the past. Her archaeological work was the catalyst that sent her daughter into the past, and she happily followed along after her by the end of the first book. But she's a bit out of place in the seventeenth century and needed more than just a life of leisure around the castle. I knew she needed her own HEA (Happily Ever After) from the start. In this book, I was able to give her just that.

A McMillan Christmas:

This book was a bit of a departure for me, but it was so much fun to write. In this book, both our hero and heroine are brand new characters, so you won't have missed anything if you are picking up this collection before reading the other books. Basically, all you need to know about this one is that you'll be introduced to several old friends throughout the book, and the castle featured in this story—McMillan Castle—is at the center of Book 3, *Love Beyond Hope.*

Morna's Magic & Mistletoe:

I can honestly say that I had more fun writing this story than any story to date. Kenna and Malcolm's story just came to me fully formed. All I had to do was sit down and let their story flow through me. Kenna is first introduced in Book 3, *Love Beyond Hope.* She is the mother of two of my heroes—Baodan and Eoghanan. She's a fighter—someone who has lost a lot but never let any of her grief kill her spirit. Her happy ending has been a long time coming. It was my honor to give it to her in this story.

I hope you love these stories and let yourself get transported to Scotland for a very magical Christmas. Be sure to check out the book list at the back of the book to see any books that you may have missed in the series.

vii

Bethany

A CONALL CHRISTMAS

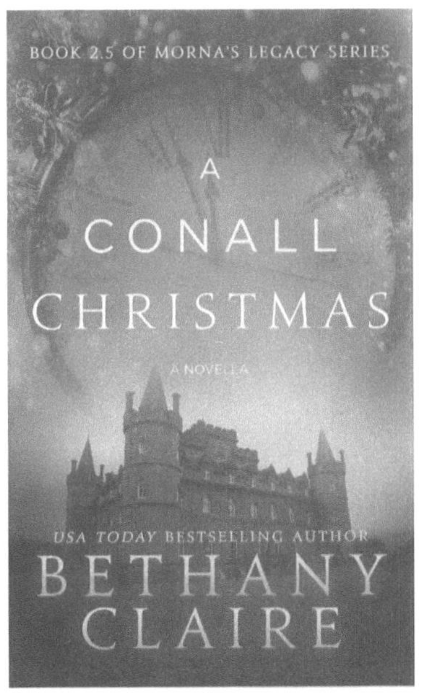

CHAPTER 1

onall Castle, Scotland - December 1646

here's nothing quite like the soft thump against your palm as you press it against the swollen belly of pregnancy, allowing the small infant tucked safely away in its mother's womb to kick at the inside of your hand. The surreal experience filled me with joy as I pressed my hands flush against my daughter's stomach, smiling widely as tears brimmed against my eyes. I'd felt the child's movement more than once, but it didn't matter. I seemed to have the same reaction every time. My baby's baby had completely captured my heart, even if it would still be weeks before I would know she could be safely delivered without the conveniences of technology and medicine from our own time.

"All right, Mom. I'm going to step away from you now. You simply cannot keep your hands glued to my stomach every moment of every day."

I smiled as Bri stepped away, grabbing the end of the blanket as she tossed the other end in my direction, signaling at me to help fold it. "Oh, but I wish that I could. I think the babe moves even more than you did, dear, and you were quite active."

"Really? Well, I sincerely apologize. I'm beginning to feel miserable."

As if to emphasize her point, she collapsed onto her freshly made bed and threw her hands up over her head as far as her dress would allow. I kicked off my own shoes, hiking up my dress as I sat crisscrossed on the end, pulling her feet into my lap and removing her shoes so I could massage her swollen and, what were most-assuredly sore, feet.

She sighed as I rubbed her, wiggling her toes as I squeezed them, and I suddenly saw her for the little girl she'd once been. She was more than ready and capable of taking care of a child, but I found it hard to believe she'd grown so quickly, not to mention that I was old enough to be a grandmother.

I continued to knead the arches of her feet and heels until she drifted. Once she snored lightly, I carefully lifted her legs so I could scoot out from under them and crawled off the bed as gently as I could. I walked to the fireplace, poking the wood until the flame took a firm root over the logs once more. I curled into a small wooden chair that sat before it as I gazed into the flames before glancing about the room.

Every inch of the castle oozed magic. It could be sensed in the air. As I sat with the fire warming my shoeless toes, I could almost feel Morna's eyes watching over us across the centuries.

No surprise really. I imagined it only made sense that magic be palpable throughout the castle. It had, after all, brought Bri and me both to live in this place and century when we'd been born hundreds of years in the future.

Before I traveled into the past, I'd been an archaeologist who specialized in Celtic finds and history. The Conall Clan was my specialty, the last twenty plus years of my life spent trying to find and solve the mystery behind who'd murdered them in December of 1645.

My continuing efforts to solve this mystery brought my daughter and me to the ruins of Conall Castle only one year ago, in the year 2013. I'd pestered her until she'd agreed to accompany me, not knowing that a spell cast by a beloved Conall ancestor, Morna, would rip her from our time and bring her into the past to live with the Conalls right before the devastating massacre.

Thankfully, Bri was meant to be here. Not only did she help them change the course of history by stopping the massacre, but she also fell in love with the man of her dreams, Conall Castle's new laird, Eoin. I'd been unwilling to be separated from my daughter, no matter how happy for her I was, and so when Bri decided to stay in this time, I used Morna's spell to travel back myself.

The thrill of an archaeologist's life is to be living with the very people she's devoted so much of her life to learn about. I now lived in a dream that was only slowly becoming reality. And, on top of it all, I would soon become a grandma.

I was as happy as I'd ever been, with only one lingering thought keeping me from overwhelming happiness. I'd always been social. I liked to date. I liked to flirt. While it had become more difficult to find a date with someone my age even in my present day time, I was certain that in the seventeenth century, men considered me hopelessly over-the-hill with one foot deep into the grave.

I would most likely spend the rest of my days alone. Something I'd realized shortly after arriving in this time, but a fact of life that took me a bit longer to accept than I had hoped.

No matter. I had much to be thankful for. Christmas time, my favorite time of the year, had arrived. I was anxious to discuss preparations for the holiday with Bri. So when I saw her stir, I stood from my place by the fire and went to stand by her side.

"What?" I knew the pitch of my voice went too high, almost squeaky, but if that old bat thought she could stifle our Christmas, she had another think coming.

"Mom, is it really that big of a deal? We didn't even notice it last year."

The hormones were messing with her head. Bri loved Christmas as much I did. I couldn't imagine how she seemed to be so fine with skipping Christmas. "Yes, it's that big of a deal! Of course you didn't notice it last year. You were all too busy trying to stop the attack on the castle. What's Mary's problem with Christmas?"

I didn't miss Bri's eyes roll before she answered my question. "She likes Christmas very much. She loves cooking. You know that. It's only that after Eoin's mother passed away, Christmas became less of an event as the years went on. Not to mention, it's been outlawed in Scotland for the last four decades."

My eyes mimicked my daughter's roll. "Darling, you know as well as I do that Christmas continued to be celebrated, just a little more quietly. Besides, who is there to enforce it when your husband is laird?"

"Well...no one really. Look, I love Christmas, but I've no desire to put Mary into more of a tizzy than she stays in constantly. If you can get her to agree to it, then I will be the first to jump on the Christmas bandwagon with you."

"Oh, I'll get her to agree. As much as she likes to fight it, I'm Mary's closest friend, and she's all bark anyhow. Go and get Eoin. While I know she will eventually get on board, we may need him to intervene in the argument she's sure to put up."

Bri nodded and laughed as I turned and left her bedchamber. It was no laughing matter. Whether the child was present or not, my first grandbaby would have a Christmas to rival any other. I would make certain of it.

CHAPTER 2

hree Days Ride North of Conall Castle

Snow built outside his window, and his creaky joints told him a bad storm brewed. Still, he left his home at this time every year. He'd not missed his trip to her gravesite once in the twenty-plus years since his beloved had passed away. He did not intend to let the snow deter his plans.

Hew walked around his small home, tidying up before his journey south. He lived alone, far away from the nearest village. He'd not seen another soul in months and that was just as he would have it. He knew his shyness held him back. It had been a wonder that he ever married at all.

He'd not expected it, the day his sister's best friend, Mae, had approached him while he chopped wood for the fire at the back of his home, grabbing his face and kissing him squarely on the mouth. He'd been a young lad then and that kiss had changed his life. Hew grew up with Mae constantly in their family's home. Mae and his sister were inseparable. While he silently admired her for years, he was far too shy to ever express the way his heart beat for her.

That night so many years ago, he'd been able to feel her watching him but did not turn to greet her, his heart pounding uncomfortably just at the nearness of her. He continued to swing his ax down into the blocks, swiftly chopping the wood into two pieces. Her hand on the lower part of his back caused him to jump, nicking the edge of the block of wood before he threw his ax to the ground and whirled to face her.

"Mae, ye startled me, lass. Ye should be inside. 'Tis far too cold for ye to be out of doors." He could remember every word spoken between them, a scene held captive forever in his mind.

She'd touched his arm then, smiling as she shook her head, dismissing his worry. "Hew, if 'tis not too cold for ye to be out here, then I doona think I shall freeze to death either. Did ye know that I shall turn ten and eight tomorrow?"

He'd stepped away from her, too many nerves for him to stand there with her hand lying on his arm. "Nay, lass. I dinna know. I shall make ye something. Carve ye a piece of jewelry perhaps?" He didn't know what to say to her—never did.

"I would like that verra much, but that isna why I mentioned it to ye."

He'd gathered the freshly chopped logs of wood into his hands, desperate to keep busy in her presence. "Nay? Why did ye then?"

He stilled when she moved to stand in front of him, blocking his path. "Will ye set all that down for only a moment, Hew? I'm trying to talk to ye if ye canna tell."

He reddened and obeyed. "Aye, lass. Why doona we sit for a moment?"

They'd moved to the pile of wood, stacked just high enough to serve as the perfect seat. He trembled as she unexpectedly grabbed his hands, but he swallowed his nerves and forced himself not to flinch away from her touch. "What is it, lass?"

"As I just told ye, I shall be ten and eight tomorrow, and I doona wish to become an old maid."

Hew couldn't still the twitch of his hand as he realized where she headed with her words. "Nay, lass, I doona believe ye will. There are many lads who would eagerly wed ye."

"Aye, I doona believe that I shall become an old maid, either. Still, most my age are already married. While yer sister is several years older than me, she was married at ten and seven. And ye are right, many lads would be willing to wed me, but I am not so eager to marry them."

"Why is that, lass? Is there no one that catches yer fancy?" It was too much for Hew to wish that Mae would answer as he wished, but to his everlasting shock, she had.

"Aye, there is one, and I willna allow him to behave as if he doesna care for me as much as I care for him a moment longer."

His heart began to beat so quickly he feared she could feel its quick pulse in his fingertips. Though a cold night, sweat beaded freely on his brow. "Is that so, lass? And who is this lad ye speak of?"

"If ye doona know, ye are as daft as yer sister seems to think ye are."

She paused and reached in quickly to kiss him. He seemed so stunned, she pulled away before he could react and kiss her properly. "Nay, lass. Ye canna mean it. 'Tis some other lad that ye mean and ye are simply using me for practice, aye?"

She laughed before kissing him once more. This time he pulled her close as she melted against him. Breathlessly, she pulled away from him so she could whisper into his ear. "Nay, Hew, there is none other but ye. There never has been. Ye are going to marry me."

He smiled against her cheek, her confidence somehow diminishing his shyness. "If ye insist, lass."

"Aye, I do."

"And what shall ye do with me once we are married?" His hands found their way to her hair, and he cradled her against his chest, pulling her into a tight embrace.

"We shall move north, find a piece of land for only the two of us, and together we shall build a home where we will spend all of our days together."

They married within a fortnight and had done just as Mae wished, moving north and building a home for the two of them, isolated from the rest of humanity. Five years flew by in a haze of love where they spent every moment at each other's side.

Eventually, they planned a trip to visit their families in Conall territory, but they left in winter and on their journey, Mae fell ill. She fought hard, but the sickness was too much. She died only two days after they arrived. He'd chosen to bury her close to there, in the land in which she'd grown up. With a broken heart, he returned to their home alone.

Hew saddled his horse, pushing away the memories of his past as he headed out into the storm. It had been many years since Mae passed and, while he would feel her absence always, his heart had now healed as much as it ever could from such a wrenching loss.

He continued to make the trip to her grave on the anniversary of her death to pay his respects, to speak to her, to remind himself that once in his life he had not been so completely alone.

CHAPTER 3

onall Castle

tried to make as much noise as I could as I made my way downstairs into the castle's kitchen where I was certain Mary would be busily working away on the evening meal. She knew it was me coming instantly.

"Adelle, ye doona always have to make such noise when ye move about. Come in here and help me plate the food."

I knew I didn't move more loudly than anyone else in the castle, but Mary was constantly looking for something to nag me about so I obliged her by being purposely obnoxious in her presence.

In many ways, Mary was the castle's most important resident. She'd worked in the castle for nearly forty years and everyone, especially Eoin and his brother Arran, accepted the cook and head maid as the castle's true boss. She ran the castle like the captain of a ship. Nothing happened within the walls without her notice or approval.

I stuck my head into the kitchen, smiling as I reached up into the shelf just out of her reach to grab the plates. I thought it best to test her mood before immediately jumping into what I wanted to discuss with her. "How are you today, Mary?"

Mary motioned at me to lay out the plates before she responded. "Ach, I'm fine. 'Tis a bonny day. I enjoy the snowfall, but I feel a bit of guilt for loving it so. 'Tis sure to mean more work for Kip in the stables to keep the horses warm."

"Oh, don't feel guilty about enjoying anything, Mary. You know that Eoin and Arran will both do whatever they need to so that Kip's load in the stables is not more than he can handle. I have a wonderful idea that I think we should all do together before the snow outside gathers too much."

"What might that be?"

"I think we should all go out and find a tree to cut down for Christmas." I looked down at the plates, busying my hands as I awaited her reaction. Perhaps if I played it off as if I didn't know her thoughts on the matter, she would be more willing to discuss it.

I glanced up as Mary turned away to grab the bread so that she could break it into pieces. "Nay, I'm afraid 'tis not possible. Lovely thought though."

Mary had never in the year that I'd known her referred to anything I'd ever said as "lovely". I was unsure of how to respond. "Umm...why 'tis not possible?"

She didn't appreciate my attempt at an accent. "Well, Christmas is no longer openly celebrated in Scotland and, after Elspeth passed away, Alasdair dinna find the joy in the season he once did. The two lads dinna grow up with it being a grand celebration."

"Do you not enjoy Christmas yourself, Mary?" Eoin and Arran's history with Christmas seemed irrelevant. Alasdair had been dead for over a year, and I couldn't see either of the men having a problem with the festivities. Their mother had died when they were very young. While Christmas might have brought up painful memories for their father, it would not have the same effect on either of them.

Mary shook her head and returned to help me with the plating of our meal. "Nay, lass. I enjoyed Christmas verra much when I was a young girl. My brother always made me the most beautiful presents. He was quite the craftsman."

"Mary." Her words surprised me. "I didn't know you had a brother. Is he...is he still living?"

"Aye lass, verra much so, but I doona see him often. He lives far away from here and is a bit shy. Always had a difficult time interacting with others. Only certain people had the ability to draw him out."

She looked down as if saddened by some memory. I interrupted her thoughts to try and lift the mood. "Are you certain he's related to you? How could one sibling end up so shy while the other does nothing but talk?"

Mary rewarded me with a quick whack on the arm as she chuckled and resumed her work in the kitchen. "Aye, I'm certain. I suppose he was shy because I never gave him much of a chance to speak. As he grew, he simply grew accustomed to his own silence."

I couldn't help but wonder about Mary's brother, about her family, and what she would have been like as a child. I felt close to my dear friend now, but I honestly knew very little about her. She was always too busy caring for everyone else that I was afraid we all often forgot about the woman within her. I shook my head, remembering my reason for speaking with her. "You have very cleverly changed the subject, Mary. If you enjoy Christmas, then why are you against us celebrating it? I'm sure you have some wonderful traditions you could share with us, and Bri and I could share ours as well."

Mary tried to hide the smile that pulled at the corners of her mouth, but I could sense her resolve dropping.

"I'll not say that it wouldna be a pleasant time. I just doona wish to upset the laddies if 'tis something that should bring up memories of their parents."

A deep voice in the doorway caused us both to turn our heads. I smiled as Eoin and Bri poked their heads into the kitchen. Eoin's strong hands rested gently on Bri's shoulders as she laid the back of her head lovingly into his chest. "It will do no such thing, Mary. Ma made Yuletide a spectacle and, while Da did try, it wasna the same after she passed. I think 'tis far past time for us to restore the celebrations to their former glory."

Mary let her smile pull free now, and I could see that the idea excited her as well.

"If that is what ye want, my dear lad, then I shall be as pleased as anyone. I only dinna want to upset ye or Arran."

Eoin moved across the room, each step accentuating the strength of his body, his hair even darker than Bri's and his eyes the color of obsidian glass. My grandchild was going to be beautiful.

He wrapped his arm around Mary, tucking her into the nook of his arm before bending to kiss her on the cheek. "Aye, I know. Ye are always watching out for us, and I love ye for it, Mary."

He released her and stepped away to regard the both of us. "Do ye think the two of ye can work together to make the preparations?"

I smiled, bobbing my head up and down enthusiastically. "Of course we can." I could sense that Mary was about to intercede with some jab as to how difficult it would be for her to put up with me so I quickly spoke again, not allowing her the opportunity. "Do we have permission to do whatever we wish?" I already had a grand idea, but I didn't want to mention it to anyone before I'd convinced Mary.

Eoin grinned and glanced cautiously at Bri. "I feel that I may come to regret this but aye, I shall not tell either of ye lassies what to do. It would be wrong of me to do so, and it would be a fruitless effort anyway."

"Absolutely right." I scooted over and draped an arm around Mary's shoulder. She glared up at me in response. "Don't you two worry. Mary and I are going to make certain this Christmas is the most magnificent Conall Castle has ever seen."

"Ye have lost yer mind if ye believe for one moment that I would do such a foolish thing and follow ye into that God-forsaken time that ye came from!"

I crossed my arms and sat down on the steps leading down into the castle's basement and spell room while I listened to Mary rant. It was impossible for her first reaction to anything that came out of my mouth to be a positive one.

"What is so important that ye would feel the need to do such a thing, Adelle? I knew ye were daft but gracious, lass, 'tis a horrible idea. What if we were unable to return home? I doona think I could stand to spend one day there."

Eventually, I interceded to stop the top of her head from exploding. "Calm down, Mary. Morna's spells are reliable. Now that we know she lives in the inn near the castle, we will go straight there to stay with her. You don't even have to go into Edinburgh with me if you don't wish. Wouldn't you like to see Morna again?"

Mary's face changed from red to white much too quickly. I was afraid I was about to have to pick her up off the ground. She extended a shaky hand in my direction, letting it hang in front of my face at eye level. "Do ye see what ye do to me? Ye have me so restless, I shall not stop shaking for days. Nay, I doona wish to see Morna again. The lass was a dear friend, but I spent the last twenty-five years believing her dead. 'Tis where the dead should stay. Good and buried."

Breathless, she plopped down next to me. I reached out to pat her on the back but quickly retracted my hand in response to the daggers she shot toward me with her gray eyes. "She was never dead, Mary. She just moved on to a different time is all. I'm sure she would love to see you."

"Nay, I doona expect she wishes to see me that much. If she did, could she not just come here herself to visit?"

I shook my head, regretting the path I'd led our conversation. I didn't know enough about Morna or her abilities to speak of her so freely. "Nevermind Morna. Don't go for her. Go for me. Surely you wouldn't want me to travel there alone?"

I was none too worried about going alone. I'd lived my entire life for the most part alone. It would be no problem for me to make the journey to my own time without her, but the temptation of watching rigid, uptight Mary in present day was a joy I very much wanted to gift to myself. It would be the best Christmas present I could ask for.

"I doona give two twiddles whether ye go alone. I hope that ye go and get stuck there. Can ye not tell by now that I'm not that fond of ye?"

I rolled my eyes at her jab. I spent most of every day at her side. If she truly didn't enjoy my company, I knew her well enough to know that she wouldn't put up with my presence. "Oh hush, Mary. If you're really so afraid to go along, that's all you had to say. I wouldn't have pressed you further. It's not good for someone your age to upset yourself with the stress of fear." I winked at her. Mary was really only a few years older than me.

Mary stood abruptly and stomped her foot like a small child. "'Tis not that I'm frightened, only that ye are foolish to do so."

"I'll make you a deal, Mary. If you go, I'll help you with whatever chore you wish for the next month."

Mary hated, more than anything, beating the bed linens. I could already see her wrestling with such a temptation in the way her eyes darted back and forth, calculating whatever prevented her from saying yes. Eventually her eyes stopped moving, and I could tell she intended to speak. "Aye, fine, but I willna wear breeches that go up between my legs. I shall stay in my dress the whole time, or I will not agree to go with ye."

I smiled. "Deal. You will look ridiculous, but it doesn't matter to me one bit as long as you come. Let's go tell Bri and then be on our way."

Present Day

*B*ri had warned me that with the castle no longer being the ruins I had once known it as in present time, it had become a popular attraction with visiting tourists. Still, I had underestimated the number of people who would be in attendance once we arrived in the twenty-first century.

Mary and I had been able to make it out of the roped-off basement undetected, but the stares Mary's clothing garnered as we made our way out were enough to rival an eight-legged horse at a zoo. Luckily, Mary remained so bug-eyed at everything she saw that she remained completely oblivious to the pointing fingers and stares.

Once outside, we began the several miles walk to the inn. Mary spoke for the first time. "Excuse my language, Adelle, but holy bugger. My head hurts something awful. I knew that it would from witnessing both Bri and yerself come through, but I dinna expect it to hurt quite so bad."

I scrunched my nose up guiltily. "Yes, I'm sorry. Morna will have something we can take, I'm certain. What do you think so far?"

"Well, I'm surprised to find that the castle looks much the same, but 'tis lighted much more and oddly."

"Yes, electricity is amazing. All homes and buildings have it."

"Is that so? As we walk along this path, it doesna look so different."

She was right, besides the gravel road leading to the castle, this part of Scotland was still very much untouched by the conveniences of modern times. "Yes, unless you decide to accompany me into Edinburgh, your shocks will be less than they could be. Morna's home will have many things to surprise you, but nothing like the city."

"Aye, well I canna say that I doona enjoy the adventure of it. Perhaps I will join ye when ye leave for the city."

We walked in silence until we arrived at Jerry and Morna's, and I was none too surprised to find both of them waiting for us at the front door.

"Ach, Mary! I canna believe it! I nearly spit up my food when my vision showed me yesterday morning that ye two lassies were on yer way to see us."

Morna charged Mary, who blanched at the shock of laying eyes on the dear friend she'd thought lost forever. She pulled the cook into a tight embrace.

Jerry made his way over to me, wrapping his rail-thin arms around my neck. "Adelle, it is lovely to see ye again, lass."

"You as well, Jerry. So Morna saw us coming?"

Morna's voice answered me as she led Mary toward us, their arms laced with one another. "Aye, I did, and I've not been so pleased by a vision in some time. I'm also thrilled to know that our dear Bri is with child, is she not?"

"Yes, and she's close to popping. Only a few more weeks, and the child will make its appearance. I simply cannot wait." I smiled, leaning in to give Morna my hug of greeting.

Morna waved us inside her home before speaking again. "I'm sure 'tis true, lass. I have something I wish for ye to take back with ye. It's an herbal potion I've mixed. 'Twill help her greatly with the pains of labor."

"Oh, thank you so much. I've been worrying myself sick thinking about the ordeal she must go through. I thought I was going to die when I gave birth to Bri, and I let them drug me up with every medicine they had."

Morna laughed. As we made our way into the sitting room, Mary's eyes bulging at every odd trinket, Morna pointed at a box in the corner, and tears immediately swelled in my eyes.

"I also retrieved something else for ye, lass."

I had to keep from running toward the large box of ornaments, each a special memory of the Christmases Bri and I spent together while she was growing up. Each year our collection grew, and each new ornament was a new, precious memory. "Morna!" I hadn't a clue how to express my gratitude.

"'Tis what ye really wanted, is it not?"

I nodded in disbelief. "Yes, but it never crossed my mind that I would actually be able to get them. I just planned to go into Edinburgh and buy a brand new set. All of this was in the States, at Bri's old place. How did you...how did you do this?"

She laughed heartily. "Did I not just make it possible for the two of ye to come here from hundreds of years in the past? Compared to that, 'twas a simple task to move these to us. Look in the other box, I also included a few other things I could sense were precious to ye."

My hands trembled with excitement as I moved to open the lid of the next box. I opened it to find an old CD player that could be operated with large DD batteries, packs and packs of replacement batteries, and our entire collection of Christmas music. Bri's baby blanket, knitted by my own mother, gently padded the Christmas items. Tears fell freely at the sight of it. "Oh my God, Morna. Are you a mind reader as well?"

Jerry interjected playfully. "Aye, she is lass and 'tis damned annoying. I canna silently begrudge her anything without her finding out about it and charming me into forgiving her."

Morna laughed and leaned gently into her husband. "I am not that good at it, but ye are quite open with yer thoughts. 'Twas easy to see the things ye desired most from your trip here."

She was spot on. There was nothing more that I wished to get. Everything I thought I would be unable to find was here. As far as I was concerned, we could make our way back to the castle immediately. But as I glanced over to see Mary gleefully playing with the running water in the kitchen, I thought better of suggesting we leave right away. "I cannot thank you enough, Morna. There's no need for me to make a trip into the city now, but would it be all right with you if we stay here tonight and leave in the morning?"

"Of course, lass. I wouldna have it any other way. I'm anxious to catch up with Mary, and I canna wait to hear her cries of excitement when we allow her to take a hot shower."

CHAPTER 5

Near Conall Castle - 1646

The wind blew icy snow roughly into his face, and Hew could barely see the path in front of him. His fingers and nose burned from the pain of the harsh wind and bitter cold. With each step forward, his horse slowed his pace.

He didn't wish to stop for the night. He was so very close to the end of his journey, but he knew that his four-legged companion would not be able to go much further. He groaned inwardly at the thought of where he knew he must stop—Conall Castle—his sister's place of residence. The castle was so close that he could make it out in the distance, its grandness evident even through the storm.

Hew knew it had been far too long since he'd paid a visit to Mary, nearly ten years by his count, possibly longer. He missed her, but he knew she would treat his arrival as a celebration. The thought of such attention caused him to cringe inwardly.

Still, there was hardly another choice. Bracing himself for the torture he knew was about to ensue, he leaned down close to Greggory's ear, whispering words of encouragement as he nudged the old horse to the right. "Just a wee bit further, lad. There shall be a fine stable and blankets to keep ye warm just ahead. I'm sorry to have taken ye out in such a storm. I shall see ye well fed tonight, old fellow."

F lames flickered in the stables, so Hew knew before he approached that someone was still at work within them. They were most likely preparing the horses for the evening, making sure they were properly tended to in the cold weather.

He rode straight into the stables without seeking permission. He knew enough of the Conalls' generosity to know that they would not protest to anyone seeking shelter for their horse on such a night.

Hew dismounted, quickly brushing the snow off of Greggory's coat, jumping at the sound of the voice in the stall at the end. "What sort of a fool would travel in this weather? 'Tis not so good for yer horse, sir. What be yer name?"

Hew's cheeks suddenly warmed. For a moment, he feared he would be unable to utter a word. He'd not spoken to another person in many moons. He swallowed, steeling himself and spoke boldly. "The fool's name is Hew. I apologize for the intrusion, but I must ask yer permission to allow me and my horse to rest here for the night. The poor lad willna be able to go much further."

A strong lad as tall as him, with long, shaggy blond hair stepped out of the stall and smiled as he walked toward him. He knew the man must be the youngest Conall brother, Arran, but the lad had been much younger the last Hew had seen him.

"Aye, of course ye can. It would be a wretched man to turn away anyone in a storm such as this."

Hew continued to rub the sleeves of his covering over his

horse's coat, doing his best to dry the animal. "Thank ye, sir. I shall help ye in the cleaning of the stables come morning in payment for yer kindness. Ye are Arran, are ye not?"

Arran reached for a blanket draped over the doors of one of the stalls and moved to help him in his efforts. "Nay, that willna be necessary. Aye, I am Arran. Should I know ye, sir?"

Hew shook his head as they worked alongside each other, warming and drying the beast. "Nay, I doona expect that ye would remember me, but I believe ye know my sister, Mary. Is she still in service to yer family?"

The strapping lad next to him patted the horse gently on the backside before casting a rather surprised expression in his direction. "Nay, ye canna mean it? Ye're Mary's brother? Well, 'tis a pleasure to meet ye. And aye, we know Mary well, but I wouldna say she is in our service. This castle is more hers than my brother's."

Hew laughed. It seemed his sister had changed little over the years. "Aye, lad, that sounds verra much like she would have it. I dread the fuss she shall make over my arrival, but I feel I must make my presence here known to her. Where can I find her?"

Arran fidgeted uncomfortably. For a moment Hew worried that perhaps his sister was unwell, but the lad recovered quickly. "Well, it seems that she herself has gone on a bit of a journey, but doona worry about the weather, we know that she is quite safe and out of the storm. I shall let her explain to ye where it is that she has gone once she returns."

Hew didn't understand what the lad meant, but he wasn't disappointed to learn that he would be able to rest before reuniting with his sister. "Ah, well, I'm certain she will be pleased to tell me all about it. She used to talk a great deal. I doona imagine that has changed."

Arran laughed and motioned at him to lead his horse into one of the empty stalls. "Nay, sir, she hasna changed. She's talked a lot for all the time that I've known her. Now, let us get yer horse settled, and ye shall follow me inside so that ye can have a room of yer own."

Hew stiffened and stopped moving forward. He would not be comfortable staying inside the castle. It was not where he belonged. He'd rather stay in the stables, with only the horses for company. "Nay, lad, I shall stay here with the horses. It would not be proper for me to accompany ye inside."

Arran insisted. "Nay proper me arse. I willna be letting ye stay out here in this weather. If Mary learned I'd done so, she'd kill me herself, I'm certain."

Hew didn't wish to be impolite to his host, but it was something he knew he had to insist on. He wouldn't sleep a wink in the presence of so many people. "I doona wish to offend ye, lad, but I simply canna stay in the castle. If ye willna allow me to remain out here, I'm afraid that Greggory and I will have to be on our way and take our chance with the snow."

Guilt filled Hew at the look of shock on Arran's face. If only the thought of company didn't paralyze him so.

"Nay, please doona leave in this storm. Mary would rather me allow ye to sleep in the stables, I'm certain. But perhaps, I can provide ye with something a little more comfortable than stable floors."

"Truly, lad, 'tis no trouble for me to stay here. I've slept in worse many times before."

Arran shook his head as he draped Hew's horse with coverings. "Just listen to me before ye say nay to it. We have a cottage not far from here. 'Tis empty, no one stays there, and ye are welcome to stay there if ye wish. Ye can build ye a fire, and there is a proper bed. Please, sir, at least stay there."

Hew couldn't deny how pleasurable a warm fire and a soft bed sounded to him. As long as it was truly separate from the castle as the lad said, he thought he could find rest for the night there. "Aye, lad. I shall gladly stay in yer cottage. I'm sorry to be a bother to ye. I appreciate yer kindness."

Arran clasped him tightly on the shoulder. "Nay, sir, 'tis no trouble. I apologize for saying so, but ye're rather a strange fellow, are ye not?"

Hew laughed at the truthfulness in Arran's words as the young Conall showed him the way to the tiny cottage. "Aye, lad, that I am, verra strange indeed."

Getting back to the seventeenth century was mildly tricky, but we managed. Because we brought with us two boxes of belongings and the precious vial I hoped would provide Bri with much relief once she went into labor, we were forced to sit on the floor of the spell room while we balanced the boxes in our laps. We chanted the words aloud together and reached over our boxes to link hands right before the spell began to work.

When we arrived back, we nursed our aching heads for a few short moments and then made our way up to the kitchen where we could hear Bri and her lookalike sister-in-law, Blaire, working together.

"We're back! What are you two girlies up to?" I set the box I carried down just past the doorway and went to give both of the girls a quick hug, lingering an extra second so that I could press my hands against Bri's stomach to see if my grandbaby would give me a quick kick. For the moment, it seemed the infant slept soundly.

"Trying to cook, but it isn't going so well. Eoin and Arran will be thrilled that yer home, Mary. They're convinced that if they have to go another day with us as cooks, they shall starve to death."

Bri winked at Mary and then bobbed her head in the direction of the box. "What did you get?"

I grabbed her hand and anxiously dragged her over so I could reveal all of the precious goodies we'd returned with. "Morna knew what I wanted. She gathered up our ornament box. Isn't it wonderful?"

Bri moved to her knees instantly, her belly getting in the way, but I knew nothing would keep her from rummaging through the boxes. Each item was as special to her as it was to me. "Oh, Mom. You're joking! This is amazing, truly."

"Yes, it is, dear. She gathered a few other items for us as well, but I'm going to wait until later to show those to you. It can just be a surprise for everyone." I placed my hand on her shoulder as I squatted down next to her as we lifted each tiny memory out of the box.

Blaire walked across the room to stand next to us. "The storm has slowed a bit. 'Tis still impossible to go too far from the main building, but not much is falling right now. Mayhap we should all go out together and find a tree to cut down for the decorations."

Bri leapt to her feet with more energy than I'd seen her exert in the last two months. "Yes, that's a perfect idea. I'll get Eoin. Blaire, you find Arran. Mom and Mary, go get Kip and meet us out back. Stat!"

She scurried off quickly, Blaire following suit. Mary and I laughed together, walking out of the kitchen so we could prepare for our outing.

<hr>

Both girls had apparently already decided that we would go tree hunting today if we returned from Morna's. The gathering of everyone went entirely too smoothly, as if they all waited on pins and needles for us to get home. The excitement of Christmas was starting to move through our merry little group.

The snow was beautiful, covering every inch of the castle grounds. I found myself wishing more than once that I'd enlisted Morna to cast us all a pair of sturdy snow boots as well, but we were all having such a wonderful time, none of us thought much about our ice-cold toes.

It took us some time before we found a tree that everyone could agree on. Many that held the perfect shape proved far too large. Some of perfect size were not the right shape. Eventually, the perfect tree stood before us. While Eoin, Arran, and Mary's husband, Kip, worked at chopping it down, all of us girls stood huddled together watching.

The landscape remained silent, save for the crack against the wood as the men took their turns driving the ax into its base. For a moment, I thought I'd imagined the soft whining sound coming from somewhere behind me, but as I listened I felt certain that I had not.

An animal, of that much I was sure, and a young one at that, made the noise. I couldn't tell what kind of creature it might be. My heart squeezed uncomfortably at the thought of anything so tiny and helpless being trapped out here in the snow.

Afraid that too many people approaching would cause it fear, I slowly crept away from the group and went off in search of the soft whine.

***

*H*ew stepped out in front of the small cottage, frowning as he looked out over the landscape drenched in snow. He'd hoped very much that he would be able to leave today, but it would be impossible. Even though snow no longer fell, he feared his horse might break a leg if he forced him to trudge through snow so deep.

He threw his arms up above him stretching and groaning at his frustration. In response to the noise he uttered from his throat, something whined not far from him. Compassion compelled him to go in search of the creature.

Turning, he draped himself in thick coverings. The chill from his ride yesterday still set deep within his bones. Grunting, he took off in the direction of the noise. He stepped only a few trees away from the cottage before he caught the dark, whimpering ball of fur at the base of the tree.

Hew bent, picking up the puppy gently as it shivered uncontrollably in his large hands. He wrapped the pup up in his own furs, rubbing his hands back and forth over the small creature to warm it. It was a miracle the creature still lived, for it must have spent the previous night out in the storm as well.

He held it closely to his chest, waiting for the puppy to stop trembling. When he felt its warm tongue start to lap at the inside of his fingers, he knew the pup was only cold, not injured. He uncovered the tiny animal, smiling as he took in its handsome features.

Hew raised him to check the gender and, finding him a boy, set him back into the cradle of his hand. The dog was fluffy with thick hair that made him look much bigger than he seemed. Dark hair covered his back but a beautiful mixture of spots of gray, brown, and black fur covered his chest and feet. Warm brown eyes oozed kindness. Small patches of light brown hair sat above his eyes, standing out on his black head, giving the illusion of brows.

"Why, ye are a handsome pup, are ye not?" He pulled the creature in close to him once more, reaching down to pick the clumps of icy snow from between the pup's paws. He stilled when another small whine caught his attention. "Ach, it seems that ye have another wee friend close by. Let's go find him together."

*I*t had not taken me long to find the source of the noise. If not for the weak bark that the creature let out as I approached him, I would have probably stepped right on top of him, the white of his fur matching the snow.

The puppy lay hidden, only his black nose and mouth sticking up out of the drift, quite close to the Conalls' small cottage. I gasped when I saw him, quickly reaching down to snatch him out of his icy home as I brushed the snow off of him with my bare hands. "Oh, you poor thing!"

The creature responded with another small bark. Once he was free of the snow, I lifted him, examining his coloring. His hair was straight but full—beautiful, but the kind of dog I was sure would shed easily. White fur covered most of his body, but his backside was black. With the exception of his white mouth and snout, each side of his face and both ears were black, too.

I'd expected the creature to squirm in my grasp but, once he became warm, he collapsed, relaxing completely, his small legs dangling on each side of my arm. I grinned as I pulled him in close. I hoped very much that Eoin would not object to having a dog in the castle because the pup would come with me regardless.

A voice behind me caused me to jump, jerking my arm so that the puppy came awake, groaning in displeasure.

"Ah, I thought I heard another one making noise. Seems our two little friends must be brothers, aye?"

I turned around to face the most handsome man I had ever seen.

"Oh my, you scared me. Hello there." I lifted my knees high as I moved closer to him. I didn't miss the strange expression that crossed his face when he heard the way I spoke. Everyone in this time did that.

"'Ello to ye too, lass. I apologize for frightening ye. 'Twas not my intention. I heard this wee lad, not far from the one ye hold in yer hands. I still heard whining so I knew there must be another close." He pointed to the black squirmy ball in his hands. The pup he held was far less content to be held than the one lying like broccoli in my arms.

I stood close to the man now and extended my hand to touch the wiggly pup he held. The dog's fur felt soft like baby hair. As I rubbed him, the man reached his hand to rub the pup I held.

"They are both fine looking pups, are they not?"

I nodded as we both pulled our hands away. "Yes, beautiful dogs. Look at the markings above their eyes. They look quite different, but they must be out of the same litter."

"Aye, lass, I believe ye are right. They are the same size and age. Forgive me, miss. My manners are not what they should be. My name is Hew. To whom do I find myself speaking?"

I reached out to shake his hand. My stomach fluttered as he grabbed my fingertips, briefly touching them to his lips. I was far too old to have such a reaction to a man, but God he was a beautiful being. "Um…" I faltered and blushed, totally out of character from my normally over-confident, over-flirty self. "Um… Adelle. My name is Adelle."

I guessed he was only a few years older than me, if not the same age. Thick, dark, wavy curls, only lightly sprinkled with salt, covered his head. He kept it cropped short unlike many men in this time who wore theirs longer. I preferred that. I didn't see the appeal in being with a man who had more hair on his head than I do.

Tall, with broad shoulders, every inch of him was covered, but I had a feeling he would not be soft like many men our age. He worked hard. It was evident in the tone of his skin and the light crease of wrinkles across his brow. A light shadow of a beard only added to the manliness he exuded.

The way he stood awkwardly after I told him my name hinted at shyness. Now that we'd introduced ourselves to one another, he seemed uncertain of how to continue the conversation.

I had to shake my head to recover, yanking my stare away from the deep green abysses of his eyes. "Um…are you from around here? Do you live in the village?"

He bent his head to glance at his puppy, finally no longer squirming as it slept in his arms. "Nay, lass. I doona live anywhere near here. I'm on my way elsewhere but had to stop here due to the storm. I am staying in this cottage here." He pointed behind him. "The Conalls were kind enough to grant me refuge from the snow. My sister lives with them and works in the castle."

Only one woman worked for the Conalls and actually lived in the castle beside myself, but there was no possible way the god that stood before me could be the brother Mary had been talking about. "You wouldn't be speaking of Mary, would you? Your sister is someone else, yes?"

Hew's eyes sparkled a brilliant green, lighting flutters in my stomach once more. "Aye, lass, 'tis Mary that I speak of. Do ye know her then?"

Stunned, I had based my mental image of Mary's brother based on her appearance and envisioned a short, round, aging bald man who talked loudly. This man was none of those things. His voice was deep, but he spoke quietly and said nothing more than required by the conversation. "Yes, I know Mary quite well. She's just around the corner here, along with everyone else from the castle. We've been cutting a tree down for Christmas. Does she know that you're here? Mary and I were away yesterday, we only just returned this morning."

He shook his head. "I doona know if she is aware of my presence yet, but I guess 'tis time that she is. Will ye lead the way there for me, lass?"

"Of course." I turned and waved so he would follow me. I felt self-conscious with my back exposed to him. With every step, I damned myself for pinning my hair up into a hideous bun before we trekked out into the snow.

The group saw me first, and Mary immediately tore into me for stepping away from their company. "Adelle, what is the matter with ye? Why did ye run off without telling us where ye'd gone? Ye could have frozen to death..."

She paused when she caught sight of her brother and moved her short, stumpy legs faster than I'd ever have thought possible as she charged through the snow to throw herself into his arms.

Hew let out a puff of air as she squeezed him and then pushed her away as gently as he could. "Be careful, Mary. Ye shall squish the wee pup I hold in my arms."

Mary glanced briefly down at the sleeping dog but was unphased by the adorable bundle. Bri and Blaire, on the other hand, immediately went to snatch the pups from each of our arms.

"What are ye doing here, Hew? I havena seen ye in years.

God, ye look good, brother!" Once Hew was free of the puppy, Mary threw her arms around him again.

"I was on my way to Mae's grave, but the storm caused me to seek shelter here. I only arrived last evening."

The sadness I'd seen earlier in Mary briefly crossed her face, and I wondered greatly about the identity of Mae. The pain showed only for a moment before Mary whirled away from her brother to face the crowd of all of us watching curiously.

"I see, and which one of ye knew he was here and dinna tell me the second I arrived with Adelle this morning?"

Bri, Blaire, Eoin, and Kip all looked back and forth at each other, clearly in the dark, while Arran glanced sheepishly at the ground. Eventually, he spoke up. "'Twas I, Mary. I apologize. I'm a fool. I got so caught up in the lasses' excitement over finding a tree that I forgot to tell ye."

I thought for a moment she would march through the snow and smack him, but her happiness at seeing her brother seemed to override her annoyance at not learning of his presence until now.

"Shame on ye, Arran, but 'tis no matter now. Why doona the rest of ye go on back to the castle with the tree? I shall join ye shortly after I spend some time speaking with my brother, aye?"

Eoin spoke as he directed us all back to the castle. "Aye, Mary. Spend as much time as ye wish. I suppose we willna starve from only one more night of Bri and Blaire's cooking. Yer brother is welcome to dine with us, but if ye wish to spend some time alone together, I can bring ye food later this evening."

I was surprised when Hew responded to Eoin instantly. "I would be much obliged to ye if ye would allow us to dine in the cottage. I shall repay yer kindness in some way."

He obviously didn't want to dine with everyone. Not that I could blame him. We were a bit much to take. Still, his quick rejection seemed a little odd. He walked over to Blaire who was holding his new puppy. After she extended it in his direction, he and Mary turned to make their way back to the cottage.

As we returned the short distance back to the castle, both Bri and Blaire squeezed in tight on either side of me while I balanced my puppy in between my open palms. The girls leaned in close so that they could hear the other's whispers.

"Mom, holy cow, would you ever have thought Mary's brother would look like that?" Bri nudged my side playfully.

I smiled, laughing as I shook my head. I leaned into her, nudging her back. "No, not in a million years would I have expected that."

"Ye did find him a handsome lad, aye Adelle?" Blaire spoke next, her voice as quiet and excited as Bri's.

"Oh yes, very much so. He's quite striking. Why do you ask?" He was married, of course. All the good ones were.

"He's a bit of a hermit from what Eoin and Arran told us. His wife died decades ago, and he lives all alone far away from anyone else. Seems a bit crazy to me, but Eoin seems to think he's just shy. Regardless, does it matter if he's crazy when he looks that good?"

I laughed loudly, garnering questioning glances from the three men walking in front of us. Bri liked to think she was my polar opposite, but she was more like her Mama than she wanted to admit. "Well, it does matter a bit, yes, but I don't think he's crazy." We were approaching the castle. "Let's not gossip anymore now, the boys will give me a hard time. I'm going to find some food for this little one to eat."

Once inside, the girls dispersed, and I carried the sleeping pup down into the kitchen while I thought on what I'd just learned about our new visitor. He was unmarried then.

And I was not displeased to hear it.

*A*ll was abuzz within the confines of Conall Castle the next day. It was decorating day and, with the visitation of her brother, Mary's spirits rose as high as I'd ever seen them. As a result, everyone else in the castle couldn't help but be merry as well.

I'd not expected us to put the tree in the castle's main entrance. I worried that with the modern ornaments we planned to put on the tree, it might raise suspicions of other castle workers. I could not have been more surprised when I made my way down in the morning to find that Eoin, Arran, and Kip had placed the tree there.

"Do you not think it would be best if we set up the tree in the basement? I won't be able to hang the ornaments on it otherwise, right?"

"Aye, ye will. Feel free to hang anything that ye wish from the tree. I willna have us hiding our celebrations. All who work within the castle know of Morna's legacy and her spells." Eoin walked up to me and bent to briefly kiss me on the cheek. "Good morning, Adelle."

I smiled, so very pleased that my daughter had found such a

wonderful man. "Oh great, that's wonderful. It will look beautiful in the corner there, next to the grand fireplace."

"Aye, it will. Look." Eoin pointed to the staircase behind me. "Here come the other lassies. Let us eat and then we will begin the festivity of decorating."

Over breakfast, I couldn't help but notice Hew's absence from the table once again. I was fairly sure he hadn't left already. The snow still had not melted enough for travel, and there was little way for him to get food in the cottage without someone bringing it to him. I didn't understand why he seemed so set against joining us in the castle. I leaned over to Mary to ask her about it. "Why won't your brother join us here to eat? He knows that he's welcome, doesn't he?"

Mary pulled one corner of her mouth to the side uncomfortably before casting sad eyes in my direction. "Aye, he knows it, but he insists on being alone."

"Why is that?" I looked down at my food so that my interest wouldn't seem too eager.

"He's painfully shy. He's spent so much time alone, I'm afraid he doesna know how to be around other people anymore."

That seemed a hard concept for me to grasp. I loved spending every second in the company of others. It was unhealthy for someone to live in such a way. It might be one thing for a person to spend time alone by their own choice, but another to feel that they were prevented from joining others due to shyness. "Well, the only way to get less shy is to practice. Will you see him this morning?"

Mary nodded. "Aye, I shall bring him something to eat as soon as we finish here before we begin decorating."

"Ask him to join us and help in the decorations. It's going to be a lot of fun. Insist on it, Mary. You can be very persuasive."

Mary chuckled but shook her head. "That may be true with many people, Adelle, but nay with my brother. I can insist until the stars have risen, and it will not persuade him to do something he doesna wish to do."

I frowned. I didn't like the thought of Hew being all alone in the cottage while the rest of us spent a joyous day decorating. "Well, will you ask him at least?"

Mary stood, covering a plate to take to her brother. "Aye, lass. I'll ask him."

*P*erhaps he'd been too short with his sister. It wasn't unreasonable for her to wish that he would spend some time with her by joining in the festivities. He would make time to see her later, when she was alone, but his shyness would have done nothing but dampen the spirits of everyone else.

Hew no longer knew how to behave comfortably in front of anyone, let alone an entire family of people who evidently were quite close to one another. He'd managed well enough when he'd bumped into Adelle the day he'd found the pup now sleeping at his feet, but that was an unusual occurrence. He would be certain to make an effort to spend a little more time with his sister before he left.

He reached down to rub on the sleeping pup, thinking back on the strangest thing his sister had told him. She'd said more than once that Adelle had insisted that he come to the castle and help them with the decorations. Why would the lass desire such a thing?

She must feel sorry for him. Any other possibility seemed too unrealistic for him to think of. There'd only been one woman to fancy him in his whole life. It wouldn't make sense for another lass to decide to do so now.

Would it?

I waited until all of the men started trimming the tree, working it into the perfect shape, before I snuck away to grab the surprise I had in store for all of them.

Mary's trip to see her brother had been quick. When she arrived back at the castle without Hew, I knew he had rejected her invitation to join us. I couldn't help the small pang of sadness that lodged itself in my chest, but I did my best to dismiss it. I hardly knew the man after all. What did I care if he chose to be such a fuddy duddy?

Blaire had already helped Bri carry the large box of ornaments upstairs, so while the men shaved away at the tree and the girls marveled at each ornament as they pulled them out of the box, I went down to the basement once more.

Opening the box, I pulled out the large boombox, flipping it over so that I could install a fresh set of batteries. Placing the CD player under one arm and a stack of CDs under the other, I made my way upstairs.

Once I got into the great room, I walked with my back toward them to shield the contents in my arms and set the player discreetly next to the fire, hidden away behind a large seat. I thought best to select a classical Christmas mix first. I was afraid anything too modern would frighten the bejeezus out of Arran and Kip, both of whom had never made a trip through time.

I started it with the volume low so that it played just loud enough to cause everyone in the room to glance around as if they were imagining the sounds in their heads. Slowly, I increased the intensity of the sound until Kip threw both his hands to his ears and looked up to the ceiling in horror.

"What in the name o' God is that? I've told all of ye, I doona like the magic that seems to go on in this place. Make it stop."

Mary laughed and walked over to grab her husband's wrists as she pried his hands away from his head. "Doona be such a fool, Kip. 'Tis not magic, only a music maker we brought back from our journey. Do ye not think it sounds lovely?"

Kip didn't answer right away. Instead, Arran spoke up, "I've never heard such beautiful noise in my life. Leave it be, 'tis magical."

Eventually, Kip surrendered and joined in with the humming and singing as we spent the day turning Conall Castle into a Christmas wonderland. The tree didn't take all that long. Then Mary took us girls downstairs to make garland and wreaths to hang up around the castle.

Though hard work, twisting the leaves and branches into some semblance of something that would please the eye, Mary, Blaire, and Bri took to it quite well. All of my projects were undisputed disasters.

I'd not been a crafty woman in the twenty-first century, where craft stores within a three-block radius sold glues and tools to help you. Without such conveniences, it was pure misery for me to even try.

After three failed wreaths and a string of garland only the *Grinch* would appreciate, I was taken off craft duty and given the measly task of hanging the mistletoe that Bri had created above the entryway into the dining hall.

Mary thought the tradition of mistletoe to be a brilliant idea. "Ye mean that if I can somehow trick Kip into standing beneath the doorway with me, he will be forced to kiss me? Why, I shall stand there all day and wait for him to pass through! I doona believe the old bugger will even remember what part of yer body that ye use to kiss, 'tis been so long since he's done so."

I laughed but, as I did so, Mary's brother crossed my mind once more. I imagined if what Bri and Blaire thought they knew about Hew was true, it had been quite some time since he'd been kissed as well. For some reason, I wished to be the person to change that for him. "Mary, would you mind if I brought Hew some food to eat after the evening meal?"

She clucked her tongue at me, knowingly. "Ach, I knew there was a reason ye wished me to ask Hew to help with the decorations. Ye have taken a liking to him then, have ye?'

I reddened—something that seemed to be happening much more frequently. I didn't like it one bit. "Well, what if I have?"

Mary laughed and looked down to concentrate on the bunch of stems in her hand. "Nothing, dear. It has been far too long since Hew has shared his company with another. Please, I would love for ye to take him his food. I doona like getting out in the snow anyway."

"Will he be angry, do you think? I don't want to upset him. I just thought perhaps I could bring some of the decorations that we didn't use, and I could leave them for him to set up at the cottage. It would give him something to do and, with the snow still piled up, I don't think he will be leaving us anytime soon."

"Right ye are, lass, and he willna be angry at all. He's a kind man, although I'll admit that he is slow to warm. But once ye reach the man he really is, behind his shyness, why..." she paused, smiling down at her wreath, "he's a man worth getting to know."

The cottage stood silent in front of me. For a moment I feared he'd already gone to sleep for the evening, but the puppy I cradled underneath my arm let out a high-pitched yelp. Within seconds, the door to the cottage flew open.

"Ach, evening, Adelle. I feared for a moment there was a third pup who had found his way out of the snow, but I see 'tis only yer little fellow."

"Ah, yes." I paused and waved Arran away now that he'd dragged the small tree we'd just cut down in front of the cottage and helped me carry the food and decorations close to the door. "Thank you, Arran. I'll make it up to you somehow."

Arran called back to me over his shoulder as he turned and made his way through the darkness, leaving Hew and I alone. "Nay, there is no need, Adelle. Be careful on yer way back to the castle."

I'd instructed him to leave as soon as he dropped off all of the items. I wanted a chance to be alone with the quiet, strange man, and I didn't want to chance that he would ask Arran to stick around as well.

Not that I should've been concerned. With the look of surprise on Hew's face, I wondered if I would even be invited inside. I lifted up the basket of food I held in my left hand as I set my pup down on the ground. He immediately ran inside the cottage to join his brother. "Um...Mary was busy so I told her I would bring you something to eat. I hope you don't mind. I also," I pointed to the items behind me, "brought some decorations. We had some left over from today, and I thought it would give you something to do, ya know, if you wanted to decorate the cottage for Christmas."

He scrunched his brows together. I couldn't tell if he was just confused or disgusted. I'd not given much thought to the fact that he was a man and probably didn't give two flips about beautifying anything. I'd simply been trying to spread the cheer. "I...you don't have to take the decorations. I can come back with Arran in the morning and get them. But at least take the food. I'll just head back to the castle now." I squatted awkwardly, whistling to my pup to come, but to no avail. The two brothers wrestled playfully on the floor with no intention of ending their little games anytime soon.

Hew surprised me by reaching out to put his hand on my shoulder. "Nay, lass, I shall enjoy the decorations. Please, come inside."

He stepped aside to usher me in, and I immediately did so, running my hands up and down over my arms to warm myself.

"Come sit by the fire while I set the table. Surely ye are in no hurry to return to the castle. Why doona ye stay and eat with me? I'm sorry if I gave ye the feeling I wished for ye to leave. 'Twas simply that I was surprised by yer presence."

"Oh." I wanted to smack myself square in the forehead at my inability to speak like a grown woman in front of him. It was absolutely ridiculous. No man, not even Bri's father, had the ability to render me speechless so completely.

"Did ye already eat, lass? If so, I shall wait until after ye have gone. Perhaps ye can at least warm yerself by the fire for a little while, aye?"

For someone so shy, he tried. I rewarded his efforts by appearing far less friendly than I actually was. I loved to talk and, by golly, I intended to do so. I set my mind to acting human again before I opened my mouth. "No. I haven't eaten."

He stood and moved to the small table, laying out the spread I'd brought for him. "Come and join me, lass."

<hr>

We ate quietly. While I searched my mind for ideas of what I could speak to him about, each time I stopped myself short. He could sense my hesitation as sometimes I even uttered a syllable only to then stop talking. He took pity on me by speaking himself.

"I apologize for the way I behaved when I opened the door. I am verra much accustomed to being all alone. Although I am a visitor here, visitors of my own are verra unexpected. Might I tell ye something?"

I nodded. "Of course."

"It occurred to me that perhaps ye keep stopping yerself from speaking because ye are worried that I might notice the odd way in which ye speak."

That had nothing to do with it, but I didn't want to object when he obviously put so much thought into it. Instead, I remained silent and waited for him to continue. He did so shortly.

"I confess that I did take note of it when I first met ye, but 'twas only after Mary told me yer story about where and when ye came from that I understood. So doona worry, lass, I willna judge the way ye speak. I'm not so good at speaking with others myself."

Surprised by his words, I smiled before speaking. Mary hadn't lied. Her brother was a kind man. "How is it that you seem to have believed what Mary told you so easily? It is hard for even those of us who have experienced Morna's magic to accept it."

"Ach, ye have found yer voice. I am glad for it." He smiled slightly.

If I'd been standing, I expect my knees would have grown weak at the beauty of it.

"I knew Morna when I was a child, and I grew up hearing stories of her powers. I know my sister well enough to know that she wouldna lie to me about such a matter. Besides, life is such that many things happen that we canna explain how or why they do. It must have been quite a change for ye to come here, aye?"

Our food was now gone, and I knew I would be expected to take my leave soon. "Yes, it was, but one I welcomed. With my daughter being here, there's nowhere else I'd rather be, and I love it here very much." I stood, pushing my chair in before walking to the door. "Why don't I help you carry these things in then I'll leave you be for the evening."

The same unreadable look that had crossed his face earlier resurfaced, and I was afraid I'd somehow upset him. He cast his palm out in the direction of the empty room. "Are ye not going to stay and help me? It seems ye have brought enough to decorate an entire village, and I havena celebrated the holiday since I was a small child. I'm afraid I shallna know what to do with all of it on my own."

I beamed and stepped out into the darkness so he wouldn't see my reddened face. "Yes, I would love to."

For someone that didn't like the company of others, he seemed to be in no hurry to rid himself of mine.

he lass must still carry Morna's magic with her for her to have such an effect on him. He'd been surprised by her slim presence at the door but was pleased to see her, blonde hair blowing wildly in the breeze, as she quickly sent Arran away. She wanted to be alone with him. While he wasn't sure why, the thought made something deep within him warm for the first time in ages.

At first, Adelle had seemed more nervous even than he felt, and it somehow helped to calm his nerves in the beauty's presence. In fact, he felt very much himself with her and talked as freely as he did with anyone.

The lass' shyness had not lasted long. After he'd asked her to stay and help him with the decorations, she'd talked with him at length, telling him grand stories of all that had happened at Conall Castle within the last months. Hew found himself for the first time wishing he had not stayed away from his homeland for so long.

When all that Adelle had brought him was set just as the lass would have it, he walked her back to the castle, his heart more sad than he would allow himself to admit that their evening together had come to an end.

"Thank you for allowing me to interrupt your evening. I hope I wasn't too much of a bother."

The lass was mad if she was unable to see how much he had enjoyed her company, but he suspected his feelings that he always kept locked deep away within him did not show clearly on his face as he sometimes wished they would.

He stared directly into her green eyes, so vibrant and alive that he couldn't help but realize how little he'd allowed himself to truly live for far too many years. She was the most beautiful woman he had ever seen, her pale face pink from standing out in the cold. He wanted to do nothing more than warm it with the touch of his lips.

"Nay, lass, ye were not a bother at all. I had a wonderful time."

Mustering all the courage he had left in him for the evening, he quickly leaned in to kiss her on her cheek. Turning before she could see his reaction, he marched back into the darkness, his heart beating faster than it had in decades.

I left my bedchamber early the next morning to join everyone in the dining hall for breakfast, still high on the endorphins that had surged through me at the touch of Hew's lips on my cheek the night before. I reminded myself repeatedly that it had only been the cheek, but it did nothing to push the giddy flurries away. What would I have done if he'd given me a proper kiss?

Visions of me pouncing him in the middle of the snow, begging him to take me right up against the castle wall flashed through my mind, and I shook my head in disgust. I was going to be a grandmother for goodness' sake.

But honestly, who was I kidding? If I expected that to turn me into a respectable, "normal" woman in her fifties, I was sure to be disappointed. I'd always been a bit young on the inside, immature some would say, and I didn't have hope that that would change any time soon. I'd given up on it ages before.

I walked into the dining hall, and I was sure my eyes widened in surprise at seeing Hew sitting at the table alongside everyone else. Doing my best to hide my shock, I sat at my usual place at the table and turned to listen to Eoin, who was addressing the table.

"Are ye finished with yer meal, lads? If so, let us be on our way. I'm not so inclined to leave Bri's side, but she was verra insistent that we make this trip."

Bri nodded and waved him off, patting her stomach with her other hand. "Yes, I was. Be gone, all of you, and have a wonderful time. The baby seems content where it is. I'm certain it will be days until the birth."

"Where are you going?" I'd obviously missed the front of this conversation, but regardless, I was not one willing to be left out of the loop.

Bri responded from across the table. "Since Christmas Eve is only days away, the men are leaving us for a few days to go on a hunt. Hew has agreed to stay with us until after the holiday. He's going to help them on the hunt. Mary says he is a fine shot with an arrow."

"Wonderful. Are you boys certain you trust us to have free run of the castle while you're away?"

Eoin laughed as the other men rose from their places at the table. "Oh Adelle, ye all have free run as it is now, do ye not?"

I had nothing to say to that. He was right. We most certainly all did exactly as we wished. Headstrong women filled Conall Castle.

As they prepared to leave, Hew walked from around the table to stand at my side, carrying his puppy that had been hidden underneath the table at his feet.

"Will ye watch over him for me while I am away, lass?" He set him next to my pup, and they instantly began gnawing at each other's faces playfully. "They seem quite attached to one another."

I grinned, nodding emphatically. I was so pleased and surprised to see that he'd decided to join the men on their hunt. "Of course. I'll take excellent care of him."

"Aye, I'm sure ye will, lass."

He turned and left without bidding farewell to anyone else in the room, even Mary, and I could almost see the steam coming from her ears.

"What did ye do to him last night, Adelle? Ye are the hussy I always thought ye were, are ye not? Why, ye have gone and soiled my brother the first evening ye spend alone with him!"

Mary waited all of five seconds after the men left the dining hall to tear into me, and my mouth fell open in response to her attack. "What? Are you mad? Of course I didn't! But even if I had, he wouldn't have been 'soiled.' He was married once before, was he not? I didn't do anything to him, save talk his ear off. He was very kind to put up with my presence."

I watched as Mary's face changed from one of anger to sheer surprise. "So ye swear to me then, ye dinna bed him?"

Whatever anger that had faded from Mary had moved into me. "Mary, if I weren't afraid you would knock me flat onto my ass, I'd be half tempted to throttle you right now. It is absolutely none of your business what I did with your brother."

"So ye did then?"

Bri and Blaire glanced nervously at one another, and I could tell they wondered if they must stand in between us to keep us from attempting to strangle one another. Both of us needed to calm down. "No, I did no such thing, Mary."

"Oh." Mary stood and walked around the room as if trying to accept my words as truth.

"Oh, is right. You should feel mighty ashamed of yourself for assuming such a thing." I leaned back in my chair, crossing my arms to show my frustration.

"Mom, in Mary's defense, Hew is her brother, and it's not as if what she accused you of would be completely unheard of with you."

I shot Bri a look that must have been frightening for she sank down into her chair and didn't say another word as we all waited for Mary to say something else.

Eventually, she exhaled exaggeratedly and moved to resume her seat at the table. "Well, if ye dinna bed him, my brother must fancy the oddest of women, because he's mighty taken with ye."

"Why do you say that?" My face warmed, and I reached up to fan myself. At least at this age, I could pass any sudden redness off to hormones.

"I all but begged him to join us as ye bid me to yesterday, and he would not come. He spends one evening in yer company, and he shows up at the castle this morning without being asked. He's always welcome o'course, but 'tis shocking behavior from him, Adelle. He even suggested the hunt. He went to Eoin early this morning and told him that he thought he'd found some great places for hunting on his way here."

"Is that so?" I looked down at myself. Damn the lack of air conditioning in this century.

Bri smiled and pointed at my face. "Mom, you're blushing. You like him, don't you?"

She skated on thin ice this morning. "Yes, I do, but I am not blushing. I'm far too old to blush. It's just very warm in here is all. I think I'm having a hot flash."

Blaire spoke up, ganging up on me with Bri. "Nay, Adelle. 'Tis not warm in here at all. I doona believe ye are having a flash of warmth. I think Bri is right, ye're blushing."

"Why don't the two of you just bugger off?" I stood and left the dining hall so that I could find some cold water to splash on my face.

They'd stayed close to the castle, finding shelter for them and their horses in the village, but the hunt had done them all good. Hew was accustomed to spending his days working hard on his land. He didn't like being cooped up in the confines of the small cottage each day.

He'd wanted to learn more about Adelle while away but had hoped he would be able to keep his growing feelings for her a secret. He'd been completely unsuccessful. It seemed all of the men had assumed his sudden eagerness to join in the castle activities had something to do with her.

As they made their way to their rooms in the inn they'd rented for the evening, Arran nudged him in the ribs as if they'd known one another forever. "Did ye enjoy Adelle's company last night? Ye must have, for I know I was unable to convince ye to step inside the castle walls."

Hew couldn't lie to him. Just the thought of her made something deep within his chest hum with an excitement he'd thought himself no longer capable of feeling. "Aye, lad. I verra much enjoyed the time we spent together."

"And ye find her a bonny-looking lass, do ye not?"

The lad was forward, but Hew expected it was how he was with everyone. Arran didn't seem the kind of man to mince his words no matter who he found himself in the company of. "Aye, she's as beautiful a lass as I ever have seen. Do ye know her well, Arran?"

"Aye. I've spent much of the last year with her. She's wonderful, a little more forthright with her words than most lasses, but I wouldna have her any other way. Mary, Blaire, and Bri are much the same way, so perhaps that is why I doona mind her so much. I find fiery lasses to be the best company."

"Nay, I doona mind it either. My wife was verra much like that. She always said whatever came to her mind. 'Twas a treasure to be with a woman I never had to wonder what she was thinking." Hew smiled, slightly surprised at himself. It was the first time he'd spoken of his wife in years that sadness hadn't crept into his heart.

"Well, ye never have to wonder what Adelle is thinking, 'tis certain. Ye shall be joining us for the meal on Christmas Eve, aye? It would disappoint her if ye dinna, and I can tell by the sparkle in yer eye when ye speak of her that ye doona wish to do that."

The last thing he wanted to do was upset Adelle in any way. He was slowly beginning to want to do nothing more than please her. "Aye, lad, I'll be there. Ye are right, I doona wish to disappoint her at all."

The men arrived back at the castle midday on Christmas Eve. The prizes of the hunt were such that I was immediately forced to join Mary in the kitchen so that we could get to work preparing the meat. Bri and Blaire somehow evaded the kitchen. I suspected they were both spending private moments with their husbands, whom they'd not seen for a whole three days.

It seemed a bit ridiculous to me that such a short period of separation seemed to cause them both such distress, but the truth was I was a little envious of the relationships they had found. I'd never had that with Bri's father. We both celebrated at the absence of the other. Even after our divorce, I'd never dated anyone long enough to allow my feelings to get all that strong.

By the time all of the food was prepared, everyone but Mary and I sat waiting anxiously in the dining hall, ready to devour the feast that was about to be placed before them. I'd just stepped into the room when I tripped on the bottom of my dress, causing me to slip forward.

I was certain I would land on the floor, spilling the precious bread basket I held in my hands, but Hew's quick hands suddenly set me right. He'd jumped up to pull a piece of garland out of his curious puppy's mouth and had passed by just in time to keep me from my fall.

"Are ye all right, lass? Mary would kill ye if ye dropped the food."

"Yes, she most certainly would. Thank you." I looked up at him, instantly lost in the greenness of his eyes. He didn't let go of my forearms, and it took Arran's voice from the table to pull us away from our locked gazes.

"Look up. Ye have both found yerself beneath the mistletoe. Ye must kiss her, Hew. 'Tis bad luck if ye doona."

Our eyes met once more. I was certain he wouldn't kiss me. It had been much for him to kiss my cheek in private. This would be too much to ask of him.

He didn't glance away. Instead, leaning in close until his lips were just a hair's width from mine, he whispered, "It seems that I must. I willna have bad luck following ye, lass."

His lips pressed warm, soft, and shy. I melted into him, nearly winding my fingers up into his hair as the butterflies in my stomach coursed through every inch of my body. Mary's voice to the other side of us caused him to pull away from me.

"Well, now ye have gone and ruined it. Now that Kip has seen what that is for, I shall never be able to trap him beneath it."

Hew laughed but leaned into my ear after Mary passed by us, whispering so that no one but me could hear him. "I intend to finish that kiss later, lass."

I smiled and whispered back, not caring about the eyes focused on us. "I surely hope so."

Christmas morning was all that I'd hoped it would be. Presents, a beautiful tree, a warm fire, and lots of love and laughter filled the castle. Together, we lit the candle to place in the window to light the way for strangers—a New Year's tradition Mary shared with us. I'd heard of the custom through my archaeological studies, but it became a treat to be an active participant in the ritual.

When Bri opened the baby blanket, she'd cried big fish tears that soon had all of the women, even Mary, blubbering like babies. The baby was to come any day now, so I'd also wrapped up the vial Morna had sent with me. Bri's reaction was just what I had expected.

"Oh, thank God! I've been so terrified for weeks at the pain. I'd about made up my mind that I was not going to let the child come out. If the medicine came from Morna, it's certain to help, don't you think?"

I suspected she was getting her hopes up a little high. While I was sure it would help to dull her pain a little, the pain of childbirth was such that there was little chance of it being a pain-free experience. I didn't imagine that's what she wanted to hear, so I simply smiled and nodded. "Yes, I'm sure it will help."

Hew had joined us but remained standoffish. I assumed he didn't want to make any of us feel guilty for not having gifts for him. I did, however. It just wasn't quite ready yet, and I didn't want him to know until later. I would need to enlist Mary's help to finish it. I'd done a fantastic job of thoroughly screwing it up.

I walked over to him, gently reaching out to touch his arm. "Merry Christmas."

He smiled, reaching up to gently squeeze my hand. "Merry Christmas to ye as well, lass. It has been many years since I have been able to witness such a wonderful celebration, but now I believe I shall take my leave and return to the cottage for awhile."

"Oh, please don't. We all enjoy having you here. Do you feel uncomfortable?"

"Nay, lass. I am surprised to say that I am verra comfortable with all of ye. 'Tis only that I have something I'd like to give ye but 'tis not quite finished yet. Would ye stop by the cottage in a little while?"

I smiled, but panic rushed through me. "Yes, of course I will." I wasn't going to accept a gift from him unless I had something to give him in return. That meant I didn't have much time to convince Mary to help me fix the disaster I tried to sew together yesterday morning.

He smiled, squeezing my hand once more before he slipped away. As soon as I saw him gone, I crossed the room to yank Mary up from her chair.

"You have got to come help me, quick. I tried to make Hew something, but I've messed it all up. Now he's going to give me something, so I need you to repair my gift to him."

"Ach, I see how he is. He will give his hussy a gift but not his sister. Did I just hear ye say ye tried to sew something, Adelle?"

Mary looked at me begrudgingly but stood. I knew she would be happy to help. "Yes, I know. Horrible idea."

"Aye, lass." Mary laughed heartily. "Ye are a fool, but I'm so happy this Christmas morning, I doona mind telling ye that I love ye dearly. Now, let's go fix the mess ye've made. My brother deserves a proper gift."

CHAPTER 14

I knocked on the door to the cottage with numb fingers and a red nose. It had started snowing once more, and the wind blew bitterly cold. He opened the door quickly, smiling wide.

"Come inside, lass. Ye and the pup both. 'Tis freezing outside."

A large fire burned from the hearth, making the room warm, almost toasty, inside. He was wearing less clothing than I'd ever seen him in, and I had to swallow hard at the sight. He wore long pants, his shirt thin linen exposing part of his chest. Chest hair poked out from the top.

Once I stood inside, he pulled me into a large hug. I breathed in deeply at the masculine scent of him as my face pressed flat against his chest. "I'm sorry it took me so long. I had to get Mary to help me finish your gift. I made quite a mess of it."

He crossed the room to grab a small box that sat in the windowsill next to the tree. "Ye doona need to give me a gift, lass."

"Well, same goes for you then. But, it seems that we both did anyway, so let's exchange them."

I didn't wait for him to give me mine before extending the two folded pieces of cloth I held in my hands. He took them, and after unfolding them, stared down at the odd pieces quizzically. "Thank ye, lass, but what exactly is it that I'm holding?"

I bent down and snatched up my puppy who snuggled next to his brother near the fire. Reaching out, I took one of the pieces from him and gently slipped it over the puppy's head, pushing each leg through the tiny holes.

He laughed loudly. "Did ye truly make a shirt for the pups? Is this a common thing where ye come from?"

I smiled. I knew he would find it silly, but there was no denying how precious both of them would look in their small, wool onesies. "Yes, I surely did. Not all that common, but a few crazy people like me do sometimes dress their dogs. You can't deny how cute they look."

He grinned, picking up the other pup as he slipped the small creation over the animal. "Nay, lass, I canna deny it. They shall be the bonniest, most ridiculous-looking pups anywhere. It seems that our gifts will complement one another."

"Oh yeah? How?"

He placed the box inside my hands. "Open it and see, lass. I hope ye like them. It has been some time since I carved anything."

I lifted the top of the wooden box gently. The box itself was exquisite, crafted by fine hands. I could only imagine how magnificent the contents inside the box would be. I lifted the small piece of cloth covering the items, and I had to choke back tears when I saw what lay inside.

Two wooden ornaments lay nestled within, each dangling from crimson ribbons, carved perfectly into the shape of a dog—a puppy to be exact. Their resemblance to the pups snuggling at our feet was striking.

I'd not had a gift so touching in many years. It wasn't the ornaments themselves, although they were certainly impressive.

The attention and thought that had gone into such a gift touched me deeply. He'd listened to me the night we'd decorated the cottage together and taken special note of my love for such objects.

His voice startled me from my gaze. "Do ye not like them, lass? I'm not so good at crafting wood as I once was. I'm a bit out of practice."

"No." I reached out to grab him firmly by the hand. "They're amazing, Hew, truly. I love them. It's only that I'm a little disappointed." I grinned flirtatiously at the concern he showed on his face.

"Disappointed, lass?"

"Yes, disappointed. I was hoping that as my gift you were going to finish that kiss you started yesterday."

He laughed, ripping the box from my hands as he tossed it onto the bed across the room and pulled me tightly against him. "Aye, I'll finish it, lass, and then I'll begin another and another."

This kiss held nothing of the shyness that had shown in his kiss the night before. His lips moved confidently against my own as one hand at the lower half of my back pulled me flush against him, his other hand winding its way into my hair.

I moaned as he pulled my lower lip deep into his mouth. He pulled away to speak breathlessly into my ear, the tickle of it causing me to squirm against him.

"Ach, lass. Doona make such a sound unless ye want me to take ye in that bed right there." He nudged his head in that direction.

While my body wanted nothing more than for him to do just that, something with Hew felt different. The feeling within me while in his presence was special, life-changing. It seemed that such a hasty act would cheapen my feelings for him. I laughed, his breath tickling my neck and back. "I'm sorry, but I can hardly help it when you kiss me so."

"Do ye wish me to stop, lass?"

"No, not at all. I like your kisses very much." I kissed him, lightly allowing my tongue to slip inside before pulling away and was rewarded with him crushing me against him once more.

He devoured me, causing my head to grow light as we breathed each other's breaths as our own. If I didn't pull away and change the subject quickly, I would allow him to take me, and something in my mind screamed that this man needed to be different.

Slowly, I closed my mouth, giving him a small kiss before pulling away. "I just thought of something."

His green eyes were hazy, nearly blurred with the lust that I was certain mirrored my own eyes. "Aye? What is that, lass? Do ye think perhaps ye could tell me later?"

I laughed and tried to step away, but he held me close to him. "No, it's very important. We have yet to name our puppies. We found them together. I think we should name them together."

He remained quiet for a moment. I suspected he was giving himself a minute to pull himself out of the thralls of his lustful thoughts. Slowly, he lessened the grip on my back and stepped away just slightly. "Aye, lass, ye are quite right. We should. I know what I wish to name the dark one."

"Really? What?"

"He's quite a masculine pup, do ye agree? His fur makes him look like an exotic beast. I think we should name him Tearlach. It means that he is a manly creature."

I smiled. I didn't think the puppy looked manly, only adorable, but he was right. As the pup grew, the fluffy hair around his head would make him look like a lion. "It's perfect."

"Ye should be the one to name the lighter one. 'Tis ye that found him."

I thought for a moment, but every name I thought of sounded too American. He needed a Scottish name that would fit his brother's. "Do you see how his tail always sticks up? It looks like he is waving a flag. Is there another word for that?"

"Aye, lass, I see. What about Bratach? It holds much the same meaning."

I stood on my tiptoes and kissed his cheek. "I think it's perfect, and with that I will take my leave. You are too much of a temptation for me to stay a moment longer."

He laughed his deep, grumbly laugh that shook his whole chest and made my knees go weak.

"Temptation, lass? Nay, 'tis ye that are the temptation. I have been alone for a long time. Ye have awakened feelings within me I fear I am too old to handle."

"You are not old. You're the same as me I'd imagine, and I am in no way old, which means neither are you." I moved to stand by the door.

"If you say so, lass. Will ye accompany me somewhere tomorrow afternoon?"

"Yes, I think I could manage that. Where?"

"'Tis a surprise, lass. I shall meet ye at the back of the castle come midday."

He opened the door to the cottage, taking my hand so he could walk me back to the castle, leaving me to wonder just what tomorrow held in store for me.

ew rose early the next morning so that he could work on carving the large piece of wood remaining from the ornaments he'd made. He hoped to make it into a sort of sled that he and Adelle could take out on their outing this afternoon.

Just thinking about spending more time with her made his heart beat quickly. He'd lived alone for so long he'd convinced himself that it was the only way to honor the memory of his late wife, to stay trapped in the memories of his short time with her. But with each day since he'd met Adele, he felt more alive. He was slowly learning that nothing could have been further from the truth.

Mae had not been a jealous woman. She knew she held his heart and lived her life with more light and love than any other lass he'd ever met. She would've wished more for him. She wouldn't have been pleased that he'd spent so many years all alone.

It saddened him that for so long he'd not seen the truth in the mistakes he was making.

All he could do now was to try and move forward, living the

rest of his life as Mae would've wished it. She would be very pleased to know that he'd found happiness once again. He could almost hear her whispering in his ear, pleading with him not to let her slip out of his grasp.

He didn't intend to let Adelle do any such thing, but he also knew it best that their afternoon spent together be passed out of doors. He was a man who'd gone too long without sharing his bed with another woman, and the next time he and Adelle were alone within four walls, he knew he would not be able to keep himself from claiming her as his own.

For this reason he worked, chipping away at the wood with as much force as he could muster, crafting it into the perfect seat for two. He was a man in need, and he needed to exert whatever physical activity he could to help keep his mind off her.

---

*E*ither Hew hadn't told Mary what he planned for us to do this afternoon, or she was damned determined not to tell us what she knew.

Bri and Blaire had insisted on dressing me, and they'd decided to place me in the finest dress I had. "Are you sure this is appropriate? I feel very overdressed."

"It's always better to be overdressed than underdressed. I believe you are the one that taught me that. Besides, we have no way of knowing do we, since Mary refuses to tell us what his plans are?"

Bri continued to pick away at my hair, doing her best to pin it into place.

Mary threw her hands up in exasperation as she screamed angrily at us. "I already told ye, I doona know what his plans are. I havena spoken to him about it. Ye are a couple of thick-headed lassies, the two of ye!"

She turned and left us, stomping her feet on the way. Once she was gone, we both burst out into laughter. "I should not have pestered her so. There. What do you think?"

Bri stepped away so that I could turn and look in the mirror. "Thank you. My hair looks nice, but I feel ridiculous in this dress. I'd rather be in jeans and a nice blouse."

Bri laughed and bent down to squeeze me while placing her face up against my own. "I'm sure you would, but those days are over, I'm afraid. At least it's not expected that we shave our legs in this time."

"Thank God for small mercies." She was right. It would have been considered quite strange for us to do so in this time and that was fine with me. I always thought it a pain in the rear anyway.

"Are you nervous, Mom? You like him quite a lot, don't you?"

I stood, wishing I could shorten the dress a good eighteen inches just so I would be able to move more freely. "A little, but every time I'm around him whatever nerves I may have had before dissipate quickly. And yes, I like him very much, which is probably foolish. Once the snow melts, he'll no longer want to stay here."

"I wouldn't be so sure, Mom. I think if he had reason to stay, he would. You may just end up being that reason."

I hoped she was right. The thought of him leaving filled me with sadness, but I would not worry about that now. Today, I was simply going to enjoy his company.

*D*amn Mary straight to hell; she'd known exactly what activity Hew had planned for us. When Hew arrived at the back entrance of the castle carrying a sled, I caught sight of Mary hiding around a corner, cackling like a banshee.

"It is not the least bit funny, Mary! Now, he will be forced to wait on me while I change. There's no way I'm going to get this dress sopping wet."

Mary stepped out from her place in the shadows, laughing as she waved her brother inside. "Oh, doona be such a grumpy bairn, Adelle. Hew, get yerself inside whilst the lassie changes."

Hew stomped his snow-covered feet off outside before following Mary's instruction, casting me an apologetic glance before reprimanding his sister. "'Twas not kind of ye, Mary." He turned to address me. "But I willna say I'm not pleased to see ye in such a fine dress, lass. Ye look lovely."

Mary piped up once again, not giving me a chance to thank him for his kind words.

"Ach, if ye find her pleasing in that, I'm sure ye shall fall over when ye see what she will come down in next. I'm certain she will use yer idea of playing in the snow as the perfect excuse to don her horrific garb from her own time. I doona see what the lads seem to see in it, but every time Adelle, Bri, or Blaire decide to squeeze themselves into their modern clothes, all the lads, my own Kip included, can hardly keep their tongues inside their mouths. 'Tis truly pathetic."

Hew's brows pulled together quizzically, but he said nothing. I ignored her as well and turned to make my way back upstairs.

I was almost out of sight when Mary called out to me. "I'm right, aye? Ye are going in search of yer 'jeans?'"

I smiled at the anticipation of ripping this burdensome dress off and sliding into the comfy denim. I screamed over my shoulder back at her. "Yes, Mary. You are very right, indeed."

---

*M*ary had also been right about Hew's reaction to seeing a woman in such clothing. It was certainly something men in this time were unaccustomed to. His mouth nearly fell open at the sight of me. Though entirely covered from head to toe, bundled up as much as I could for our snowy activities, I suddenly felt self-conscious under his gaze.

"Ach, lass, I doona know if ye should trust yerself with me when ye look as ye do. Do women truly dress in such a manner commonly where ye come from?"

I laughed and marched out into the snow ahead of him. "Oh yes, all of the time. This is quite a conservative outfit, I assure you. Would you rather I went and put my dress back on?"

He caught up to me quickly, throwing his arms around me from behind. He kissed me roughly on the cheek, his facial hair tickling my ear. "Nay, lass. I wouldna let ye go and change even if ye wished it. Come. I found a bonny hill near the cottage that shall be perfect for sledding."

Excited by his choice of activity, it rather surprised me as well.

He was much more fun than he'd originally let on. Taking his hand in my own, we made our way to the snowy hill.

The lass meant to torture him. No other explanation for dressing the way she had made sense. He could make out the shape of her bum in her trousers, and what a fine bum it was. Round and full, just like a woman's should be.

If the lass spoke true, and there seemed no reason why she would not, he imagined men in her time spent a good portion of their days walking about quite uncomfortably, such a feast for their eyes laid out in front of them daily.

Hew breathed in deeply through his nose, hoping the chill in the air would cool the fire that burned inside him. Thankful when they reached the hill, he promptly placed the sled he'd built down into the snow and instructed Adelle to sit in the front so that he could join her on the back end.

Pushing off hard, they flew down the snowy landscape, both of them howling with delight as the cold wind rushed across their faces. When the sled finally reached the bottom of the hill, it stopped rather abruptly, uprooting both of them from their seats, sending them tumbling out into the snow.

They landed in a twisted pile. Adelle was on top of him laughing so hard that the trembling of her chest shook his own.

"Are ye all right, lass?" Their fun would be spoiled quickly if his idea caused her harm.

She smiled brightly, bending to quickly kiss him on the tip of his nose. He found himself wondering how a lass could manage to keep her teeth so brilliantly white. They were stunning, just like every other part of her.

"Yes, I'm fine. Let's go again!"

She leapt off of him and was halfway up the hill before he could manage to roll over and climb his way out of the snow.

CHAPTER 17

"Wakey, wakey..."

Bri's voice lured me out of a deep sleep. I awoke to find Bri and Blaire sitting on either side of me, grinning in anticipation.

I rolled onto my stomach, shielding my face from the both of them, groaning as I spoke. "What do you want? Just leave me alone. I'll wake up sometime tomorrow."

Bri stuck her hand into my hair, mussing it about so that I would turn back over onto my back. "You missed breakfast. So did Hew. Mary's not pleased with either one of you, and she said that you will just have to wait until evening to eat because she wasn't going to warm anything for you once you woke up."

I obliged her and rolled over, sitting myself up so that I was eye level with both of them. Endlessly hungry, I could out eat almost any man. No way would I wait until evening to eat. "Like hell I will. I am more than capable of feeding myself. That bossy biddy will not dictate when and what I eat."

Bri looked over at Blaire who laughed knowingly. "What did I tell you, Blaire? I knew she would say something like that."

I cleared my throat to draw her attention back to me.

"Hicumm…excuse me. I'm right here you know. Now, what are the two of you doing in here?"

I knew well enough why they'd come, but Blaire obliged me by answering my question. "Why do ye think we have come? We wish to hear all about yer afternoon yesterday."

I couldn't help but grin thinking back on the day. It had been a wonderful afternoon and ages since I'd laughed so hard. My stomach would be sore for a week from the effort of it. I ached from head to toe, bruised from the many spills I'd taken into the snow, but every tight muscle was worth it. "Well, we honestly didn't do much of anything except sled down the giant hill near the cottage about a thousand times."

Bri smiled as she held on to her swollen belly. "Did you have a good time?"

"Aye, o'course she did. She canna keep from grinning." Blaire winked at me but pointed to my face in concern. "Ye seem to have had a wee bit too much fun though, Adelle. Ye are mighty red."

I reached up and touched my face, flinching at the pain. My cheeks felt quite swollen. There was little in the way of sunscreen in this time, and I'd not thought to cover my face, even after I learned we were to spend the day sledding. "Oh my, I'll have to see if Mary has any herbal salve I can put on this to calm it down a bit. How bad do I look?"

"Completely terrible."

My eyes widened in surprise. With each passing day Bri grew more uncomfortable in her pregnancy, and she was becoming increasingly blunt with her words. "Ouch. Thanks, Bri, but I suppose it's my own fault. I really didn't think about sunscreen at all."

Blaire glanced at Bri with shocked eyes and did her best to comfort me. "It isna all that bad, Adelle. It shall heal itself eventually."

"Eventually?" That was not okay with me. It needed to be completely healed by tonight. After our afternoon of sledding had concluded, Hew had very seriously and nervously asked that I dine with him in the cottage this evening. He said he had something very important he wished to tell me.

"Aye." Blaire looked at me nervously.

I knew it wasn't her fault, but she could tell I was agitated by her response that it would take some time to heal.

"I know that 'tis not pleasant for ye, but it shall take at least a week for ye to look like yerself I'm afraid."

"Awesome." I didn't know what else to say. Nothing could be done for my stupidity. I would look scary as hell when I arrived at the cottage this evening. Perhaps we could dine outside in darkness. Even if we both froze to death, it would be preferable to frightening the poor man to death with the abomination which was now my face.

"*A*re ye certain, brother? Ye havena known her verra long. 'Tis no small decision to decide to leave the home that ye have known for so long."

Hew moved about the cottage nervously. He knew it was a rash decision, but nothing had felt so right to him in a good many years. He loved the lass greatly, and he would tell her so tonight. "Aye, Mary, I am certain. There is naught left for me at home, and there hasna been since the day Mae left me. 'Twas foolish of me to stay there so many years after her death. It pains me to think on all the joy I have missed because I was too frightened not to be alone. I wasted much time."

His sister reached out and lay a comforting hand on his arm. "Nay, brother, ye dinna waste time. Things happen as they are meant to. If ye truly feel the way ye seem to about Adelle, then I doona believe ye were meant to leave yer home until now. If ye had, it wouldna have been her that ye found."

Mary's words comforted him. It was a kind way of thinking of all the mistakes he had made. Regardless, he was thankful he had met the lass now. "Aye, Mary. I canna imagine not knowing the lass now. If I agree to work here at the castle, do ye think that Eoin and Arran shall agree to let me make this cottage my home?"

He smiled as Mary laughed. He should've expected such an answer from his fiery sister. "There is no need for ye to ask either of them. Ye are welcome to stay here because I say so and that's all the permission ye need. Both of the laddies know it and have since they were bairns. 'Tis I that am truly laird over Conall Castle."

"I believe ye are right, Mary. They all seem to bow at yer feet, regardless of the hard time ye seem to love to give them. Now, allow me to walk ye back to the castle, Lady Laird. I have much to think on. It will take me some time to think of just the right way to say what I must."

"What in the bloody hell is the matter with ye, Adelle? Take that covering off the top of yer head."

I knew I looked ridiculous, like a cheap Halloween costume with the gauzy fabric over my head, but there was no way I was taking it off. I was a vain woman, and I wasn't afraid to admit it. Whatever he had to say to me, he could say it to me as I was or not at all. "No, I will do no such thing."

I stepped into the cottage past him, setting the growing Bratach on the floor as he went and joined Tearlach in their usual game of "who's the toughest brother?"

He shut the door to the cottage and walked around to face me, frustration clear on his face. "Ye look ridiculous, lass. I wish to tell ye something important, and I doona wish to address ye covered like a wee ghost."

I glanced up at him, only barely making him out through the small holes in the fabric, but it allowed me to see his perfectly perfect face. I spoke a little more loudly than necessary. "How is your face not red as a beet? You were out in the same snow and under the same sun that I was in yesterday, and there is no sign of it anywhere on you!"

He laughed, understanding. "Ach, I see. Did the sun blister yer skin a bit, lass? I should have insisted that ye cover it, but I dinna think of it. I spend much of my days outdoors. I suppose it has grown accustomed to such sunlight."

"Well, how wonderful for you. Let's eat." It wasn't only the way my face looked that put me in a sour mood, but the pain from it felt something awful. I'd never been burned so badly in my entire life.

"It shall be mighty hard for ye to eat properly with that covering ye. Just take it off, Adelle. Do ye really think that I'm so concerned with the way yer face looks?"

I nodded emphatically. "Of course you are. All men are."

He rolled his eyes, sat down at the table, and started eating immediately, not waiting for me to join him. He responded in between mouthfuls. "Suit yerself. Eat if ye wish. If ye truly believe that, Adelle, ye havena been around the right kind of men. I like yer face verra well, but 'tis not my favorite part of ye."

"Oh, fine. So you're a boob guy, I suppose? Maybe you prefer the 'arse?'" I mimicked his brogue, not sure why I felt the need to provoke him so.

"Yer 'boobs,'" the word sounded strange on his tongue, "and yer 'arse' are not so impressive, lass. 'Tis yer mouth that I enjoy verra much."

My brows met in the middle of my eyes underneath the veil. "My mouth? My lips are quite thin. You have strange tastes."

He stood, and I thought perhaps I had pushed him too far.

"Aye? And ye are a bloody fool, Adelle. I dinna mean yer lips. I mean the shocking words that ye always seem to form with them. I have never known a lass so forward."

I looked down, embarrassed. "Yes. I know. That's always been a problem. It's a bit of a turn off, isn't it?"

He frowned once more and came to crouch down next to me,

taking my hands into his. "I doona know what ye mean by 'turn off' but nay, I love the way ye speak verra much. Now, I willna tell ye what I must with that damned cloth covering yer head."

He yanked it away before I could grasp it. He reeled back in disgust, almost falling backward onto his bottom. "Ach, lass, ye look dreadful. Never ye mind, I doona wish to say what I once wished."

My eyes widened with shock and pain. He quickly scrambled up on his feet to gather me into his arms, laughing softly. "Oh, lass, forgive me. Doona look so upset. I couldna resist it after ye berated me such just a moment ago. Ye look mighty fine, lass. Ye always do."

I didn't pull away from him but rolled my eyes. "No, I do not honestly think I look fine. My face is so red I look like I was born on the sun, and it's quite swollen as well."

"Doona tell me what I think, lass. I wouldna lie to ye. I doona care if the redness never fades, although it shall. I would still think that ye looked mighty fine. Now, hush, and let me tell ye what I wished to when I asked ye to come here."

I relented. I didn't believe a word he said about my face at the moment, but I didn't wish to argue with him anymore. I was eager to hear what he had to say. "All right, fine. What is it?"

He stepped away and sat on the edge of the bed, holding my hands so that I would sit next to him. "I've decided that once the snow melts, I am not going to return home."

Hope fluttered in my chest. I'd spent every second trying not to think of the day when he would leave here and praying each night that the snow would stay forever. "Really? Why?"

"Do ye really not know the answer to that question, lass?"

He looked into my eyes. I could see all that he wished to say deep within them, but I desperately wanted him to say the words. "Maybe, but I won't know for sure until you tell me."

He took a deep, shaky breath. He was nervous, but I was not about to intervene and let him get away without saying what he felt. I'd let too many men do that before. If he meant it, he could find the strength to say the words. "I...I know that I havena known ye long, Adelle, but it doesna take so long for the heart to know what it wants. I'm in love with ye, lass. Verra much so."

I smiled, staring deep into his eyes, as tears I held back threatened to fall. I must have remained quiet for one moment too long for he spoke again, his voice shaky.

"I doona expect that ye should feel the same so quickly. Perhaps 'twas rash for me to tell ye so soon, but I have spent too many years alone. I willna deny myself love a moment longer if I can have it."

"No." I reached up and lay my hand against his cheek. "No. It wasn't too quickly at all. I love you too, Hew."

"Do ye truly, lass?"

"Yes, I do. I think I loved you the first moment I saw you in the snow, holding that sweet little puppy firm against your chest." I leaned forward and kissed him but had to pull away at the pain that shot through my lips at the pressure.

"Ach, lass. I'm verra sorry that ye are in such pain. Doona kiss me now. I hope there shall be plenty of time for that later."

"There's nothing for you to be sorry about, and yes, I do too."

His face grew serious once more. For a moment I was worried.

"I willna return from where I came from, but before I make this my home, I must finish the journey I started. I must bid Mae farewell one last time, lass. I hope that ye doona mind."

I shook my head, surprised that he thought I might. "Of course I don't and of course you must. When will you leave?"

He looked out at the snow, black in the darkness, as he hesitated before answering. "At sunrise. I know that the snow isna melted yet, but it hasna snowed more in days. I am anxious to finish my journey so I can begin a new chapter in my life."

Something twisted uncomfortably in my stomach, but I could not determine its source and did my best to push it from my mind. "You will be careful, yes?"

He smiled, rubbing his hand gently up and down my back. "Aye, lass. Of course I will. I have something most precious that I must return to now."

I wished to stay with him until morning, but I left him shortly after learning he would leave at sunrise. I wanted him to be rested before traveling out in the snow. He'd sent both pups with me, leaving Tearlach in my care for the duration of his journey.

I slept fitfully. While I tossed wildly throughout the night, both pups slept soundly, snuggled tightly into my side in the bed with me. They didn't move all night, only rising right at sunrise. Just as the sun broke over the horizon, they stood on all fours in the bed. Looking toward the window in the direction of the cottage, they whined mournfully.

The knot in my stomach returned.

CHAPTER 19

Hew left right at sunrise just as he'd planned. It was not a far journey to Mae's resting place. In fair weather he could have made the trip there and back in a day, but with the snow still so deep, he knew it would take him at least two.

Just two days away from Adelle seemed too many. He wondered if she'd been disappointed that he hadn't asked her to marry him. He hoped she was not, for he intended to do so as soon as he made it back from bidding Mae one final farewell.

He wished to marry Adelle with all his heart, but some small piece of him would not allow himself to ask it of her when Mae still lingered in the back of his mind. He knew she would have been pleased for him. He'd come to that realization soon after he arrived at Conall Castle, but he wished to spend a few moments alone with Mae so that he could truly put the past behind him.

The day trickled by slowly as he lost himself in a sea of past memories. Memories of loneliness and the choices he'd made that had caused him to be so. A new future lay ahead of him. He couldn't wait to embrace it with all that he had.

He stopped often to allow his aging horse to rest and to clean the icy chunks from the horse's hooves and coat. He asked much of his beloved beast to accompany him on this trip. His horse was old. Hew knew the animal would not make it another year. It seemed appropriate that Greggory's last journey be the last time he would journey to Mae's grave, as well.

Slowly, dark descended over Hew and the great beast. He knew he should stop for the night, but no good place offered shelter from the snow. He knew there to be a small village just outside of the Conalls' territory. So against his better judgment, he nudged the horse on, praying with each soft kick of his heels that his companion could make it into the village.

It happened quickly. The horse stepped upon a rock buried out of sight, deep within the snow. He heard the creature's leg snap and did his best to throw his own leg over the side so that he could dismount before the animal fell, but Hew was not quick enough.

Just as he threw his leg over the side, Greggory fell in the direction he dismounted, pinning him beneath. As his own elbows sunk into the wet snow, they crashed roughly into the same rock that had felled his horse. His left shoulder dislocated on impact.

Pain coursed through him. The weight of his horse on top of him knocked all the breath from his lungs. The stars in the sky melted together, turning into darkness as he lost consciousness.

Present Day

"Morna...Morna, wake up, lass!" Jerry shook his wife's shoulder with as much force as his thin arms could afford. He watched terrified as she tossed in her sleep, making noises as if she were injured. He could see her eyes darting back and forth beneath her closed eyelids, and he held his breath in fear until she opened her eyes to look at him.

"I must gather my spells. They are in need of us once more."

Jerry sighed in relief, his whole body trembling from the remnants of his worry. He'd seen his wife often stir during fits of her dreams, but never so much as he'd just witnessed. For a brief moment, he'd worried that it hadn't been magic that caused her to do so but perhaps old age.

He had every intention of passing from this life before his beloved. He knew he would not be able to live a day without her. "Ye scared me to death, Morna. I was afraid...well, I doona wish to speak of what I thought."

He smiled against her hand as she lay her palm against his cheek, knowing what he meant well enough. "'Tis not a worry ye should have. I shall not leave this world until I am good and ready to, and that willna be for a long time. Come."

She stood and waved at him to follow her. He did so without question. His wife carried a great burden, one he was eternally grateful he didn't possess. "What is it, lass?"

"A lad I knew as a child has taken a fancy to Adelle, and he finds himself in need of help. I must warn them, send Adelle the dreams that were just shown to me so they may have a chance of reaching him in time."

She didn't stop to explain more to him, and he didn't ask any further questions. This was an urgent matter, but he didn't worry over such things as his wife did. He'd yet to see one of her spells go awry.

CHAPTER 20

I'd slept so little the night before Hew departed that I would have been on edge the next day even if the pups had not chosen the exact moment of his departure to whine as if wounded. I spent the entire next day sick with worry, and it exhausted me. My only relief was that my face no longer ached, and the swelling had diminished greatly throughout the day.

As I traveled upstairs to my bedchamber, a pup under each arm, I was sure I would spend another sleepless night worried over Hew. Much to my surprise, a sense of drowsiness so strong that I felt halfway asleep by the time I reached my bedchamber door overcame me.

It seemed a great effort to change into my nightgown. As soon as my head hit the pillow, I fell asleep.

I woke in the middle of the night with sweat beaded on my brow. The covers were off of the bed, mangled on the floor as if I had fought a great battle in my sleep. Screaming had pulled me out of the horrific dream I was having, and for a moment I thought I had heard my own yells.

I felt the need to scream now. Visions of Hew crushed beneath the weight of his horse, unable to scoot from beneath the animal, burned in my mind. I stilled in the bed, sitting up so that I could listen.

For a moment all remained quiet, but it took only a second before another scream ripped through the castle corridors.

I leapt out of the bed. Bri. She must have gone into labor sometime in the night. I could only hope that it was just starting, and I had not missed being there for her.

I burst into her and Eoin's bedchamber, relieved to see that Mary was already making preparations, ordering others about while Blaire administered Morna's mixture to Bri.

I ran to her side, giving her my hand as she squeezed it tightly with an incoming contraction. "How are you? Is everything well?"

She grunted in between words, determination set in her face. She was beyond ready to get the child out of her. "Yes, as well as it can be, I believe. Will you get out there and tell Eoin he better get his ass in here this second? I don't give a damn if it's unusual for men to stay at the bedside during delivery. If he misses the birth of his child, I shall never forgive him."

"Of course." I had to pry her fingers loose and turned to Mary only briefly before leaving. "Is she close, or do we have some time before the baby arrives?"

Mary must have been able to tell something else distressed me for she answered me quickly, waving me on to whatever other task sat on my mind. "Nay, she isna as close as she wishes. We have some time still."

I nodded and ran out of the bedchamber, nearly running into the three men – Eoin, Arran, and Kip – huddled together in the hallway. I knew I must do as Bri bid first. Although I was certain my dream had meant something, I couldn't know for sure that what I had seen had been real.

I grabbed Eoin's arm and pulled him away from the circle, smacking him lightly as I scolded him. "What on earth do you think you are doing? You better get in there with Bri right this instant or I am going to drag you there myself."

He looked back at me nervously. "I am afraid to, Adelle. I doona think I can bear to see her in such pain, and I couldna live with the guilt if something happened to her and the babe."

I softened, feeling sorry for him. It was easy for women to forget what a terrifying ordeal childbirth was for the father. "Nothing is going to happen to them. Morna's drink will help with the pain soon and all will go well. Trust me, if you miss this, Bri will not understand. Go. Now."

He nodded and hurried down the hall, leaving me to turn my attention to Arran and Kip. "I need to ask something of both of you. I know that you may think me mad, but please I beg you, listen to me before you dismiss me."

Kip stood silently, giving me an expression that I knew meant he dreaded whatever I was about to tell him. He knew it would only mean more work for himself.

Arran nodded and reached out to lay a reassuring hand on my shoulder. "Aye, of course, Adelle. What is it?"

"I had a dream, a terrible one. I've never had one quite so vivid. It was dark, and Hew was lying on his back in the snow. His horse had fallen on top of him, crushing him, and one of his arms hung oddly to his side." Saying what I'd seen out loud made it seem more real to me. As I finished, my voice cracked. I couldn't keep a tear from falling down my face.

Arran glanced quickly at Kip and then back at me. "Do ye think that he is in danger, lass, or did ye only have a dream that has upset ye?"

I shook my head. "I don't know, but I'm afraid that he might be. I know it seems crazy."

Arran squeezed the shoulder he held under his hand. "Nay, it isna crazy. We have all seen too much of what Morna can do to think so. Kip and I will ride at once."

"Thank you. I'm sorry to send you, but I can't leave Bri right now."

Arran was already moving down the corridor, Kip following silently behind him as he called back to me. "Of course you canna. Doona worry. We shall find him in time."

I believed that they would. They had to. I couldn't bear to think otherwise.

Once Morna's medicine worked its way through Bri's system, her screams lessened substantially and things began moving rather fast.

She dilated more quickly than Mary had expected. Much to her dismay, she was forced to enlist the help of each of us to help in some way. Blaire did whatever Mary asked of her while Eoin and I sat on either side of Bri, coaching and calming her with each set of pains.

When it came time for Bri to push, I watched in awe and astonishment at her strength. It was a miraculous thing. The love that filled the room in the moment the tiny bundle arrived into this world was enough for me to momentarily push away my worries over Hew.

While here, there was nothing I could do, and my heart nearly burst through my chest when I held my granddaughter in my arms for the first time.

I'd heard it said before that grandchildren filled you with a kind of love that was not even matched by your children. I'd always thought it a crazy notion, but as I latched on to her tiny fingers, I finally understood.

To hold a little human, one that came from a very piece of me, allowed me for an instant to believe that I would truly live on forever, in Bri, in her daughter, and in whatever children this child would one day have. It was all that one could ask for in life, more than I ever thought I would receive.

"Mom, you're crying more than I am, more than Eoin."

I glanced over to see Eoin practically blubbering in the corner and laughed as I carried the child to Bri's loving arms. "I don't care. I have never seen anything more perfect in my entire life."

Bri smiled, bending to kiss her daughter's head. "I know. Me either. Where's Arran? I'm sure he's ready to meet his niece."

I didn't wish to burden any of them with bad news, but I knew I must tell them. "It's nothing to worry over I'm sure, but I had a dream about Hew. I became worried that perhaps something had happened to him on his journey. Arran and Kip rode after him to make sure that he is all right."

Bri looked up at me closely, clearly seeing past the calm façade I was doing my best to put on. "Go."

I shook my head, dismissing her. "No, I'm not going to leave you so soon. You just had a baby for goodness' sake."

She raised her left hand and shooed me from the room. "Mom, go. Everything is fine here. I know you need to be there. Just promise me you'll be careful."

I couldn't deny she was right. I bent quickly to kiss her and the babe on the forehead before turning to leave the room. "I will."

I ran to the stables, mounting the first horse I saw and took off at full speed away from Conall Castle.

'd left the castle before sunrise, and it neared dusk when I found them. The vision before me was just as I'd seen it in the dream. I had been right. I was certain it was Morna who'd sent it to me.

"Is he..." I could hardly force the words out of my mouth. "Is he alive?"

"Aye, lass. I am verra alive and intend to stay that way."

When Hew's voice answered, the relief that washed through me was enough to nearly bring me to my knees.

My legs were shaky as I approached him, the adrenaline that had allowed me to ride to him so quickly suddenly receding. I knelt next to him, grabbing both sides of his face as I examined him for injuries. I spoke to Arran and Kip behind me, "Why haven't you moved the horse off of him? He's going to lose his legs if the horse stays on him much longer."

"We only just arrived as well, lass. Ye must have been riding verra quickly to have caught us."

Hew reached his right hand up to touch my face. The other arm still dislocated. "Nay, lass. If I hadna thrown my shoulder out of place, I would have been able to scoot out from under him. I willna lose my legs."

"I'm glad to hear it." I stepped out of the way so that Arran and Kip could get on either side of him. Together they lifted him, avoiding his injured shoulder so that they could pull him out from under the horse whose breathing was shallow. My heart winced in sadness at the creature's pain. His suffering would have to be ended.

Once his legs were free, Arran had me move to Hew's right side so that I could hold him down and steady while Kip secured his feet. Once he was as still as we could get him, Arran asked him to bite a rag as he jerked the shoulder into place. It was a horrible sound but after the initial pain, the relief became instantly visible on Hew's face.

With help, the two men pulled him to his feet. After a few moments of allowing his blood to recirculate, he moved about to get his footing under him.

Eventually, he turned to address all of us. "I am verra grateful for yer help. I hate to ask it of ye, but would ye all mind riding ahead a ways, only for a few moments?"

"Why?" The word slipped out quickly, but as I looked at the way he stared down at his horse, sadness in his eyes, I knew.

"It must be I that end this for him, and I wish to do it alone."

Silently, we turned and left him.

He'd not taken long. Once he joined us, we made plans to stay in the village where Hew was heading when his horse had fallen. Close to Mae's grave, Hew was determined to complete the journey he had intended.

Although I couldn't stand the thought of leaving him alone once again, I understood his need to do this one last time.

*A*rran, Kip, and I had been at the small inn a few hours when Hew arrived. He said little as he entered, only asking which was his room and leaving us in the dining hall to retire for the evening.

We followed him shortly, separating as we each made our way to our rented rooms. We were all exhausted. I couldn't blame him for not wishing to speak with us when he'd arrived. I was just happy to know that he was safe.

He'd suffered much the last few days. He was sure to be sore, tired, and heartsick at the loss of his beloved horse, not to mention the melancholy I knew he must feel after having visited Mae's grave.

For this reason, I expected it to be Arran or Kip at the door when I heard a soft knock right as I blew all but the last candle out for the evening. Instead, when I opened the door, Hew stood before me, his eyes hungry and in need.

CHAPTER 23

"You should be in bed. You're injured and it's been a long day."

He didn't answer me, only moved into the room shutting the door behind him. He reached out to me with his good arm, pulling me close to him as he kissed me desperately.

After a moment, he pulled away breathlessly. "Doona tell me what I should do, lass. I had to see ye."

He released me and I stepped away, hoping that putting some distance between us would dim the fire he'd lit within me. It did nothing to help. "Is everything all right?"

"Aye, lass. Will ye marry me?"

The words caught me off guard. He spoke them so quickly, I wondered for a moment if perhaps he hadn't meant to say them. "What? What did you just say?"

It took him only two strides until he stood before me, clasping tightly onto both of my hands. "Ye did hear me, lass, but I shall ask ye again. Will ye marry me, Adelle?"

A pleading in his eyes nearly broke my heart. After everything, he still worried that I might say no. "Yes, of course."

"Really, ye will, lass?"

105

"Aye," I mimicked his brogue in jest, reaching up to kiss him gently before standing on my tiptoes to whisper into his ear. "I want nothing more than to be your wife."

At once, the hunger I had seen in his eyes when I opened the door returned. He kissed me wildly with no sort of restraint. He held me flat against him as he groaned into my mouth and dug his hips into me. I moaned at the sensation.

"I'm verra pleased to hear it, for I dinna wish to bed ye if ye werena to be me wife. Now that ye are, I doona believe I can wait until we are married. But I willna touch ye if ye doona wish it."

"You're joking, right?" My fingers immediately flew to help him in the removal of his shirt. It felt like I'd been waiting years to see what lay beneath it, and I couldn't help the sharp intake of breath the sight of him caused me. He was beautiful, perfect, and now he was mine.

He laughed at my hastiness. "Tit for tat, lass. Turn yerself around."

He did his best to untie my laces, but his shoulder was still so sore that he could scarcely use one of his hands. "Go get in the bed," I demanded.

He shook his head, taking my order for a dismissal of his ability to make love due to his injuries. "Nay, lass. I am well enough to bed ye. Thinking of doing so was the only thing that kept me from succumbing to the icy cold that tried to lure me into death. I doona care if me shoulder bothers me. I need to be inside ye, Adelle."

"Oh, don't worry. You will be. Take off your clothes and go get in the bed."

He laughed but obeyed. I had to restrain from reaching out to smack his beautiful rear end as he took off his clothes. There was age to his body, no doubt, but I wouldn't have wanted him any other way. To me, it only added to his masculinity.

"Ye are a bossy wench, are ye not?"

I didn't answer him, only grinned wickedly and nodded as I

slowly untied my laces. I reveled in the way his jaw dropped with every increasing inch of skin that revealed itself to him as I slowly removed my dress.

I gave him a moment to gaze upon me, the adoration in his eyes enough to make me feel as if I was the most beautiful woman on earth. I moved across the room to blow out the last candle. As darkness engulfed the room, I slipped into the bed with him, straddling myself atop him to care for his tender shoulder.

I leaned forward, my bare breasts pressing up against his chest. I kissed him, moaning as he dug his fingers deep into my hair and tugged my head backward, exposing my neck as he kissed me along my collarbone.

I squirmed astride him and when he could stand it no more I raised up so that I could descend upon him. We moved together gently, both of us absorbed in the newness of one another.

It didn't matter that the candles weren't lit, the room was ablaze with our love for one another.

CHAPTER 24

We were married in the great room of Conall Castle on New Year's Day surrounded by all of the people we loved most in the world. The vows were simple, but I'd never meant anything more than the few words we spoke to one another.

"I doona know where life will take me, but I choose ye to be at my side. From this day forward, my soul belongs to naught but ye. I now bind meself to ye in the present and for all the times to come. Together we are now one."

I didn't know where the vows came from, and I'd undoubtedly messed up the accent badly, but Hew didn't care, and neither did I.

As he leaned in to kiss me, baby Ellie Adelle Conall, named in honor of Eoin's mother, Elspeth, and myself, squealed as if she'd been pinched. Our pups howled loudly in response.

A happy chaos surrounded us, and it was just as we wished it.

I had been right. It proved to be the best Christmas that Conall Castle had ever seen.

A MCMILLAN CHRISTMAS

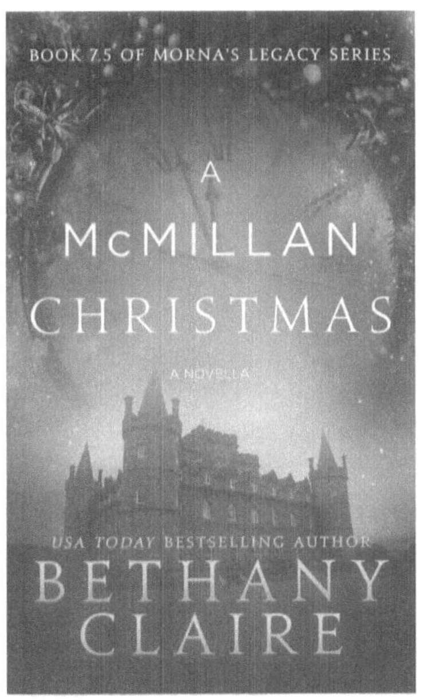

CHAPTER 1

On An Unknown Road In Scotland—December 18, 2016

I could barely see the road in front of me. Thick snowflakes the size of quarters fell so quickly that my windshield wipers couldn't keep up. Just as soon as one layer of snow was brushed away by the blades, another fresh coating took its place. To make matters worse, not only did the cheap tires on my standard rental feel less than secure on the icy Scottish roads, I was also helplessly lost.

The journey from the airport to my grandparent's new home in the Highlands was—according to them—supposed to take me three hours, tops. It was now two in the afternoon, and I was already on hour five of my drive.

The sudden vibration of the cell phone inside my coat pocket rattled me so much that I quickly pressed on the brakes and steered into the first pull-off I approached.

Pulling the phone out of my pocket, I hurried to answer before it sent my grandmother to voicemail.

"Hey, Gram. I know I'm late, but the weather is growing increasingly nasty as I continue north. In all honesty, it may be days before I get there. The visibility is very low and..." I trailed off as broken segments of my grandmother's voice interrupted my speech.

"Harper...Harper...I canna hear ye. Where are ye?"

Of course the reception was bad. As soon as I reached the edge of Edinburgh on my way out of the city, my signal dropped. Her phone call was the first sign that any reception had returned. It was part of the reason I was lost. Not only was the rental car place out of GPS navigation systems, the cell service was so nonexistent that I couldn't use the Maps app on my phone to get directions either.

"Gram, I'm going to call you back. I'm in a hole. Let me drive to the top of this hill, and I'll try to call you back."

I didn't wait for her answer. Ending the call, I shifted the car into gear and slowly made my way to a point of higher elevation ahead. It took longer than expected. I was forced to pull over four times for oncoming traffic. On the long, winding, one-lane road, I appeared to be the only one headed north. It only confirmed what I already knew—coming to Scotland was a mistake.

I suspected it the day I booked my ticket, knew it deep down when I boarded the plane, but watching all of northern Scotland fleeing south confirmed it completely. I was cold, frustrated, and near tears. I pulled over once again and returned my grandmother's call.

"Gram, is this any better? Can you hear me?"

"Aye, I can hear ye just fine. Do ye know where ye are?"

I didn't have the slightest clue. Five years had passed since my last visit to Scotland, and I'd only ever been in this part of the country with Kamden. At the time—fool that I was—I'd been too wrapped up in him to take much notice of what was going on around me.

"I really don't. I had to wait two hours at the rental car place, then all they had was a compact standard with no GPS. I've done my best to follow your instructions but, honest to God, I don't know how any of you get around. Nothing is clearly marked, and the weather is so bad I'm not sure I would be able to see the proper signage even if it was there."

Now thoroughly worked up, I struggled to take a deep breath and forced my tone to soften before I spoke once again.

"I'm sorry, Gram. I'm just ready to see you guys. Everything is fine. I'll get there eventually. It just might be midnight. Keep the lights on for me. Did you know the weather was supposed to do this?"

I should've checked it myself. I knew that Scotland had plenty of snow this time of year. Truthfully, too many memories had been playing through my head while packing for the weather to cross my mind.

Gram's long pause was answer enough. Eventually, when I said nothing, she relented.

"Aye, I knew there was a chance, but they hardly ever get it right. I was worried that if I told ye, ye wouldna come. All of this is my fault. I canna tell ye how sorry I am. Yer grandfather told me I should tell ye, but I just wanted to see ye so badly. Now I've had ye fly all the way to Scotland and 'tis verra likely I willna be able to see ye anyway."

Gram's voice trembled, and my heart squeezed uncomfortably. I hurried to reassure her.

"Hey, it's okay. You can't take responsibility for the weather. Of course you'll get to see me—it just may be tomorrow instead of tonight. It will be okay. We are still days away from Christmas, and I'm staying through the New Year."

"Oh, my sweet girl, ye doona understand. I tried to call ye as soon as I saw that yer plane had landed to tell ye to get a hotel at the airport where ye could stay until ye got another flight home, but it never went through."

"A flight home? Why would I book a flight home?"

"Harper, we are completely snowed in. The road to our house is impassable, and I expect it to get far worse before it gets any better. Most of Scotland will be buried under snow come morning."

My grandmother continued to talk, but I no longer listened as her words replayed in my mind. Snowed in? Impassable? What was first an annoyance now presented itself as a real danger. At this time of year, it would be dark in only a handful of hours. If the vast empty land that lay behind me was any indication of what lay ahead, I doubted I would be able to find lodging anywhere close. If the road to my grandparent's house was impassable, then surely many other roads would be, as well.

"Harper, can ye hear me? Are ye listening?"

The worry in my grandmother's voice pulled me back into our conversation.

"Yes, I'm sorry. I'm listening. I'm just…I'm not sure that I'm going to be able to find anything before I reach roads that are too covered in snow, and I don't think I have enough gas to keep my car warm overnight."

The quick shuffle of the phone as it shifted hands told me just how frightened my grandmother must be for me. She'd never been one to handle any sort of crisis well, and my grandfather, God bless him, was always there to step in and save the day for her. If only all men were as wonderful as him.

I smiled as his deep, calm, and reassuring voice came over the phone.

"Ye and yer grandmother are cut of the same cloth. Both of ye lassies take a deep breath and calm down. Do neither of ye have any faith in me at all? I willna let ye freeze to death in the snow. If we can figure out just exactly where 'tis ye are, I'm certain I'll be able to think of a place ye can go. I know this country as well as I know the moles on my arm. If ye truly are good and lost, why I'll find myself a snowmobile and will go in search of ye."

I smiled at the confident humor in his voice. He must've been just as worried as Gram, but he hid it well. I would've given just about anything to see him zooming over the snow-laden countryside astride a snowmobile right then.

"Okay, thank you for that. I've no doubt that you would come and find me if it truly did come to that, but let's hope it doesn't. I really have no idea where I am. How do you expect me to tell you?

"Firstly, bundle yerself up real nice and leave yer car running. Ye have winter hiking boots on, aye?"

"Yes."

"Brush the snow off the top of yer hood and climb atop so that ye may see better. Keep yer phone shielded in the hood of yer coat and tell me what ye see."

The prospect of stepping out into the freezing cold didn't thrill me, but I knew that in order to pinpoint my location, I would have to get a better grasp of my surroundings. I touched on the speakerphone and lay my phone on the dash so that I could ready myself for the wintery air that awaited me outside.

"All right, give me just a second. Can you hang on? Don't hang up. I'll let you know when I can see something."

"O'course, lass. I'll not be going anywhere until we've seen ye safely settled somewhere this night."

With my coat zipped, head covered, and gloves on, I placed the phone in my pocket, reached in the backseat for the window scraper, and stepped outside. I'd only been parked for ten minutes, and several inches of snow were already accumulated on top of the car. It took some effort to brush the bulk of it off. Once I managed, I climbed up onto the vehicle and reached back into my pocket for my phone.

"Okay, I'm here. Let's see..." I stalled while taking in the landscape around me. I sat parked at the top of a hill with a deep valley to my left and high terrain to my right. Rolling, snow-covered hills lay ahead. "All right. I just drove up a pretty steep climb so if I look behind me, it's a deep slope down. To my left is a large valley. There are no buildings or landmarks that I can see from that direction. Ahead is a winding road with three distinct dips and peaks. To the right, it's pretty much just straight mountainous terrain. I hope the snow doesn't cause any rocks to slip because I'm pretty certain I would be toast if any fell."

There was a brief period of silence. I could just imagine Gramps stroking his thick beard with his thumb and pointer finger as he tried to picture all that I told him.

Eventually when he spoke, his tone was filled with even more humor than before.

"Did ye say there are three distinct peaks in the road ahead?"

I lifted my hand to my brow to block some of the snow and strained to make certain.

"Yes."

"Turn yer head upward. Is there a rock at the top of the mountain that resembles a monkey?"

The snow made it difficult to see, but if I concentrated, I could make out the hint of such a shape. A memory tugged at the edge of my consciousness.

"Yes. The snow blurs it a bit but, yes, I do think I can see it."

"Lass, I know just where ye are. I believe ye know, as well."

The memory returned full force. I'd looked over this exact deep valley and stared up at the monkey rock once before.

I knew exactly what lay ahead—McMillan Castle...and the man who broke my heart.

CHAPTER 2

M *cMillan Castle*

Everyone would be surprised to see him—Alfred, the tour guide; Henderson, the ticket salesman; Margaret, the cook; even the castle dog, Sileas, would find his timing surprising. It would be the first time in a decade he'd come home before the end of the castle's tourist season. If the weather predictions were correct, McMillan Castle was about to see the worst snowstorm of the past one hundred years, and he had no wish to make everyone that worked there spend Christmas trapped in the castle with him. Those with families should spend it with their loved ones. It wouldn't be his first Christmas spent alone.

As he pulled into the driveway of his old home, Kamden McMillan slowed his car to a stop, rolled down his window, and waited patiently for Henderson to recognize him as large, wet snowflakes floated into his car.

"Hello. Welcome to McMillan Castle. 'Tis a mighty cold day, but in my humble opinion, ye are about to embark on a discovery of the most magnificent castle in all of Scotland. Ye have come on a verra fine day, as well. Our head cook, Margaret, has prepared her special Christmastime bread pudding. Ye willna want to miss it. After yer..."

Kamden watched as Henderson glanced up for the first time.

"Wha—what are ye doing here, Kamden? Why dinna ye tell me it was ye? I wouldna have kept blabbering on so."

He laughed and reached through the window to shake his old friend's hand. "I was enjoying yer sales pitch far too much. While I believe ye are over selling the experience, I appreciate yer efforts to bring people through the gates."

"Are ye staying through the holiday then?"

He nodded and shifted the car back into gear as Henderson opened the gates.

"Aye. What time does the next tour leave? I've got a mind to lead it myself."

"Oh, ye should. Everyone would love it. Ye've ten minutes to make yer way to the front doors. Best ye say hello to Margaret first, or she'll be right angry with ye."

"Aye, she would. Not a one of us wants that, do we? I shall enter through the back so that I can see her first. It's good to see ye. I'll visit with ye more at close today. I wish to meet with everyone in the sitting room this evening. Today shall be the last day of the season."

He drove away quickly so that Henderson couldn't question him. There were several cars already lined up behind him. If he got out of their way, perhaps they could make the tour he planned to lead.

The road from the gates to the side of the castle stretched the length of the large pond that lay in front of the castle. So many stories of magic were associated with the freezing cold waters of McMillan Castle—not that he believed in magic. If he did, he would certainly be calling upon it now, pleading with it to give him one more chance to make things right.

He shook his head to clear his mind as he neared the castle's side entrance. Melancholy thoughts would not help him give his castle guests the tour they deserved. Turning off the car's engine, Kamden hurried inside, stomping on the doorway rug to remove the snow from his boots. He could smell Margaret's baking and happily followed the smell.

When he entered the kitchen, Sileas, who lay happily at Margaret's feet hoping to catch some kitchen droppings, spotted him and let out his signature whine as he bounded toward him nearly knocking Margaret's feet right out from under her.

"Why, ye naughty dog. Do ye mean to make me break a hip? What are ye carrying on about?"

Kamden extended his arms wide as Margaret saw him. He braced himself for what was sure to be a rough impact as she ran toward him. He hugged her close as she reached him.

"I dinna expect to see ye for at least another week. Is the weather what has brought ye here?"

Of course Margaret would guess his reasons for coming early.

"Aye, but I mustna stay and visit just now. I've a mind to lead the last tour today. Do ye think Alfred will mind?"

Margaret kept a hand on his lower back as she ushered him from the kitchen.

"No, not at all. I expect he'll be verra pleased. He's come down with a bit of a cold. His voice has nearly left him completely. In truth, yer timing couldna be better."

"Good." He paused, the suggestion of his comment sinking in. "Not good that he's ill. Good that he will...eh, never mind. Ye understand what I mean. I canna wait to taste yer pudding. I'll see ye later."

Kamden bent to kiss her cheek and hurried to find Alfred before the castle's last Christmas tour.

*O*n The Road To McMillan Castle

"*I*s this outing truly necessary, Morna? I know ye feel that ye are rather invincible, and I suppose ye actually are, but 'twould do ye good to remember that I am not of the supernatural. If we crash on these icy roads, it could do me in."

Morna laughed as she sped across the snow-laden countryside, not reducing her speed a bit at her husband's words. After all the times she'd used her magic to bring people together through time travel, he should be accustomed to her shenanigans by now.

"Jerry, we've already discussed this. Of course 'tis necessary. Do ye really think I would be dragging either of us out in this weather if 'twas not? I have spent so much energy tending to the needs of my family that reside in the past that I've done a rather poor job of tending to relatives in the present. There is a lad verra much in need of my aid this evening."

"Does this lad know that he requires yer help?"

"Of course not. Do they ever? I hardly see how that matters at all, Jerry."

Jerry laughed. It pleased Morna to know that he didn't plan on being miserable for the entirety of their outing.

"Ye are right, love. It matters not. What of the lass—does she live in a time already past? Do ye mean to send him back?"

Time travel was her signature spell. While a form of it would be employed for her next pair of destined lovers, she had a new twist up her sleeve for this night.

"She lives verra much in the present—a modern lassie for a modern man. Aye, they will both travel backwards though in a different way than before. 'Tis a new spell. I verra much hope it works."

"Ye know it will work. They always do."

Morna could sense that Jerry was tense as she slowed her speed and turned into the driveway leading to the castle. The gate and ticket booth were closed and not a single car could be seen past the gate.

"I think we've arrived too late, Morna. It looks as if they've closed for the day. Mayhap longer than that if this weather keeps up."

She refrained from rolling her eyes at him. How had he not already guessed that she'd ensured they would arrive at precisely the time she intended?

"Jerry, I can see the castle is closed. 'Twill do little to keep us from entering. I wish to speak to the lad, and I'll hardly be able to do that if the castle is crawling with tourists."

"Aye, fine, but how do ye expect to explain yer sudden intrusion into the man's home?"

"Ye of little faith, Jerry. Why doona ye just wait and see? Follow my lead. I'll have us both back home in time for supper."

CHAPTER 3

"*H*as everyone cleared out? Ye dinna rush them, did ye?" Kamden directed his question to Alfred as all of the other castle workers began to fill the entryway. He knew the man felt terrible from the redness of his nose and the pasty pallor of his cheeks, but he'd specifically instructed that no tourist be ushered out of the castle until they were good and ready to leave. If he was going to have to close a full five days early, then he would allow the last tourists of the season as much time as they wanted to wander around inside.

"No rushing was required. I believe everyone can tell the weather is about to take a turn for the worst. I think they were all ready to seek shelter elsewhere."

"I doona doubt it." Kamden leaned to the left of the large doorway, glancing out the paned windows at a sea of white stretching beyond the front lawn of the castle all the way to the pond. The frosty waters of McMillan's pond were already beginning to freeze. By Christmas, it would be frozen through. "Where is Margaret?"

"I'm right here. Hold yer horses, ye impatient man. While

everyone else's work ends when the last guest leaves, mine never ceases."

Kamden smiled and gratefully took the steaming mug of coffee Margaret extended in his direction.

"Aye, while what ye say is usually true, it is no longer the case. Not this winter. I have come home early to see this place shut down until well after the New Year. Weather reports predict record-breaking snowfall and ice. I willna have a one of ye out here putting yerself in danger. Nor will I have tourists wandering out here during such a mess. I simply want to meet with all of ye to tell ye to have the verra merriest of Christmases and to leave here at once. As always, I appreciate everything ye do for me here, but I can manage just fine for the time being without ye. Doona forget to pick up yer bonuses next to the doorway before ye leave. We will open back up in March."

Kamden knew the only protest would come from Margaret. Everyone else would be thrilled to spend a few more days with their loved ones before Christmas. What Margaret didn't know was that once he told her the surprise he had in store for her, she would be just as ready to abandon him as the rest.

"Ye surely canna mean me, as well? What will ye do for food? I willna leave ye here to starve. I believed I was to have five more days to prepare and freeze enough food to keep ye fed and well for the next month. I need that five days. I willna be leaving until my work is completed."

"Margaret, if ye insist on staying, ye may go to the kitchen and do what ye can for the next few hours. I'll see everyone else off, settle myself into my chambers, and then I'll discuss yer early departure with ye in private. Make no mistake, I'll be seeing ye safely home before dusk."

He could see from the way her stance shrunk just an inch that she believed there was no point in arguing with him. Her surrender would be short lived. He had no doubt that by the time he went to see her in the kitchen, she would be ready to debate the matter with him once again. He waited until she turned and left the room to bid everyone else farewell.

"Ye are a fine man, Kamden. I would've sat at my post without complaint until the end of the season, but I did fear that the loss of my toes would be the price I would pay for my loyalty to ye. Thank ye for yer kindness."

Kamden knew that Henderson joked, but the man's words brought up a valid concern.

"Is there no heater in the ticket booth? Ye should have said something long before now."

"Aye, there is, but every time I open the window to greet the next guests, all the warm air disappears."

"We will come up with a better solution for ye before we open again. For now, go and ready yer home for all of the grandchildren I know must be headed yer way."

"Aye, they are. I canna wait to squeeze them."

The old man's build was broad and harsh, but his face and smile were friendly, and he never looked happier than when he spoke of his grandchildren.

The impending sadness of a Christmas spent all alone would be worth it to him if everyone he cared for could fill their holiday in the company of those they loved most.

Kamden opened his arms to hug Henderson. As the old man left, he said goodbye, one by one, to those that worked to keep his castle and home a wondrous delight for all its guests.

After he saw everyone save Margaret gone, he turned to grab his jacket, intent on gathering his belongings from his car. Instead, as he walked outside, he was met by an elderly couple making their way to the front door of the castle. Snow swirled around them, and they both looked like they were about to blow over from the force of the wind. Too shocked by their sudden appearance to say anything else, he hurried to offer them assistance.

"Let me help ye. 'Tis too cold for either of ye to be out in such weather."

The couple, both seemingly battered by the wind and snow, said nothing as he moved in between them and placed an arm around each to help them walk.

He glanced back at the castle gates as they moved together and was surprised to find them standing wide open. Henderson's car was already gone. It was unlike him to leave without making sure the gate was secured.

Once inside, he released his grip. The woman, after taking a moment to dust snow from her coat, spoke for the first time.

"Oh thank ye, lad. We had no idea the weather would turn so ghastly. No wonder we seem to be the only tourists here this day. Please tell me ye are still giving tours."

Kamden quietly took them both in for a moment. They'd appeared so frail to him as he watched them trudging through the snow up to the doors, but now as they stood brushing themselves off, they appeared anything but.

"Doona ye watch the news? This weather has been forecast for some time."

Kamden couldn't help but think that the old woman was a little too quick with her response to him.

"We doona have a television. Ye know how the forecast goes anyway. It seems they are only right half of the time."

While that was true, it still did little to explain their presence. Did they not notice the empty ticket booth even if the gate was open?

"Well, I canna disagree with ye. Excuse my rudeness, but ye must have passed the ticket booth on yer way here. Dinna ye notice that it was unmanned? I'm afraid that we've already closed for the winter season due to the weather. Allow me to escort ye safely back to yer car. I suggest ye hurry home and tuck in for the storm."

Neither of them moved at his suggestion. By their

expressions, he didn't think they were surprised to hear that the castle was closed.

"I did see that the ticket booth was closed, but seeing as the gate was open and it is so verra cold outside, I simply assumed that ye had moved sales to inside the castle. Surely, even if ye are closed, ye willna turn us away for we are here now and drove three hours to reach ye. My husband loves Christmas, and he has looked forward to seeing McMillan's Christmas decorations all year. Ye willna disappoint him, will ye?"

Kamden eyed the old man and saw nothing that resembled disappointment on his face. If anything, he looked rather amused at his wife's ramblings.

Regardless, the woman was right about one thing—they were already here. What would it really hurt for him to give one last tour of the season? If anything, Margaret would be thrilled to have two more people with whom to share her bread pudding.

"Right ye are. Why doona ye hang yer coats and follow me? I'll see that ye have the grandest of all tours."

cMillan Castle

Normal group tours of the castle lasted exactly forty-five minutes. Alfred would show each group of visitors around the main common areas of the castle, bring them down to the castle kitchens, and then upstairs to see two of the castle's twelve bedrooms. The tour always ended in the great room. During warmer months, a tour of the castle gardens was also provided. Even during the Christmas season, when slightly more time was taken to explain the various decorations in each room, tours never lasted longer than an hour.

This tour, however, with its talkative and questioning couple, had already gone on for an hour and a half. Eager to see Margaret off before nightfall, Kamden eventually turned to address the elderly couple behind him, intent on informing them that their private tour had come to an end.

"And now, we've reached the end of our tour. All of the rooms past me are my own private chambers and are not open to guests.

It would help ease my worry a great deal if ye would allow me to escort ye to yer vehicle so that ye may travel home before the weather grows worse."

The woman—who he now knew was named Morna—spoke as if he'd said nothing about ending the tour.

"Private chambers, ye say? Why, I've always wondered how a modern man would live in such an ancient castle. Surely ye have yer own rooms done up differently than the rest of the castle?"

He answered hesitantly. The woman seemed to be an expert at extending conversations.

"Aye...they have been altered significantly."

Kamden didn't miss the ornery lift of the old woman's smile. Dread filled him.

"Would ye mind ever so much if I looked inside? Ye giving us a tour made my husband's night, but this would truly make mine. If ye will only let me inside for a moment, I promise ye we will leave straight away."

Under most circumstances, he would have denied the woman's request. No guests were permitted inside this wing of the castle, but he knew there was really no harm in letting her look. He'd yet to unload his belongings from his car so he knew the room would be in pristine condition.

His arms were crossed, but he lifted a hand to point one finger in Morna's direction.

"Aye, fine. Ye may look but then ye must leave straight away. I willna have ye stuck out in this weather. And please doona take any photographs inside these rooms."

"O' course. Thank ye."

Morna smiled brightly at him as he reached to open the door to his living quarters. It stretched the length of the hallway. Rooms for any personal guests he might have lined the other side of the hall.

An idea occurred to him as he ushered them inside, and he

hurried to follow through on it in order to ensure their quick departure from the castle.

"Why doona the two of ye look around in here all ye like? I trust ye not to touch or take anything. While ye look, I shall go and start yer car and bring it directly to the front door."

Morna's husband, Jerry, stepped toward him, whispering so that Morna couldn't hear.

"God bless ye man, for this and for putting up with my wife for these last hours. Ye are a saint among men. I would've turned us both away at the door."

Kamden smiled and gave the man a firm pat on the back. He'd known all along that the old man cared little about seeing the inside of his home.

"It was my pleasure. I'll meet the two of ye downstairs."

Kamden wasn't sure he should allow the couple to leave. The snow fell so thick and heavy that he doubted Margaret's ability to make it home, and she only lived a mile away. This couple had much further to go. Still, when he offered them a room, they refused it, and for a reason he couldn't quite explain, when the old woman told him she could manage the trip home just fine, he believed her.

She hugged him tightly before they left. There was a grandmotherly grip to her hug that made him feel as if he'd known the eccentric woman all his life. Despite the poor timing and odd circumstances of their arrival, he found himself rather sad to see them go.

"What are ye doin' just standing out there? They passed through the gate long ago. Come inside and let me show ye what I've prepared for ye."

He turned toward Margaret's voice, brushing the snow off of his arms and shoulders as he walked.

"I'm sorry it took me so long. I dinna expect them to stay for hours. It would have been best if I'd denied their request for a tour."

"Oh, doona say that. 'Tis Christmastime. I'm sure yer kindness meant much to them. I've only managed to prepare a week's worth of meals for ye. I would really prefer it if ye let me stay here until Christmas Eve so that I may see ye better settled. I truly doona mind."

Kamden smiled. He couldn't wait to see Margaret's excitement at his news.

"Ye canna stay. Someone awaits ye at home."

He watched as Margaret's brows rose high on her forehead, but she showed no excitement as she eyed him suspiciously.

"Who? Doona tell me 'tis Emily and the babe. I may fall over from joy if it is."

Kamden took a step closer to her—just in case she actually did.

"I hope that ye doona fall, but I'll catch ye if ye do. Aye, 'tis Emily, the babe, and yer new son-in-law, too. I picked them up at the airport early this morning and saw them to yer home before I came here."

Margaret's arms came around him in an instant. He could feel her sobbing as he held on to her tightly. Her daughter lived in Australia with her new husband and baby, and Margaret had yet to meet either of them.

"Doona cry or ye shall make me cry, as well. I couldna verra well allow ye to miss the child's first Christmas, could I? Now, ye needn't show me a thing as I know verra well that ye have left detailed instructions on how I should heat everything. Gather yer things and let me see ye home."

Margaret pulled away just enough so that she could grasp both sides of his face. Tears filled her eyes as she looked up at him.

"I willna ever be able to thank ye enough for this kindness.

Why doona ye join us for dinner? It breaks my heart to know ye plan to spend Christmas here all alone."

"No, ye need the time with yer family. I will be just fine here. It willna be my first Christmas alone. I've grown rather accustomed to it."

Margaret stepped away and frowned as she reached for her purse.

"No one should grow accustomed to such a thing. There is another out there for ye, I know it. 'Tis only that ye must open yerself up to the possibility of love again. Otherwise, it will never find ye."

He appreciated Margaret's optimism, but he knew that there was only one lass that would ever hold his heart, and he'd ruined any chance he had at holding hers long ago.

"Perhaps ye are right, though I doona think I'll open myself up to it this Christmas."

He turned without another word, leaving her to follow after him.

n A Now-Known Road

"Gramps, I appreciate you helping me figure out where I am. Can you please hand the phone back to Grandma?"

I couldn't talk about this with him. Grandfather had always been far too fond of Kamden—even after the debacle of our breakup. He wouldn't understand my dismay over having to go back to the place where everything had fallen apart.

He said nothing, but I could hear the phone switch between their hands once again. Gram's tone was immediately empathetic.

"Harper, before ye say anything, I want ye to realize that I really doona think ye have any other choice for tonight. I know that does little to make it any easier. 'Tis only that I know ye, and I'm worried that ye will dig in yer heels and try to make do in the car overnight rather than go to the castle. Ye'll freeze if ye do that. 'Tis far too cold."

Most nights, she would've been right, but just a few minutes exposed to outside air had caused my joints to ache from the cold. I knew I had no choice.

"No, you don't need to worry about that, but yeah, it doesn't make it any easier. What am I supposed to say to him? I haven't seen him in five years. He's probably married by now. What if his wife is there with him? What if he has children there?"

The thought alone was enough to make my head spin and my stomach cramp uncomfortably. It would be hard enough to see him alone, but if someone else was there—a wife or a girlfriend—the liquor cabinet would need to be well-stocked to see me through this storm.

"Harper, he isn't married. Doona ye think I would've told ye if he'd gotten married?"

I didn't really know. It had been so long since I'd seen either of my grandparents and even when I spoke to them, they were both careful to never mention Kamden.

"Oh. Okay, well, good. Still, what do you think he will say? I know he will let me in, but I hardly think he wants to be snowed in with me for days on end."

"Sweetheart, if ye would stop speaking for more than three seconds, I could calm yer worries. Kamden willna be there. I saw Margaret a week ago, and she said that he wasn't due to arrive at the castle until Christmas Eve. With the weather the way it is now, I verra much suspect that no one will be at the castle."

A breath I didn't know I held released at my grandmother's words. The castle was empty. Not only would I have a beautiful, warm, safe place to stay for the night, but I could enjoy it all without dealing with my ex-boyfriend. Sure, I would have to stare down plenty of ghosts of Christmas pasts in the castle, but I could manage the memories. I wasn't so sure that I could manage facing Kamden.

"Are you sure?"

"About what? I am fairly sure that Kamden willna be there, though I admit that I canna say for sure that no one will be at the castle. Though anyone that might be there will let ye inside. Only the Grinch himself wouldna let someone in on a night like this. Now, get off the phone with us and get yerself to the castle. Let me know when ye get there."

"I will. I'm sorry that I won't make it tonight. I'll get there as soon as I can."

"There is nothing for ye to be sorry for, Harper. We will see ye when the weather clears—whenever that may be."

As we bid each other farewell, I buckled my seatbelt and took off for McMillan Castle, hoping with each passing mile that the castle would be unattended and that Kamden hadn't moved the back door's spare key.

McMillan Castle

A hot bath would fix everything. His nose burned from exposure to the cold, and his legs ached from trudging through the snow. Nothing could have prepared him for such a long walk back. If his own car couldn't make it the mile back from Margaret's house, he was surely glad he'd insisted on bringing her home himself rather than letting her take her own car. Now, his car remained at Margaret's home, and Margaret's car was stowed safely inside the castle's old stables. Not that it mattered—no one would be going anywhere for days.

He very much hoped that the elderly couple from before made it home safely, for in this sort of Scottish weather, it wasn't safe for a single soul to be outdoors.

It took a long while for the bath water to run warm, but eventually steam began to rise. Kamden undressed quickly, placing the stopper in the bottom of the large copper, claw-foot tub as he slipped inside. He wished for every hot, scalding drop to touch his skin. He didn't remember ever being so cold before.

As the heat thawed him, thoughts of Harper swam through his mind. Baths always made him think of her. So did airplanes, scones, black and white films, and truthfully, just about everything else. He wondered what she was up to now—where she lived and whom she now shared her life with.

He wondered what she would think about the man he was today.

Sileas slept happily next to the tub. As the chill in his bones thawed, he closed his eyes, perfectly content to relax this way for the rest of the evening.

The spare key was gone, the old lock replaced with a numbered touchpad. I eyed the numbers nervously. The castle was surely hooked up to some sort of security system, not that I believed anyone would come and investigate a break-in during this weather. Even so, I didn't have any real desire to listen to sirens all night while I tried to sleep.

Kamden was a man of habit, of tradition. He never changed anything unless forced to do so. The rigid walls in every area of his life made him feel secure, and they are exactly what pushed me away.

I wondered what prompted him to change the lock. Had it been our break-up? Surely he hadn't worried I would ever break in. Although, as I looked at my current situation, I realized that perhaps that was no longer quite true.

My fingers hovered nervously over the keypad as I thought back on any important dates in Kamden's life. His birthday, his parents' anniversary, the year the castle was built—none of the combinations worked.

If the lock was like most, it would only allow me a few more tries before triggering the alarm system. On a whim, I typed in the only other date I could think of, the one date I was almost certain Kamden would no longer remember—the date of our first day of college—the day we met. Kamden and I both started college later than most people. There were just too many adventures we each indulged in before getting serious about our careers. It was our unique but shared early adulthoods that attracted us to each other in the first place. To my everlasting surprise, the lock clicked open. Into the castle I stepped.

***

Sileas' sudden leap from the floor sent Kamden's eyes flying open, and water sloshed onto the floor as he sat up in response to the dog's high, eager whine at the closed bathroom door.

"What is it, boy? 'Tis only the wind. I'm sure ye've never heard such a sound in yer life. I know I haven't, and ye are much younger than me. Come here and sit down. Everything is fine."

Rather than calm the dog, his words only seemed to aggravate the great beast further. He whined even more loudly at the door. As if begging Kamden to let him out, he ran over to the tub and jumped up on its edge, pawing to get his attention.

"All right, all right, I'm coming." He stood, reaching for the warm towel hanging on its heating rack. He dried quickly and reached for a robe to cover himself as he opened the door to the bathroom.

Kamden expected the dog to calm once he realized no one was on the other side. Instead, Sileas took off like a rocket, out of the bedroom and into the hallway. He could hear the dog running and barking all the way downstairs. He knew the dog's sounds well. It was the same noise he made when Kamden came home only hours earlier.

Someone else was inside the castle. Someone the dog knew well.

I heard the dog coming only seconds after I stepped inside and closed the back door. I recognized his heavy footsteps and the distinct sound of his whine immediately—Sileas.

I couldn't help but smile as I hurried into the castle's main entry to greet him on the stairs. For the first two years of his life, Sileas and I had been the best of friends. It wasn't until he bounded up and into my open arms that I realized how much I'd missed the big, drooling beast.

I held and rubbed him, smiling and near tears at the joy I felt to see him once again. It took a long moment for realization to set in. No one would have left Sileas here alone in such weather. If Sileas was here, it meant someone else was as well.

I stood nervously and slowly lifted my eyes to the top of the staircase. Rather than the welcoming face of Margaret or Henderson, I was met by the tortured and shocked gaze of Kamden.

Suddenly, freezing to death in the car didn't seem all that unappealing.

*M*any possibilities passed through Kamden's mind as he followed Sileas. Perhaps Margaret and her family lost heating or electricity in the storm and needed to seek shelter at the castle. God help them if they trudged through such weather with the baby. Perhaps Henderson realized he'd left the gate open after going home and came back to make certain it was closed. At least a dozen thoughts crossed his mind, but he never expected to round the corner and find his very own ghost of Christmas past staring up at him—Harper.

Five years without a word or a whisper of her, and now she stood on his stairwell.

"Ye cut yer hair."

If she wasn't standing before him, Kamden would've smacked his own forehead for saying something so stupid to her, but they were the only words he could muster. Just as it always had, the sight of her left him gobsmacked. Her hazel eyes, the shiny honey tint to her hair, the smattering of freckles across her nose, her beauty never ceased to make him smile. Her shape was different, firmer somehow, but overall she looked like the same beautiful woman. But she wasn't the same. Nothing was the same. He could see it in her eyes—the unfamiliar way she looked at him. They were now little more than strangers.

He couldn't imagine why she was here.

"Yes, I cut it some time ago. Look, I..." She hesitated and he saw her swallow. For a moment, he thought she might cry. It caused his chest to tighten in response.

"I never would have come if I'd known you were going to be here."

He didn't know how to speak to her. He feared whatever he said wouldn't relay how he truly felt—what he truly meant. "What are ye doing here then?"

Sileas balanced on his hind legs with his paws on the sides of Harper's hips, begging for her attention. Kamden looked on, waiting for Harper's answer. She continued to love on Sileas while she answered him.

"Trying not to freeze to death in this weather. You're pretty isolated out here. I didn't have many choices. I didn't expect you to be here. If anyone was here, I expected it to be Margaret or Henderson."

Of course she would come here if stranded. Anyone would. But what was she doing in Scotland? He didn't expect her to ever set foot in the country again. He remembered her swearing to as much the last time she left.

He took two steps down the staircase. Harper took two steps backwards.

"Aye, any other year, ye would have arrived to find them rather than me. I came home early when I heard reports of the storm. I dinna wish for anyone else to be stuck here because of it. They say it could last for days."

She nodded. An uncomfortable silence followed. They both realized what this meant. They would be alone here—together— for days on end. Facing their past was now inevitable.

*I*f not for the reassuring touch of Sileas' paw against me and the ability for me to hide my hands beneath the thickness of his coat, I knew Kamden would have seen me shaking. I hated it. How could he still have such an effect on me? Years had passed. Why was I not stronger? Why did the sight of him still seem to undo me so completely?

I could barely hear him over the sound of blood pumping in my ears. His voice sounded muffled and foggy. As he stepped toward me, I instinctively stepped back. I wasn't frightened of him, I just no longer knew how to interact with him. Everything about us standing across from each other felt foreign—as if I'd broken into a stranger's home to find the owner still there. It might have well been just that for the cold distance that lay between us.

One night in the castle with him would be hard enough, but only a fool would believe that the snow would be gone by morning. It would be days, possibly longer, before I would be able to leave here. It would take a miracle for me to make it to my grandparents' house by Christmas.

He stepped toward me once again. As if pulled by strings, I stepped back.

"I would never hurt ye, Harper."

I knew that. Yet I couldn't seem to control my body's need to distance itself from him in that moment. I planted my feet, grinding them into the staircase determined to not take another step as Kamden continued down the stairs to pass me. I could see the hurt in his eyes as he passed, but there was something else there as well, something that I couldn't quite put my finger on— something extraordinarily different about this man I'd once known so well.

It took his voice to bring me back to the present.

"I'm going to the kitchen. I've not yet looked at what she left, but I know Margaret cooked like a fiend this afternoon. Ye must be hungry, and ye look exhausted. Let's get ye something to eat."

I'd been both of those things earlier, but the shock of seeing Kamden shook me enough to make me forget my growling stomach and weary eyes. Adrenaline still coursed through me, making me shaky, nauseous, and wide awake.

Kamden was so calm and apparently unshaken by the sight of me. His reaction rattled me even more. While I hoped he would be gone, deep down I knew there was a possibility he would be at the castle. For him, this was his home. Nothing would have given him cause to believe I would come walking in the front doors in the middle of a snowstorm.

With Kamden gone, Sileas returned to all fours and headed for the kitchen. Reluctantly, I turned and followed him, speaking to my old friend as we went.

"Are you going to be the buffer between us, Sileas? I think we may need one. I fear that before this night is over, both of us will be in tears."

Sileas let out a knowing bark in response. Even he could foresee the inevitable trouble that would result from the two of us being locked up all alone here.

In a flash of horror, it occurred to me as I entered the kitchen to see Kamden flinging contents of the freezer onto the center island—his robe hanging half open—that his state of dress for this time of evening was unusual for him. Had I interrupted something? Was he not alone here?

I'd not noticed his robe on the stairwell. But looking at him in his current state of dress, I felt foolish to have assumed he was alone. Gram's assurance that he wasn't married shouldn't have caused me such relief. Unmarried didn't mean alone. I should know that better than anyone. Kamden and I were inseparable for years, but we never married.

Just because I'd lived like a virtual monk for the past years didn't give me reason to believe that Kamden had done the same. Of course he hadn't. Men are terrible at being alone. And as much as I hated to admit it—his looks were enough to ensure that he never needed to spend a Christmas alone unless he wished it.

"Kamden, do you need me to leave here? Margaret's home isn't far. I'm sure she would let me stay with her. If I've interrupted something, I can go."

He froze with one hand on the freezer door and another

buried deep inside it. He lifted his head and looked over his shoulder at me, his expression confused.

"What?"

"The way you're dressed—is someone else here?"

The lump that rose in my throat as I asked the question infuriated me. I hoped the fear hadn't come through in my voice. Kamden hadn't belonged to me for years. There was no reason for the thought of him with someone else to make me so emotional.

He glanced downward and smiled for the first time since my arrival.

"No. No one is here, though I doona expect ye will believe what I was doing when ye got here."

"Oh really? What were you doing?"

One corner of his mouth pulled up into an ornery grin that caused my stomach to flip over with a familiar sense of need. His smile always did me in.

"I was taking a bath."

I relaxed a little at his smile, and it seemed to me that some unseen wall crumbled between us. Not that it would make much difference—dozens more would have to be demolished for things to ever be normal between us again. Even if we were snowed in for a month, it wouldn't be enough time to accomplish that.

Still, it seemed that a pathway for communication was now open—one where I wouldn't have to worry about every little thing that I said to him. I hoped he felt the same way.

"No." I said the word on a shocked, disbelieving breath. I'd known cats who liked baths more than Kamden McMillan. "You hate baths."

I was a bonafide bath aficionado, but no matter how many times I tried to convince Kamden just how wonderful a bath could be, I'd never been able to get him to take one—even with me.

He flushed slightly but quickly turned away, burying his face in the freezer as he continued to rummage through its contents.

"They are not as terrible as I once thought them to be. Tonight, after trudging through the snow the mile from Margaret's house, one seemed especially appealing."

"Why did you walk all the way from Margaret's house?"

"I knew her car wouldna make the trip, so I parked it in the old stables and drove her down in my own. By the time I left, my own car dinna see fit to make the trip either. I was forced to walk back."

I shivered just thinking about it. It was a miracle he'd been able to manage it.

"Did that squelch any dreams you had of hiking Everest?"

He laughed and leaned back to close the freezer.

"Aye, 'tis funny that ye mention it. I was thinking just that about midway through the hike."

It didn't surprise me. Our thoughts usually followed along the same wavelength. Except when it came to matters of the heart.

Unless some miracle had occurred within the last five years, I knew that Kamden didn't have a clue what to do with any of the dishes he was so hurriedly placing on the center island. Even with Margaret's instructions, he would either burn the food or undercook it. With the initial surge of adrenaline subsiding, the growl of my stomach returned. I was far too hungry to let Kamden prepare the food.

"Why don't you let me pick something and start warming it up? You can go finish up your bath."

I moved from the doorway and made my way over to the island, not waiting for his answer as I began shuffling through the bags of frozen meals scattered on the counter.

"Aye, ye know better than to let me deal with the food. Thank ye."

I stilled as his hands gripped my arms from behind. Before I could turn or say a word, I felt his lips gently touch the back of my head.

"Harper, 'tis good to see ye."

He stepped away and left quickly, leaving me alone in the kitchen. I didn't breathe until I heard his footsteps ascending the stairs. When I finally exhaled, my breath shook with need.

I slumped over, leaning my elbows on the counter and covered my face with my hands.

I was in so much trouble.

Morna's Inn

"Jerry, come and see what I made wee Cooper for Christmas. 'Tis quite a bit larger than I intended, but I doona think it will be able to hold all the magic it needs to if I make it any smaller."

She could hear her husband's footsteps coming up the stairs, and she waited to say more until he entered. When his hands gently touched her shoulders from behind, she lifted it up for him to see.

"What do ye think? Will he like it?"

"It...'tis verra interesting. What is it meant to do?"

"Allow me to show ye."

She waved him back, knowing Jerry well enough to know he wouldn't wish to stand near her while she transported the gift backwards in time. It was an easy enough spell, one she used regularly for the letters she and the young boy sent back and forth to one another. While letters had always served the two of them just fine, Christmas was a time of magic. Why shouldn't she fill the young boy's life with just a little more of it?

"What exactly are ye showing me? Now that Cooper has the gift, how am I supposed to see what it does?"

Morna twisted and glared at her husband as she shook her head.

"Old age has made ye impatient and cranky. Give the child a moment to find it, will ye?"

Morna could sense the second Cooper picked up his gift, and she reached beneath her desk to retrieve her end of their new communication device—a small compact case, much like one she used to powder her nose. From the outside, Cooper's looked like little more than a pocket watch. Inside, it would connect him straight to her.

She popped the case open and smiled as Cooper's face appeared before her.

"Whoa, Morna, what is this? It's awesome."

"'Tis a new way for us to communicate. I made it small enough to put in yer pocket."

He frowned, and his little lip twisted uncomfortably.

"I don't have pockets."

"I bet if ye asked Isobel nicely, she could sew ye some. Doona ye think?"

"Yeah, that's a great idea. And she won't tell anybody what the pockets are for either."

Morna could see that Cooper sat on one of the castle's stairwells. What she meant to tell him, all of his family needed to hear.

"Are ye alone? If so, can ye go and gather everyone around? I need yer help this night."

Without saying another word, Cooper snapped the lid shut. She waited patiently for him to return. When he did, he was surrounded by all of McMillan Castle's residents—Mitsy, Baodan, Eoghanan and Grace, even Jane and Adwen stood in the background.

Grace spoke first, her tone gently admonishing.

"Morna, you spoil him. The letters are enough. You know that he'll never give you any peace now."

She ignored Grace. She would never cease to spoil Cooper whenever she could.

"As ye all know, I've a penchant for matchmaking. I canna help it. 'Tis my calling and it allows me to indulge in my intrusive and meddling nature. There is a descendent of yers, a man who has ended up far more alone than any in the room with ye will ever have to be. He misses his family, and he needs a second chance at love. I mean to show him the magic this night, and I wish for him to have access to it from now on. Ye all can give him part of the family he craves. I canna bring back what he lost, but I can connect him with what I can. Will ye welcome him?"

The response was no less than what she expected. It only took a few minutes for them to work out all of the details. She bid them all a Merry Christmas and a quick goodbye. When she turned to face her husband, he looked baffled and exhausted.

"How do ye ever dream up such schemes? Ye doona intend to only send the lad through one travel, but two? I fear ye have a better chance of putting him in a psych ward than mending his heart."

Morna hoped Jerry was wrong, but she couldn't deny that she was more nervous about this spell than most. Never before had one of her subjects endured two entirely different travels in such a short period of time. She just had to hope that the man and his lass were of sound mind and body. For if not, her Christmas would be spent repairing damage rather than enjoying festivities with her husband.

CHAPTER 8

*K*amden changed and left his room quickly. It wasn't until he walked into the castle's great room and met the portraits of past McMillans face-to-face that shock set in. Thoughts moved slowly through his mind and his limbs grew suddenly heavy. Unable to continue his path toward the kitchen, he leaned against the room's back wall and slumped to the floor. He always sat with the room's portraits when he needed guidance. Now he needed their reassuring presence to reaffirm his sanity.

Had what he remembered really happened? Was Harper truly standing in his kitchen right now, warming a meal for the two of them after all this time? The chances of it were so slim that it seemed impossible. And yet, he knew that it was true.

He knew it if for no other reason than the fact that Sileas refused to follow him upstairs. If it were only the two of them in the house, Sileas would have been on his heels every step. But if Harper was here, Sileas would choose her company over his any day of the week. The castle dog adored her—always had. Although, he couldn't think of anyone that didn't adore Harper. In all the years he'd known her, he'd never heard anyone say a bad word about her.

She tried to hide her shaking hands from him, but he saw them before she slipped them into Sileas' coat. It was the first place his eyes had gone—his effort to measure if Harper's surprise at seeing him was genuine. Strong emotion of any kind always caused Harper's hands to shake. Nervousness, excitement, even anger would send her hands bouncing. They validated everything she told him—she never would have come if she'd known he was here.

At first glance, the briskness of Harper's tone and stiffness of her stature made her seem like a stranger, but once she joined him in the kitchen, he knew she was still the woman he knew and loved. He was glad for it. In his mind, nothing about her needed changing.

She was still the same bright, funny mind reader she'd always been. He loved how she could pick up on his thoughts before he said them. Just as he was about to suggest that she cook instead, she offered. It was always that way with her. She knew and understood him on an intuitive level that no one else in his life ever had.

In this dreary, dreadful storm, fate had blessed him with another chance. He was not the same stupid, frightened man of five years ago. He wouldn't let her slip through his fingers once again.

He would have to tread slowly with her. While Harper's strength still shone just as brightly through her hazel-colored eyes, there was hurt in them as well. Hurt he'd caused. Hurt that would take time to heal.

He hoped the storm would give them both enough time to return to one another.

hirty minutes after Kamden went to change, I remained alone in the kitchen. While I'd never known him to take more than ten minutes to ready himself for anything, I understood why he took his time to join me. We both needed time to process. I was appreciative of the time alone.

After looking through the food that Margaret left, I chose an American favorite—meatloaf. The first year I dated Kamden, Margaret made it her mission to convince me of the merits of good Scottish cuisine. She never made anything other than traditional fare and quite stubbornly refused to let me cook. Despite her efforts, I never warmed to Scottish food.

By our second year, she started to believe that I was in it for the long haul and reluctantly began incorporating dishes that she knew were more suited to my tastes. They just so happened to be Kamden's tastes as well. For as much as he loved fried, fatty, dreadfully unhealthy foods, he should have been born in America. To everyone's annoyance, his body didn't seem to change one bit no matter how much junk he put in his mouth.

In the years since I left Kamden, much about my own diet had changed radically. While I'd never been overweight, I'd never been skin and bone either. My mother always called me "squeezable." Seeing as I didn't find anything wrong with the way I looked, the label never bothered me.

Once I left Scotland, heartbroken and angry, I needed an outlet—something to burn off all of my pent up energy. I found cycling and eliminated most of the crap from my diet. With time, my soft physique turned into a sculpted *I-bet-I-can-kick-your-ass* bod that helped to reinforce the *don't-come-near-me* vibes I worked so hard to put off. Pushing people away allowed me to control my own life, and it kept me safe from any other emotionally-stunted men that might wish to break my heart.

If someone had asked me only days before if I enjoyed my life of solitude, I would've said yes. Albeit, I have no doubt it would've sounded rather unconvincing. Now, I wasn't so sure about anything. I didn't know if it was just nostalgia or some long locked away part of my heart struggling to break free, but part of me longed to be the girl I used to be. I wanted to be the easygoing girl, the "squeezable" one who knew love and wasn't afraid of it. I wanted to be the girl that went to bed wrapped in the arms of another. Since I knew there was no chance of that girl returning to me tonight, I decided to at least allow myself the meatloaf.

Standing in his kitchen brought back the memories I knew were inevitable upon coming here. I doubted many people on earth were as complicated as Kamden McMillan. He was always kind, attentive, and funny with me and everyone else around him. In all our time together, I never saw him be unkind to any of his employees. Even as overwhelmed as he'd been during our first year together while he was trying to save this place, even with all of the pressure of being a full-time college student with a castle estate to run, he stayed level headed, thoughtful, and kind.

Kamden and I did everything together. We talked endlessly about everything. Everything, that is, except love. Kamden didn't speak about love in any context. I never heard the word come out of his mouth once. I understood why. The pain of growing up with a cold-hearted, closed-off toad made him weary of emotions. At least that's what he told himself and anyone that ever asked about it.

In truth though, Kamden showed love unlike anyone I'd ever known. He showed his love for his home by tending to the castle during some of its toughest times. He showed his love for his education by sticking with school despite all of his obligations here. His employees knew that he loved them by his countless acts of kindness toward them. If one of the castle workers needed their water heater replaced at their home, he would be the first person to see it fixed. When one of his tour guides found out she was expecting, he saw to it that she didn't lift anything heavier than five pounds until she went on leave. He was just that sort of guy.

I knew that he loved me, too. I never doubted it. He showed it in how he listened, expressed it in how he made love to me. I told myself that knowing he loved me was enough. I was careful to never tell him that I loved him either. I showed him in everything that I did and said, but if he wasn't willing to say the words, then neither was I. We continued like that for years. Until the day that he proposed.

On that day, our silent agreement suffered a swift, clean break. As much as I loved him, as much as I knew he loved me, in that moment, I needed to hear the words. I simply couldn't say yes without them.

In my joy at seeing him down on one knee, the words *I love you* slipped out of me easily—like I'd said them to him a thousand times. In my mind I had. I didn't even realize that I'd made a mistake until the smile fell from his face and his grip tightened on my hands. When he should've reciprocated my words—in that moment more than any other—he closed himself off to me completely—all while continuing to slide the ring onto my trembling finger.

My heart shattered in the middle of that awful silence that hung between us, and I realized that for me, knowing wasn't enough. I deserved more than he offered me in that moment.

Tears streaming down my face, I handed the ring back to him, walked over to where his car was parked and—leaving him stranded in the middle of a snowy field—I drove away. Some part of me always expected him to realize his mistake, sort through his issues, and come bring me back. He never did.

The memory no longer hurt the way it used to. For the first few years, each time I would play that scene over in my mind, I was filled with a mixture of heartbreak and rage that was so potent it would bring me to my knees. But with time, the feeling of loss decreased, and any anger that I felt for Kamden dissipated.

Kamden never meant to hurt me with his silence. If anything, I think my confession of love broke his heart, as well. I'm not sure he realized what he felt for me was love. He believed himself safe with me. Once I said the words to him, his illusion of safety shattered. He'd fallen into the most powerful emotion any person can feel, all without his knowing it.

I stood peeling potatoes when the sound of Kamden's voice in the doorway caused my fingers to slip, sending the blade skimming across the end of one of my fingers.

I screamed and looked down to see blood saucing our side dish.

CHAPTER 9

Kamden was beside me in an instant, ushering my hand into the flow of water he turned on as he reached for me.

"I'm not much in the mood for potatoes. Do ye mind if I throw them in the bin?"

Our eyes met as I glanced up at him, and we both burst into laughter.

"I should never be allowed around anything sharp. Yes, throw them in the trash."

He stepped away to clean up the mess on the counter while I washed my hand. When he returned, he rested one hand on my lower back while his other moved to guide my hand away from the running water.

"Ye need to bind this. Hold a towel against it. I will go and grab a bandage. What did ye choose?"

Once exposed to air, the sliced skin burned quite badly. I gripped it tightly and tried to ignore the fact that it still bled profusely.

"Uh, meatloaf. Is that all right?" My voice sounded strained and aggravated. I'd always been a big wimp when it came to pain.

With his hand still on my back, Kamden steered me out of the kitchen, up the stairs and to a giant leather couch in the middle of the great room. A fire burned next to it.

"Aye, I love it. Sit here. I'll return in a moment."

As soon as I relaxed into the sofa, Sileas jumped up and cuddled into me. I could still feel the touch of Kamden's hand on my back. Nervous, needy pinpricks raced up and down my spine. He was going to need to keep his hands off of me if I was going to manage to keep a level head over the course of the coming days.

Attraction didn't erase the past. Attraction didn't mean that Kamden could offer me all that he couldn't years ago. Attraction was little more than a physiological response to the memory of our shared intimacy. It was normal, natural, and completely ignorable.

By the time he returned with gauze and bandages, the bleeding had stopped. I attempted to pull the supplies from his hands, but he resisted as he crouched down in front of me close enough that his knees bumped up against the edge of my shoe.

"I'll do it. 'Twould not be verra easy for ye to manage on yer own."

Hesitantly, I extended my hand and braced for the warmth of his fingers as they touched my own. My hands began to shake on impact, and I could see a grin begin to spread from the corner of his mouth. Damn him. He thought my shaking was a sign of arousal. And it was, but I sure didn't want him knowing it.

"They're only shaking because it stings. You know how I am with pain."

"Aye, 'tis true I've not known anyone with as low a pain tolerance as yerself. Though, I was there when ye broke yer femur bone in two and yer hands dinna shake a bit then."

"You're an ass."

I didn't mean to be snippy with him—the words just slipped right out.

He laughed, and his next words only left me feeling more

exposed. "I'm sorry. I doona mean to tease ye. 'Tis only that it pleases me to see that ye doona hate me completely."

He was taking a gamble with such logic. He knew that hate or anger could cause my hands to shake just as much as attraction, but I didn't see how arguing the point would help me. To continually deny it would only make him think I wanted him even more.

"I don't hate you, Kamden. I never did."

"Even when ye left?"

"Even then—especially not then."

My hand was now tidily wrapped, but he didn't release his grip.

"We need to talk, Harper—about all of it. I think we owe each other that much."

I agreed. I just dreaded it. In our current situation, a heart-to-heart was inevitable.

"We will, but only after I have food and several glasses of wine in my tummy."

I pulled my bandaged hand away from him, stood, and went in search of some wine.

---

*H*e loved the way she looked when tipsy. Harper's bright, wide smile grew even warmer than usual, and the speckled flush of her cheeks only seemed to enhance the honey color in her hair. She was on her third glass of wine, but for the ease of her movements and the ever-growing thickness of her words, it might as well have been her fifth.

She ate more than he did at dinner, but he expected it was the only meal she had eaten all day. After so many hours in the car, she was probably dehydrated to boot. He would have to take the bottle and put it away soon. While it was tempting to sit back and let Harper get totally soused, he didn't wish for her to wake with a terrible headache come morning. More than that, he wanted her honesty, not drunken confessions of feelings she'd rather withhold from him. He wanted nothing from her that she wouldn't freely give.

He stopped after one glass. He wanted a clear head when speaking with her, to say everything he wanted and be of present enough mind to hear everything she had to say.

He saw his chance when Harper stood to examine the fireplace, wine glass still in hand. For the briefest of moments, her back was turned. He stood quickly and grabbed the bottle.

"I'll be back. I'm going to put the wine away. Then, may we talk?"

She waved him on without protest. When he returned, she held a small envelope and curiously extended it towards him.

"What is this?"

His first inclination was that one of the castle staff had picked up their Christmas bonus and then in the middle of saying goodbye to everyone, set it upon the mantle and left it, but as he reached for it, he could see that it was addressed to him. He read the words aloud.

"To McMillan Castle's master. I wish you the happiest of Christmases." His brows pinched in confusion. "Is this from you?"

"No."

She laughed as she answered him and drew the word out humorously. He thought she looked a little unsteady on her feet and gently guided her over to the couch.

"Well, let's find out who it's from then, shall we?"

The letter was closed with an old-fashioned wax seal. In the center of the wax were the initials M.C. It opened easily. As he joined Harper on the couch, he read the words silently to himself.

Dear Mr. McMillan,

Let me begin by giving you our most profound gratitude for the special tour you gave my husband and me this afternoon. It was a joy to see the love you have for this place. I personally know some of your ancestors very well, and it would please them immensely to know that their home has been so well taken care of for so many generations.

Now, onto the real reason for my letter. You, fine sir, are a practical man. I know this because I knew the man who raised you. I knew the man who raised him and so on and so on. I could go for so many years past it would make your head spin. McMillan men are sound of mind and immensely practical in all things. I beg you to let go of that practicality. For a world of miracles and magic awaits you this night.

So, are you ready? You must promise me to rid yourself of doubt and criticism before you continue. I'll give you a few minutes...Ready? Here we go.

As you know, my name is Morna. I'll not tell you what I am for I see no real need to go into it here. All that's important is that I care for you more than you know. I am so very sorry that your childhood was not filled with the love you deserved. As with most of us, our pasts shape us into the people that we are, but our pasts do not have to define our future.

Five years ago, you allowed that broken little boy to ruin the relationship with the woman you were meant for. You allowed your past to define your future. Broken-hearted little boys fear love. Grown men do not.

I know that my words may sound harsh, but I canna find it in myself to apologize for them. Sometimes those that love us need to shake the stupid right from us. Is that not what happened the night you dreamed of Baodan McMillan and his fair wife, Mitsy? That's right, lad, I know all about it for I was the one who put the dream in your mind to wake you up. And wake you up, it did. You learned your lesson and I am glad of it. Now, what you need is a second chance.

So now, enough with the lecturing—I'm ready to gift you a little Christmas magic.

I don't usually deal in the business of wish granting, but if you look to the earliest portrait in the grand hall, you will see the bonniest of your ancestors. His name is Cooper, and we are the dearest of friends. He often comes to visit me in this time. While he always says it is to see me, I know the truth—he really just misses his television and Disney movies.

Just last week, Cooper was over and we were watching the story of Aladdin and his big, blue genie. Have you seen this one? If not, I highly recommend it. I know I digress, but this genie gave me an idea. There always is a nice ring to things that come in threes, so I will follow the genie's pattern.

I'm gifting you three wishes: one for you, one for sweet Harper, and one that the two of you must make together. Your wishes must be made before going to sleep this evening. To make your wishes, do the following:

1. Upon the letter's completion, chunk this note straight in the fire. Harper need not see a word inside.

2. Say your wish aloud.

3. Have Harper do the same.

4. Repeat together.

5. Rest peacefully knowing that tomorrow will be a very different day for you both.

I've only one warning. Heed it well. For the love of all that is good in this world, wish for what you know you want the most. You've already made your wish a hundred times. Just wish for the same thing tonight. If you screw this up like you did your proposal five years earlier, I shall have to come and visit McMillan Castle once again, but this time it won't be the friendly, nosy, old lady version of me you saw this afternoon. It will be the angry, distant second-aunt (or whatever I am to you) version that is good and ready to slap, rather than shake, the stupid out of you this time.

That's right. We're related. Surprise!

Jerry says hello and to tell you that he had nothing to do with any of this.

Good luck and Happy Christmas.

Morna Conall

Even with one more glass of wine in my system than was wise, I knew I'd never seen such a strange look on Kamden's face. The expression lay somewhere between fright and amusement. I couldn't figure out which one was the overwhelming emotion. Whatever the letter contained, he had no wish for me to see it. As soon as he finished reading it, he stood and chunked it in the fire.

"Was it that bad? Who is it from?"

"Ach, 'tis nothing. I closed the castle earlier today due to the weather. Just as I sent everyone away, an old woman and her husband showed up and asked if I would give them a tour. She was the strangest woman I ever met, though I dinna think her insane until this moment. I doona know why I burned it other than the letter said that I should."

He might as well have been speaking Mandarin for as little sense as all of that made, and I didn't think my slightly intoxicated state had anything to do with why I found it confusing.

"Why would she want you to burn the letter? And why is she insane?"

Kamden said nothing until he reseated himself. With Sileas still laying on the couch, I judged it safe to join him and sat on the other side of the dog.

"I doona quite know how to begin. I canna explain how she knew some of what she did."

I could see him working through all of it in his mind. His thick, beautiful brows were pulled in tightly, and he rubbed his forehead with the tips of his fingers—something he only did when he was tired.

"Why don't you start at the beginning? Talk through it with me."

It suited me just fine if we spent the evening discussing his mysterious letter and the crazy lady who left it for him. If he was distracted, perhaps he would forget to discuss anything related to us.

"Aye, fine. Oddly enough, the letter was just as much about ye as 'twas me."

"Great." When I heard the ridiculously sarcastic response to his statement escape my lips, I knew I was more into my cups than I thought. It was exactly what I was thinking, but I never intended to say it aloud. "Let me go get a big glass of water first."

He laughed and stood before I could move from the couch.

"I'll get it. I need one, as well."

It took less than a minute for him to return. He came back with two glasses of water and some aspirin for me. I smiled in thanks and quickly took the preventative painkillers.

"Okay, start at the beginning. How in the world could that woman know anything about me?"

As soon as Kamden twisted so that we faced one another on the couch, Sileas—the traitor—jumped up and went to lay by the fire. The space between us immediately seemed much too small, but I knew that moving would make my discomfort obvious.

"Well, she couldna know anything about ye. That is, unless she truly does have the powers she claims to have. Ye know as well as

I the stories people tell about this and several other castles throughout the Highlands."

I expected I knew the stories far better than Kamden. While he grew up having the stories whispered to him by his grandfather's workers, I had intentionally learned as much about the tales as I could. In the end, resurrecting the rumors were what saved McMillan Castle after the death of Kamden's grandfather. People love believing there's the chance of magic lurking right around the corner. If they can go and explore a place where magic supposedly actually exists, they're all over it. Much to Kamden's chagrin, I'd been right that he should use the tales to his benefit.

Where the stories originated from, no one knew, but they all had to do with the castle's ability to send its residents back and forward through time. At least for several generations, that is. At some point, the ritual to ignite the time travel got muddled, and over time it changed so much that it no longer contained its power. By the time I started my research into the old stories, the old tale claimed that in order to travel backward, one had to gather a rock and spin three times while holding the rock above your head, all while standing outside on the castle's highest tower. Upon completing your spins, you had to chunk the rock into the castle's pond. This method didn't work. I knew. I tried it dozens of times with countless castle tours I helped lead during weekends and summers here with Kamden. It was the highlight of every tour.

You could see in the eyes of every tourist that some small part of them always hoped it would work. I'd always been one who enjoyed whimsy. Kamden hadn't. To even hear him suggest that the old woman might have whatever "power" he referred to was startling.

"Power...as in some sort of magic? You don't believe in anything like that."

He blushed slightly and something in my stomach flip-flopped in response to how attractive he looked when embarrassed.

"Ye are right. I never did. Though the night ye left, something happened that I've not told a soul. For if I couldna explain it to myself, I knew no one else would be able to help me sort through it either. This woman knew about it. I canna see how she could've known."

What intrigue—Kamden McMillan experiencing something that didn't fit into one of his tight, rational boxes of logic. I couldn't wait to hear more.

"What happened?"

He scooted closer—too close—so close that our knees touched. Then with absolutely no hesitation, he reached for my hands and gathered them into his own. My chest tightened and my breathing escalated. The only saving grace was that he held onto my hands so tightly they couldn't shake. At least there was that to save me from total humiliation.

"I'll tell ye, but it all relates back to ye. So first, I'll say what I've been trying to tell ye since I saw ye on the stairs a few hours ago. I know ye well enough to know that yer eagerness to speak of this letter is an avoidance tactic. Aye?"

"Maybe." I would give him no more than that.

He smiled and released his grip on one of my hands to reach up and brush a strand of hair away from my face. I drew in a shaky breath and closed my eyes, hoping every minute he would stop before I melted into him.

"Did ye know that until ye, Margaret was the only person in my life to tell me she loved me? I'm sure my parents did, but I doona remember them at all. And Margaret told everyone she loved them. I always rather thought she must not really know what love is either to use the word so freely. My grandfather raised me on his own. Not once did he ever say those words to me. The only time I ever heard him utter the word love was the day he told me just how dangerous such emotion was. 'We lose the things we love,' he said. 'Best not to love at all.'"

I never met Kamden's grandfather. He passed away just one

week after we met, but I'd heard enough stories about the old man to form an unfavorable opinion of him. Still, to imagine a young boy growing up without ever having had that validation broke my heart completely. I couldn't imagine it.

"I'm so sorry, Kamden." The words fell short of what I felt, but I knew that my apology was not what he sought anyway.

"Ye doona need to be sorry, Harper. I am the one who is sorry, though 'tis no excuse for what I did to ye. I always knew better. My first love was a lass who lived just down the road. I was no more than fifteen. I loved her. I truly did. I knew it without doubt. If I remember correctly, I told her so only three months after our first date. My love for her dinna frighten me a bit. I remember thinking what a sad, lonely man Grandfather must be to have closed himself off so completely. I never bought into Grandfather's delusions about love. Through my whole life, I've allowed love to drive almost every decision I've ever made. It served me well until I met ye."

I didn't know what to say to that. If he meant to make me feel better about anything that had passed between us, it wasn't working.

"Kamden, are you trying to tell me that you couldn't return my feelings because you still love your first love more than you ever loved me? If so, that's totally fan-freaking-tastic, but there was no need for you to tell me that now. It just sort of rubs salt in the wound."

I tried to pull away from him, but he didn't allow it. Instead, his hands moved from mine up to my arms where he gripped me tightly.

"Harper, 'tis not what I'm saying to ye at all. I canna even remember that girl's last name. I told her I loved her on month three and by month five, I was with someone else whom I loved just as much. Do ye know the difference between the love I felt for those that came before ye and the love I've felt for ye since the first moment I saw ye?"

I was at a disadvantage. I couldn't move away from his grip, and the need in his eyes was as telling of his feelings as my shaking hands were of mine. Any resolve I had to resist him was crumbling by the second.

"No."

His voice was hoarse and gritty, and there was a sense of desperation in it that caused my eyes to fill with tears.

"I've always known what love was. But before ye, the loss of love was worth the risk. I could fall in love, lose it, and survive. I knew from the start that wasn't the case with ye. I knew if I loved ye and lost ye, I wouldna survive the grief of it. But at the same time, I couldna keep myself away from ye. I thought that if I kept ye at a distance and never admitted it aloud, I could protect myself from my grandfather's miserable fate. I was a fool, Harper. Denying love does nothing to prevent pain. It only makes it worse, for 'tis the loving that makes pain bearable."

He could sense that I no longer wished to pull away. His hands moved from my arms to my face where he brushed away my tears before leaning in to place his lips on mine.

He knew he should stop himself. There was still so much he needed to say to her, so much he needed to explain, but God, she felt good pressed against him. Her desperation seemed to match his own. She opened herself to him, easily accepting the swift dip of his tongue as he explored her mouth with an insatiable hunger.

He lost himself when she moaned beneath him. As he slid his hand over her breast, all thoughts of conversation left him. It was only when she stilled and pushed him away that any sensible thought returned.

"I'm sorry, Harper. I—" She interrupted him before he could say more.

"You don't need to apologize for anything. I think...I just don't think this is very wise."

It was entirely wise. Kamden had no plans of ever kissing anyone but her for the rest of his life. Though he knew he couldn't say that to her—not yet. She was already too flighty around him. Instead, he nodded in agreement, lifted himself from on top of her, and pulled himself together as much as he could.

"Ye are right." He could only vaguely recall the last words he said to her before the kiss. Luckily for him, her memory seemed to return more quickly.

"What made you realize all of that, Kamden? You referred to something that happened the night I left, but you never said what it was."

The dream—at least that's what he thought it must be. Though it was so unlike any dream he'd ever had that he found it difficult to believe that was truly what it was.

"Do ye remember my fondness of these portraits?"

Harper twisted to look at the row of faces behind them. The movement exposed her neck to him, and by the light of the fire, he could see how flushed her creamy skin still was. It caused his groin to ache dreadfully.

"Yes. You told me once that you would talk to them all the time growing up. That if you had a problem, you would come to them and somehow just talking things through in their presence helped you to sort things out."

He smiled. She never forgot anything.

"Aye, and it always did. The night ye left, however, 'twas not enough to speak to them. I needed to hear back. I was alone here. I sent everyone away shortly after ye left, spent the evening raging in front of these portraits, damning them for not being more help, damning my ancestors for dying and leaving me here to sort all of this out on my own. I drank too much and fell asleep by the fire. In my dreams, I was amongst them." Kamden paused and pointed to the earliest portrait so Harper would follow his meaning. "Not with them in reality. It was more like seeing the movie of their lives playing out in my mind.

"I saw Baodan McMillan's heartbreak at the death of his wife. I witnessed the betrayal of his brother, and I understood his pain. But then I watched as he moved out of that darkness, toward love once again.

"Whether any of what I saw actually happened to these people, I suppose I'll never know. What I do know is that seeing my own kin suffer such heart-wrenching loss only to open his heart up to the possibility of pain once again showed me that not all McMillans are destined to end up like my grandfather. Love was a choice for this man. A choice he made while already knowing true loss.

"Distancing myself from ye at the same moment I asked for yer hand did nothing to protect me from pain. All it did was betray the trust ye placed in me by offering me yer heart. I loved ye, Harper. I was simply too much a coward to say it.

"I will be a coward no more. I loved ye then, and I love ye now. And these words now will not be the last time ye hear them cross my lips. I shall tell ye every day until ye forgive me—every day until ye believe them and know in yer heart that I am not the same man I was then."

CHAPTER 12

believed him. I believed he meant every word he said. That didn't mean it was enough to change anything. He could tell me he loved me every day until this blasted snowstorm came to an end and then call and tell me he loved me every day after, and I doubted it would ever shift what was now broken inside my heart.

What Kamden didn't realize was that his confession of love didn't change anything for me. I always knew that he loved me. I knew the day I left—I was just no longer willing to be with someone who refused to say it aloud.

Five years of stifled heartbreak and anger erupted from me in one quick motion. Before I knew it, the little wine that remained in my glass splashed onto Kamden's face as I stood from the couch and glared down at him.

"You're an idiot."

Kamden's big green and infuriatingly beautiful eyes nearly bulged right out of his head as he tried to wipe away the wine with his fingers.

"Of all the ways I imagined that going, I dinna ever imagine that."

"Case in point, Kamden." My voice dripped with sarcasm.

He stood, his eyes shocked and angry as we glared at one another.

"Just what exactly did ye find so offensive? Forgive me, but I canna see it."

"I know that you 'canna' see it." I hated myself for poking fun at his accent. It insinuated that I didn't like it, and we both knew that wasn't true. But I was too wound up to reign myself in now. Calm had no chance of finding me until everything was out in the open. "That's exactly the problem. The day I left...was that the first disagreement you ever had with anybody in your life?"

I didn't wait for him to answer. I didn't really care.

"I walked away from you that day because I'm not foolish enough to agree to marry someone that won't tell me they love me, but I didn't realize this relationship was over until four weeks passed without a word from you.

"I stayed in Scotland for four weeks waiting for you to work through your shit. All while genuinely believing that once you did, you would come and find me. I left word with Margaret about where I would be, and I waited for you. You never came. Even after I went back to the States, I kept expecting you to show up."

I was screaming at him, sobbing in between shaky breaths. I didn't realize until that moment just how much pain I had carried with me all these years.

Kamden looked horrified and suddenly much older than he was. I couldn't tell if he wanted to gather me up in his arms, or turn and run into the blowing snow and hope for the best.

When he said nothing, I continued. Now that I was speaking about all of it, it felt like opening an artery, and I couldn't seem to stop the flow of words.

"Why didn't you come and find me? The second you woke up from that dream and you knew your mistake, why didn't you come? Do you think I wanted to take that stupid job in Boston? I didn't. I wanted to be here with you. And now...how am I supposed to feel after everything you've just told me? It would've been easier if some grand revelation hadn't come to you. Then I could go on believing that the reason you never came for me was because you were still just as broken as you were then.

"Now, though, I know that you weren't broken. You just didn't love me as much as you thought. For apparently, it never even crossed your mind to ask me to come back to you."

I couldn't deal with the conversation a moment more. Whatever he could say in response to me, I knew it wouldn't make me feel any better.

Turning away from him, I gently clicked to call Sileas to my side, and I walked from the room.

"Where are ye going?"

Kamden's voice followed after me. I could hear his steps approaching, but I didn't look back, and I didn't say a word until I reached the room across from his. I would spend the night here, without my bags. I couldn't bear to say another word to him until there were walls between us.

Once inside, I slumped back against the door, waiting for the questions I knew were bound to come from the other side. I could feel him out there sitting just opposite of me. He waited. When he finally spoke, his voice sounded just as tortured as my own.

"Harper, I did look for you. I looked everywhere."

Margaret would never lie to him. She was the closest thing he'd ever had to a mother.

"I wish that I could believe you."

"I've never lied to ye."

"I don't know what you've done. Not anymore. I'm tired. I just want to go to sleep. Please leave me alone."

"Aye, fine. I wish that we could go back in time—to our last days together. I would do things so differently."

I didn't answer him as I stood and moved to the bed. Instead, I whispered my response so that only I could hear.

"Oh Kamden, I wish we could, too."

———

_B_etrayal surged through him as he walked away from Harper's door. Witnessing her pain was heart-wrenching, but to hear her say that she'd wanted him to come for her? Nothing could have hurt him more.

He went to Margaret the moment he woke from his strange dream so many years ago because he knew that Harper wouldn't have left without telling someone where she was going, but Margaret told him that Harper didn't want to be found, that she never wanted to see him again. When he sought out her grandparents, they had moved. Margaret told him that they'd gone to somewhere in the States to be with Harper. He'd had no reason to distrust her.

Despite Margaret's misgivings, he still searched, but Harper never told him about a job offer in Boston. Without anything to go on, his search got him nowhere. Years he'd lived thinking she hated him, thinking she never wanted to see him again. All the while, every day he left her out in the world alone he was breaking her heart all over again.

Margaret's betrayal felt as if his only tie to any sort of family had just been severed completely. It baffled him.

He crawled into bed like an animal, a sense of desperation clinging to him so tightly that no thought of Morna's instructions crossed his mind as he drifted off into an angry sleep.

His last conscious thought was one of family—a wish that those who helped him once before would give him guidance once again.

CHAPTER 13

I stood in the back corner of the castle's kitchen watching as Margaret chopped away at a heaping pile of vegetables. I called to her, but my voice sounded distant. She didn't respond. She didn't seem to see me either.

I lifted a knee to move but couldn't step forward. Baffled, I tried again but to no avail. Something invisible prevented me from moving. I called to her again, but my voice only reverberated off whatever unseen wall stood between Margaret and myself. Panic blossomed inside me. Just as I opened my mouth to scream, Henderson entered the kitchen. I paused— Sileas was at his side, and the dog was visibly younger than he truly was—he was little more than a pup.

The sight of Sileas relaxed me. I was dreaming. Of course I was. It made sense. The invisible wall, the sound of my own voice coming out strained and distant—it was like one of those nightmares where you open your mouth to scream and nothing comes out. Only, this dream was lucid—I knew that I was dreaming. My thoughts in no way seemed sleepy or distorted.

I remembered reading about such experiences in college— lucid dreams often allowed the person to manipulate his or her own dreams. Now that I was aware I was sleeping, there was no reason why I should still be blocked by the invisible barrier. I lifted my knee and leaned forward only to be thrown backwards against the counter once again.

I still couldn't move. Maybe one had to be practiced at lucid dreaming to alter the state of their dreams. Whatever the case, at least I knew that this state of frozen suspension would end.

Henderson's voice filled the room, and knowing there was no longer any harm in being unable to move, I stopped trying to fight against the barrier in front of me and listened in.

"What did ye just tell him, Margaret? I've never seen Kamden so upset."

"I told him precisely what he needed to hear. Someday he will thank me for it."

I watched on as Henderson spread his hands flat against the island and leaned forward to look down at Margaret's small stature.

"And what did he need to hear? I hardly think that is for ye to decide."

Margaret shifted uncomfortably on her feet, and a sense of knowing spread through my limbs. Sileas' age should've clued me in sooner. This dream was the time right after I left.

"I told him that Harper dinna wish to see him again and that she dinna tell me where she was going."

"Is it true?"

Margaret's silence caused Henderson's face to flush bright red.

"Do ye know what ye've done, Margaret? Do ye think lying to the lad will stop him? He'll just go to her grandparent's house. Then he will know ye lied. He will never trust ye again after that."

When she answered him, Margaret's tone sounded pleased. For the first time, I found myself glad for the barrier. Without it, I feared I would've lunged for her neck.

"Do ye think I'm such a fool? I thought of that. Harper's grandparents are away for the holiday. They went to the States to see her parents. When they return, they'll be returning to their new home up north. They've just sold their place in Edinburgh."

Henderson's question reflected my own.

"Why would ye do such a thing? They love one another. What place is it of yers to keep them apart?"

"I've been the only one to watch out for that boy for his entire life. He never had a mother. Someone needs to act in his best interest."

"He'll be thirty next week, Margaret."

"That matters not. Harper knew what she was getting herself into when she started dating him. He treated her like royalty. If that wasn't enough for her, then good riddance—he deserves better than to be humiliated and left out in the cold."

"Neither of us know what happened between the two of them last night. Ye know the lad as well as I do. He's a good man, I'll not say otherwise, but he can also be a damned fool. If I were a betting man, I'd wager that the lassie had good reason to leave. Regardless, none of this is our business."

If I ever saw Henderson again, I would kiss him for his defense of me.

Margaret set her knife on the counter and crossed her arms in defiance.

"Ye are right. None of this is any of yer business at all. What I say to Kamden and what I doona say is of my concern, not yers. Will ye tell him?"

"Aye, I will. I'll not let yer petty meddling interfere in their lives."

Margaret's voice lifted three octaves to a screeching tone that caused Sileas to whine.

"Petty? Meddling? I care for him, Henderson. His heart is broken. If that is what Harper did to him, I doona ever want her around him again."

"I thought ye liked Harper."

"I thought I did, too, though it seems I dinna know her. He could've done nothing to deserve such treatment."

Henderson shook his head in disgust and turned to leave the room, but Margaret's voice stopped him before he took his first step.

"Wait. I thought I would give ye the opportunity to agree to keep this secret, but ye have not done so. If ye tell Kamden any of this, I shall tell Kamden yer little secret. Do ye really think he would keep ye on here if he knew ye'd taken half of last month's ticket sales for yerself?"

When Henderson faced her, the redness in his cheeks was gone, replaced by a sickly whiteness that made me fear he would drop to the floor.

"How do ye know about that?"

She laughed. I found myself disliking her more with every word.

"How could I not know? I make the deposits each week when I go to get groceries. I see how many guests come through these doors. The money hasna added up for some time. I doona know what caused ye to do this, but I know the sort of man ye are. I know that if ye would take from Kamden and this castle, ye must be in dire need of it. I doona want to do this, but if ye tell Kamden what I've done, I shall tell him straight away."

"Fine. I thought I knew ye Margaret, but ye can rot in hell for all ye have done. I'm sure I shall join ye for being yer accomplice."

As Henderson left the room, the barrier in front of me gave way and my mind began to spin.

The dream was over.

He stood before his ancestors but apart from them, an onlooker on the past and nothing more. He could see and hear them but not interact as he wished. He wanted more than to see their lives play out in front of him. He wanted to speak to them, to know that he was not so alone and that some of his family was still available to him.

This scene was different—earlier than the events he witnessed before. On second glance, he could see that this dream wasn't in the past at all. Or at least, it wasn't as far back as his dreams took him last time. There was a car behind him and three people stood in front of him.

He knew them all. Morna stood on the banks of the pond with her husband a few paces behind her. Next to them stood a red-haired woman with an ornery glint in her eye.

Mitsy—the lass he watched Baodan McMillan fall in love with during his dream so many years ago. But what was she doing in the present with Morna and Jerry? Did that mean the tales about his ancestors were true? That Baodan had married a woman from the future? How had he not picked up on that as he watched their story play out before him last time?

Dozens of questions raced through his mind. Yet he knew he was unlikely to find answers to any of them.

Sarcasm dripped from Mitsy's voice as she spoke to Morna and Jerry.

"Oh, right. How stupid of me. Are you joining me, or am I jumping on the crazy train alone?"

Kamden had no idea what exactly she referred to, but his eyes moved to the smooth rock in Mitsy's hand. The stories always referred to the use of a rock. His pulse quickened as he watched the scene play out before him.

Mitsy turned away from the old couple defiantly.

"I don't need to practice."

She reared back, flicked her wrist, and let the rock loose.

Kamden watched as it bounced off the water. Once. Twice. Mitsy turned to speak.

"See, three times..."

Before she could finish her sentence, Kamden watched as the lass disappeared.

Everything went quiet around him. As he stood still in the distance, Morna and Jerry got in their car and drove away.

Kamden knew all of this could be a dream and nothing more, but if it wasn't, he now knew how to use the magic that eluded his ancestors for so long.

The surroundings around him whirled together. Kamden knew his dream was approaching its end.

cMillan Castle—December 19, 2011

I didn't wake once the dream ended. For several more hours, I enjoyed a dreamless sleep, content to be warm in the bed with Sileas by my side. I woke to a surprisingly bright beam of light hitting me in the face. Yawning, I stretched out my legs and raised my arms above my head and out to the sides in the hopes some movement might pull me from the deep sleep. When my right arm hit something solid, I screeched and flew out of the bed so quickly that my ass hit the floor with a big thud.

Scampering to my feet, I looked at the bed. Kamden lay sound asleep. My first impulse was to scream at him, to whack him with a pillow and shoo him from my room, but then my brain caught up with my eyes, and I realized that Kamden wasn't in my room. I was in his.

Wine was the devil's poisoned apple. If three glasses of wine got me so wasted that I unconsciously stumbled into Kamden's room in the middle of the night, I would never touch the stuff again.

The sunlight continued to ping the back of my head. Twisting on impulse, I turned to look in its direction. When I saw outside the window, I reached out a hand to steady myself against the windowsill.

As expected, snow covered the ground outside, but rather unexpectedly, the dangerous accumulations of snow, the piles and piles of it, were gone. The sun was out, and any sign of the storm that sent me to the castle for shelter was gone.

I gripped my head as I fought the overwhelming confusion that gummed up all other thoughts in my mind. How could the snow have melted so quickly? By the time I fell asleep, I was entirely sober. How then had I ended up in Kamden's bed without memory of it? If I was going to sleep with him again, I sure as hell wanted to be able to remember doing so.

The sound of footsteps in the hall sent me into a panic. It was only when Sileas barked at the approaching sound that I looked at him for the first time since waking. Just as in my dream the night before, Sileas was young. Remnants of puppy still clung to his little face, and his bark didn't have the same deep tone that it had now.

None of it made sense. Perhaps I was still sleeping? Only in this dream I wasn't frozen in place. On the small chance that it was true, I hurried back to the bed, crawled inside, and pulled the covers all the way over my face and shut my eyes as tightly as I could manage.

Nothing happened.

Instead, the footsteps of whomever approached Kamden's room now stopped right outside the door, and someone was calling for me to answer it.

"If the two of ye are still abed, I can let Sileas outside. The last day of tours starts in an hour. Ye know how Sileas likes to greet the guests."

With Kamden still snoring beside me, I crawled back out of the bed and very hesitantly walked over to the door where I cracked it open. The second I did so, Sileas was off the bed and running down the hall.

"Whitney? Is that you?"

I'd not seen the young housekeeper since leaving Kamden, but she didn't look a day older for it. She looked back at me with an expression of confusion that matched how I felt.

"Aye, o'course 'tis me. Are ye and Kamden still leading today's tour together? Alfred said that ye were, and when I told him that the two of ye were still asleep, he almost came up here to wake ye himself. I told him 'twas best if I did so."

"Oh. Well, thank you." Terror dripped down my spine, but I couldn't see how letting Whitney in on my own insanity would help matters. With as much coolness as my shaky voice could manage, I responded matter-of-factly.

"Yes, we will lead it."

Then, I closed the door in her face and stood there with my hand still gripping the bedroom doorknob until I could no longer hear her footsteps retreating down the hallway. Once she was gone, I locked the door and ran over to Kamden where I gripped onto both of his shoulders and shook him as roughly as I could.

That's when I really knew I'd entered the twilight zone. My arms could scarcely lift him even a few inches off the bed. All of my strength was gone. I glanced down at my arms, my legs, and to my horror, my slightly pudgy mid-section.

"Kamden. Kamden. Wake the hell up. Something...something is going on here and I am freaking out."

He stirred, but my nudging did nothing to wake him. I stomped toward the bathroom, reached for the rinsing glass next to the sink, filled it, and then walked back over to the bed. Without hesitation, I threw the water in his face. His eyes flew open as he gasped and sputtered and sat up in the bed.

"Wha...why do ye keep doing that to me?"

I'd forgotten all about the wine incident from the night before.

"Just wake up. Something is happening to me."

The panic in my voice must've concerned him for he was up and out of the bed in an instant, reaching for my arms as he tried to calm me.

"What is it? What's wrong?"

I pulled away and pointed toward the window.

"Go and look out the window."

I was certain my hands had never shaken so violently in my life. It took me crossing my arms to still them as I watched Kamden move across the room. He looked out the window for a long moment. When he finally turned towards me, unbridled confusion etched his face.

"How long did we sleep?"

"I don't know, but that's not the only thing, Kamden. I woke up this morning in your bed. I have no recollection of coming in here last night."

His brows raised as he sat on the bed.

"Ye dinna come in here last night. I would remember that."

I threw my hands up in exasperation.

"I would remember it, too, but I'm telling you, when I woke up, I was lying next to you in that bed."

Kamden's fingers moved to his forehead, just as they'd done while reading his letter the night before.

The letter. Some far off question begged me to acknowledge it, but I was far too shaken up to think about it just now.

"That's not even close to being all, Kamden. Look at me."

His hand dropped from his face, and he looked up.

"What about ye?"

I approached him while motioning to my untoned arms. Then I dramatically pointed toward my gut.

"I did not go to sleep looking like this."

"I like the way ye look. Always have."

"That is not the point. You know that I didn't look like this when I went to bed."

For the first time since waking, Kamden smiled. Really smiled. A big, goofy grin that made me want to slap him. I screamed at him in exasperation.

"What is the matter with you? Do you think this is funny?"

"Aye."

I did hit him then, lunging toward the bed as I whacked his arm in frustration.

"It's not funny. Something seriously weird is going on here."

"Aye."

I felt sick. Dizzy sick. So sick that I feared I would vomit right on top of him if some sort of sanity didn't find its way into my psyche soon.

"I swear if you say 'aye' one more time, I'm going to throw myself out that window. What is going on?"

Casually, as if it were the most normal thing in the world, Kamden said, "Morna's letter was true, lass. Our wishes worked. We went back in time."

CHAPTER 15

I listened quietly for a long time as Kamden explained to me the contents of the letter he received the night before. I knew that while he'd attempted to explain everything last night, it all derailed after our kiss and my reaction to his confession. Every bit of it was hard to believe, but I couldn't very well argue with the reality of it as I was living it. By some strange miracle or curse—I guess only time would tell which one it was—Morna's magical letter sent us back to our last Christmas together.

"There is only one thing I doona understand. Ye made yer wish whether ye knew it or not. Ye said that ye wished ye could believe me. I made my wish, unknowingly as well, before I went to bed. I wished for my family to help me once again, but we never made a wish together. How then, did we end up here?"

I replayed the events from the night before over in my mind and I knew right away.

"We did make a wish together. You just didn't hear me. I didn't really want you to. When you told me that you wished we could go back to our last days together, I whispered that I wished so, too."

"Ah."

That pleased him. I could see it in the way he grinned at me. An unusual feeling of closeness filled the space between us. I expect it was the fact that whatever this strange turn of events might mean, we were going through it all together.

"Did your wish come true?"

He crossed his arms.

"I'm not sure. In the midst of sleep, I thought aye, but now I see I'm missing one verra special component of the magic."

"Meaning?"

"Much like the dream I had five years ago, I watched events of a past time happen before me. Though, this time, I watched the real time travel ritual take place. We've been doing it wrong for a verra long time."

"I know."

I laughed, panic subsiding with each moment we spent talking through the crazy that was this day. As unbelievable as every bit of it was, I no longer found it worthy of window-jumping panic.

"How's it done, then?"

"First, we must have a magic rock spelled by the same Morna who left us the letter. Then, 'tis really rather simple. There's no need for climbing up the tower or spinning in circles. Ye simply skip the stone across the water. On the third bounce, ye disappear."

Any normal day, it would've seemed absurd. Today—not so much.

"Of course. That's much more sensible than the way we always did it with the tourists. Problem is, you don't have a magic rock."

He stood and disrobed in front of me without a second thought.

It should've shocked me to see him standing there in his underwear, but knowing the time we were now in somehow made it seem okay. In this time, we were together. In this time, I saw him naked all the time.

"Precisely. Alas, I doona have a magic rock." He stepped away and moved into the bathroom where he reached into the shower to turn on the spray. "Would ye like to join me?"

I swallowed hard as he removed the rest of his clothing and stepped inside. I shouldn't look, but he just made it too easy.

"Uh no, better not." I had to raise my voice so he could hear over the water.

"Suit yerself. What about ye? Did yer wish come true? Is there any chance that ye believe I looked for ye now?"

I started to answer him, but he interrupted me as he opened the shower door and leaned outside to speak.

"I canna hear ye. The glass is all steamed up now anyway. At least come and sit in here and tell me."

"Fine." I walked backwards into the bathroom and stood still just to the right of the shower door. Just thinking about my dream enraged me.

"Yes, I believe you. I had a similar dream to yours. It was the weirdest experience of my life. You need to fire Margaret."

He hesitated and then said rather sadly, "So, 'tis true then? I had hoped there was another explanation."

I knew it must pain him to hear of Margaret's betrayal. He loved her dearly.

"Yes. I'm sorry, Kamden."

"What did ye see?"

I told him what I could, omitting the parts about Henderson's transgressions. Margaret had been right about one thing—he would never steal unless something extreme was going on in his life. If Kamden had remained ignorant of it for over five years, I saw no need to deliver one more piece of hurtful news to him now.

When I finished, Kamden turned off the water. Before I could move away from him, he stepped out of the shower and wrapped his arms around me. I gasped and tried to break free, but he clung too tightly.

"Kamden!" I shrieked at him. "You're wet. You're soaking my clothes right through."

He laughed into my ear. My entire body came alive as his warm breath traveled down my spine. His naked body pressed flat against my back, and I had no desire to move away.

"These are yer night clothes. Ye must shower and change if we are to lead today's tour. If we are correct and we really are back five years in the past, 'tis the last tour of the year. We gave the group quite a show last time. Let's not disappoint them this time around, aye? Then once everyone is gone, we will sit down and try to figure all this out."

Years of misunderstanding and hurt still lay between us, but two very important things were already healed inside my own heart. First, Kamden loved me and he'd said it. Two, it had never been his choice to stay away from me.

It certainly wasn't everything, but it was something. Standing there with him, his arms wrapped around me, my nightgown becoming more see-through by the second, I didn't have the strength to fight him anymore.

It was a new day. A new time, even. Perhaps, this was our second chance to get things right.

Twisting, I faced him and wrapped my arms around his neck.

"Is it too late to take you up on the shower offer? We have to be downstairs in half an hour. I might be able to get ready more quickly if you help."

He groaned as I kissed him. Much to my surprise, he quickly pulled away, though there was a smile in his voice as he left the bathroom.

"I'm afraid 'tis, lass. Ye know how I hate to leave our guests waiting. Doona worry, I'll make it up to ye later."

I took a deep breath, turned the water to cool, and breathlessly jumped beneath its spray.

I couldn't wait to get this tour over with.

pproximately twenty-five minutes later, Kamden and I were both dressed and ready to head downstairs for the tour. I remembered this day well. I could even remember the faces of most of those we would soon see downstairs for the castle tour.

Most castles in Scotland closed for the winter season. As I knew firsthand, travel wasn't especially easy in the winter, and it wasn't the peak of tourist season anyway. McMillan Castle benefited greatly from most other castles being closed. While tourism was definitely down in the winter, there were always some visitors keen to visit the country regardless of the weather or time of year. By decorating McMillan Castle with gorgeous Christmas décor and throwing in some holiday activities with the tour, the castle quickly became a must-see destination if visiting Scotland in the winter.

"Are ye ready for this? Do ye remember enough to help lead it? If not, I can manage on my own. Ye could experience it as a guest."

I knew he meant the offer as a kindness, but I couldn't help but feel a little insulted. I loved this castle as much as he did. I didn't imagine that I would ever be able to forget its history.

"You just wait. You won't be able to tell that I missed a single tour. I remember everything."

I left the bedroom first. I wanted to gather up the guest roster from Henderson before the tour started. It was always nice to have the guests' names in front of me. More often than not, I could guess the name that belonged to each person just by looking. It was a special talent that annoyed Kamden to no end. It was always my favorite thing about the tour.

I was keenly aware of how strange it was that all of this felt normal to me. Walking down the castle's staircases and corridors, gazing up at the Christmas décor as I made my way to the front entrance, it felt as if the last five years never happened at all. For now, I didn't even really care.

It was nice to be back in an easier time before everything fell apart. Even if I woke to find all of this was a dream, even if it all went away tomorrow, I could see no harm in enjoying it while it lasted.

All thoughts of joy went away the moment I stepped into the main entryway. I expected to see Henderson coming through the front door with the list of names. Instead, Margaret stood in his place holding the clipboard and pen.

"You." I hurled the word at her like an insult as I stomped over in her direction.

She couldn't have looked more confused. Assuming I joked, she mimicked me, pointing a finger in my direction and with a shocked tone she said, "You."

I didn't smile or laugh. Instead, I ripped the clipboard from her grip and stood there angrily.

I wanted to scream at her, to tell her she was fired and toss her stuff right out the front door, but I knew it wasn't my place to do so. Margaret was not my employee.

Kamden was only a few steps behind me. While I expected

him to—at the very least—treat Margaret with the same icy coolness I had, he instead gathered her up in a big hug and kissed her cheek before pulling away.

"Good morning, Margaret. Is it not a fine day? What are ye doing in here? I expected ye to be in the kitchen."

She smiled at him, and my blood boiled. I knew what traitorous thoughts lay beneath that smug smile of hers.

"Aye, 'tis lovely. Though it seems the world has gone topsy turvy today."

She had no idea.

Kamden looked around as if looking for something amiss.

"What do ye mean?"

"Alfred is in the kitchen watching the scones for me, and I've taken over Henderson's position."

"Where is Henderson?"

"He is helping one of the guests change a flat tire."

"Ah. Do ye think he can manage it on his own?"

Margaret nodded and nudged her head toward the door.

"O'course he can. The two of ye have a tour to lead. The group is waiting just outside."

I couldn't believe how polite Kamden was being to her. It should've upset him even more than me.

"Margaret, would ye mind welcoming everyone inside while I speak to Harper a moment? We just want to practice our entrance."

Margaret agreed, and before I could say a word, Kamden dragged me into a dark hallway on the other side of the entrance hall.

"What were ye about to do to Margaret before I came in here?"

I crossed my arms and didn't blink as I answered him.

"Fire her sorry ass."

He laughed but quickly gained his composure as he lowered his voice to plead with me.

"Harper, doona ye remember where we are? As of now, Margaret has done nothing to deserve yer hatred of her. We canna verra well punish her for something she hasn't done."

"But she will do it. We already know that she will."

He placed his palms on either side of my face and kissed me gently before pulling away to look down into my eyes.

"No, she willna do it. For things are not going to happen the same way they did last time. Besides, I doona believe there was malice in Margaret's choice."

I wanted to believe him. While I was willing to enjoy things as they came, neither of us could know for sure if we had any power to change how things occurred between us last time.

"You don't know that."

He didn't seem shaken by my lack of faith.

"Aye, I do know. Things are already different. Five years ago, 'twas not Margaret that greeted us at the door, and none of our guests punctured a tire on the way up here. If those changes can happen, so can many others."

Perhaps he was right.

"Fine. I will say nothing to Margaret, but I mean nothing. I don't want to see or speak to her and that's exactly what I'm going to do."

He kissed the tip of my nose and took my hand as we went to welcome the tour.

"As long as ye doona insult her or pull her head off, I doona care."

When we stepped into the entryway, a dozen tourists stood waiting. I was good with people, but Kamden came alive in front of strangers. His warm welcome had them all smiling and laughing before he even introduced himself.

We played off one another well. Kamden stuck to the history, and I filled in the yawn-worthy stuff with all the tales of whimsy. It was a good group—not too big, not too small—and all the faces were exactly the same as five years before. With a quick glimpse at the roster, I remembered each of them.

Kamden always saved the great room for last. It was by far the most breathtaking room in the castle. From its large fireplace and portraits to the massive Christmas tree at its end—it was a guest favorite every time.

It took only seconds for me to spot it when we entered the final room on our tour—the velvet sack sitting right above the fireplace where Morna's letter had been the night before. I didn't falter in my story as I walked over to the mantle and pointed to the portrait of Kamden's father to direct their gaze in another direction as I reached to grab it.

It was heavy, and I knew right away what it was. Sidestepping over to Kamden, I gently placed the bag in his hands. He looked at me and mouthed his question, "What is it?"

Shrugging, I walked away to finish my speech, but when I looked back at him from across the room, I knew I was right.

A big, smooth rock lay in the palm of his hand.

CHAPTER 17

The moment he concluded the tour, Kamden moved to Harper's side.

"Meet me in my study. I'll show the guests to the kitchen and leave them with Margaret. I wanna speak to ye about this."

When she nodded and took the rock from his hand, Kamden turned to see the group downstairs. It took some time to corral them. Many wanted pictures with him by the tree. Others wanted him to sign their souvenir books. It was unusual for the owner of such a great castle to interact with guests. As much as he wanted to speak with Harper, he wouldn't deny them the unique experience of having some time with him.

"If ye are all ready, I'd like to take ye to the castle's kitchen. It is the most updated part of the castle—a necessity to keep our dedicated cook, Margaret, happy. She's prepared some special treats just for ye. Then, our usual tour guide, Alfred, has arranged sleigh rides around the pond for all of ye. If ye still wish to take pictures in the great room, doona worry. Once ye've finished all other activities, ye are free to wander around the castle on yer own, just as long as ye are out of the castle by five this evening. At that time, Harper and I will be leaving for a verra special trip. Christmas Eve will be our fifth year together. I plan to propose."

He smiled at the anticipated "oohs" and "awws" from his guests. Knowing they would have time to wander on their own seemed to do the trick, and they gathered around him without delay as he led them downstairs.

Margaret waited for them at the bottom, a basket of scones in her arms, the kitchen bar lined with mugs of hot chocolate.

"Do ye and Harper wish to join in? I've prepared a mug for each of ye."

He stood by Margaret's side while the group filed into the kitchen. Once all were inside, he turned to speak to her.

"Thank ye, but no. We need to finish packing for our trip. I'll see ye before we leave."

She waved him on, and he rushed toward the study.

He couldn't wait to cancel their trip.

His family awaited both of them in the past.

I never doubted that a magic rock would show up somewhere. Not after my wish was granted in my dream and our mutual wish was granted when we woke up in the past. The rock's appearance seemed inevitable.

Five years ago, Kamden and I left for a trip to the swankiest and most secluded resort in the Highlands. I suspected that this time around, Kamden had other plans in mind. He always longed for family. If this rock truly had the power to bring them to him, he would take it.

Kamden's study lay on the ground floor of the castle at the very end of the primary corridor of the staircase. It ensured total privacy when he wished to spend hours going over the books or, as was usually the case, just wanted a moment to breathe.

I roamed around the room taking in all the memories of years past. Photos of our college years together were scattered around the bookshelves that lined each wall. While each one made me smile, they were also a reminder of all that crumbled between us the day I left. I hoped Kamden was right. I hoped things could be different this time.

"I like that one of ye."

I didn't know he entered until I heard his voice behind me. I leaned into him as his arms came around me. He bent to rest his chin on my shoulder as we gazed at the photo of me in my cap and gown.

"You can't be serious. You can tell I've been crying—my face is all red and puffy."

"I never saw anyone less eager to graduate college. Ye loved every minute of it."

I had. College brought me to Scotland—the only place in my life where I ever felt truly at home.

I pulled away and went to pick up the rock sitting on the desk. It could've been my imagination, but it even felt magical.

"So...we're not going north, are we?"

He smiled and shook his head.

"I called and cancelled our reservation as soon as I left the guests in the kitchen. I wish to take ye on another trip instead."

"Do you think it will work?"

I hoped that it would. His disappointment would be overwhelming if it didn't.

"Aye. I do. I canna see why the witch would leave it for us if it wouldna. I doona wish for the staff to know about it. We shall have to resort to trickery."

"Trickery, huh?"

He had everything planned. He was quick that way. He could come up with plans on the fly with ease.

"Aye. They will wish to see us off. The staff is staying on until Christmas Eve even though our last tour is now done. I say we leave in the car as planned, then take the back road to Margaret's house and park the car in her old shed. 'Tis unused, I know, and I doona believe she's opened it in a decade."

Nothing sounded less appealing.

"If we do that, we will have to walk a mile back here. It will be freezing."

He nodded apologetically but didn't back down.

"Aye, 'twill. But if we park the car on the side of the road, someone will see it. I doona wish for them to be concerned about our wellbeing. We will wait until dark to skip the rock. That way, we will be able to leave unseen."

At least we wouldn't be hiking in the middle of the snowstorm of 2016. As long as we bundled up, we would be fine. Uncomfortable, but technically fine.

"Okay. How long until we leave in the car?"

Kamden glanced down at his watch.

"Two hours."

"Great. Are we packing?"

He thought about it for a long moment before answering.

"I doona think so. What do we have that would belong in the past? I say we just go with the flow, lass."

Laughing, I agreed. It was all rather exciting, really. Wherever the rock sent us, I supposed it would be an adventure. The past years of my life had been much too void of risk. I would make up for it now.

"All right. I've got something I need to take care of. Do you think Henderson is back in the booth?"

He eyed me suspiciously.

"Aye, I expect he is closing everything up. Why?"

"Good." I pulled him toward me and kissed him until both of us were breathless. "I'll meet you in our room in an hour. Maybe you can make up for abandoning me in the shower, then?"

That distracted him enough to stop his questions.

I took off in search of Henderson.

I heard Henderson's chair shift from inside the old ticket booth the moment I knocked on the door, but it took me calling out for him to answer.

"Henderson, it's me, Harper. Let me in. I'm freezing out here."

There was another slow shuffling sound and then, finally, he opened the door.

"Harper, what are ye doing out here? Ye should've told me it was ye from the first. Almost every day we have some guest try to come in after I've closed the booth. I'm accustomed to ignoring the knock on my door."

"I just wanted to come and see how you were doing. Mind if I sit?"

He must've been suspicious of my answer right away, but he said nothing to indicate he was. Instead, he smiled and ushered me to one of the two chairs that sat inside the tiny space. In peak months, Kamden hired seasonal help to man the other booth window.

"How did the tour go? It seemed a fine group."

"It went great. Maybe the best one ever."

The old man smiled, his crooked, yellowed teeth just barely peeking out in the middle of his silvery beard.

"I'm pleased to hear it."

An awkward silence settled between us. I loved Henderson, but I'd never really had much conversation with him outside of normal niceties. It was odd for him, too. His eyes roamed around the interior of the booth uncomfortably.

Eventually, I decided it was best to be frank with him. He wouldn't appreciate anything else.

"Can I ask you a question?"

"O'course, ye can."

"Henderson...are you in some sort of trouble?"

Whatever he expected me to ask, it hadn't been that. His mouth visibly opened and closed at least three times before he answered.

"How did ye know?"

I couldn't very well tell him the truth. Instead, I tried to come up with the most believable lie. The only thing I could think of was to tell him that I'd been making the deposits. There was a chance he would know that wasn't true, but it was the best thing I could think of in that moment.

"Margaret's been so busy lately doing her usual end-of-year assessment of the kitchen and preparing food and goods to hold Kamden over for the next few months that I volunteered a few weeks ago to take the deposits into town and pick up the groceries for her. Did you know that I majored in accounting in college? It doesn't take long for me to see when numbers are off."

Even that was a lie—I held a degree in Shakespearean literature, but I didn't know how Henderson would ever be able to call my bluff on that.

He crumbled the minute I asked him the question. The pain and guilt on his face was so evident that I moved to gather him up against me as he started to cry. My heart broke for him. Before I knew it, I sat there and cried right along with him. I said nothing.

There was no need for me to. In a moment, he would gather himself and explain. Whatever the reason, I could feel nothing but sorrow for whatever position he was in.

When he did lift his head, he apologized profusely.

"I'll pay every bit of it back, I swear to ye. Did Kamden send ye because he was too angry to speak with me himself? I doona need my last paycheck. I shall gather my things and not ever come back here again."

I reached for his hands and tried to reassure him with my grip.

"Hey, it's okay. Kamden doesn't know anything about it. He's not angry, and I'm not either. We know you, Henderson. I just want to know what's going on so I can help."

"Nothing could justify the trust I've betrayed. My reason matters not."

I continued to insist.

"It does to me."

For a long while, I thought he wouldn't tell me. He sat thinking for the longest time, then he pointed out the booth window toward the building on the other side of the trees.

"Last month, Kamden asked me to take out the old snowmobile and get it running again. He thought there would be enough snow to use it this year. So, I spent two weeks working on the machine, and I finally got it running. Problem was, I dinna know how to drive it. I turned it on, but instead of backing it out of the barn, I plowed it through the front."

My hands flew to my face in shock.

"Did it hurt you?"

He shook his head and the tops of his cheeks uncovered by beard turned bright red.

"No, though the barn is in right bad shape. I couldna tell Kamden, for he would've fired me and rightly so. I would've fired me, too. I doona make enough to pay for its repairs on my own. I've pulled aside a little this month to cover the cost. Though, I never would've done so if we had not had the busy summer that we did. I swear it to ye."

I would've burst out laughing if not for the distraught look on Henderson's face. I truly expected him to confess to some sort of gambling addiction, not for him to tell me that he was so prideful that he would rather steal than admit to a mistake. If it could even be called stealing—the money was going right back into the castle.

"So, you're not even using the money for yourself?"

He looked appalled by my question.

"O'course not. What sort of a man do ye think I am?"

"A stupid, prideful one. Kamden would never fire you for something like that, and you know it. You were simply too embarrassed to tell him."

"Aye, I am. Please doona tell him, Harper. I'll pay the castle back. 'Twill only take me some time."

"You won't do any such thing." I pulled my checkbook out and looked him straight on. "How much have you taken?"

"I willna allow ye to pay for this, Harper."

His arguing was pointless. I held the upper hand and he knew it.

"Yes you will. How much?"

He looked down shamefully.

"Three thousand pounds."

Swallowing, I tried to hide my astonishment as I wrote him a check.

"Cash this, put the money back in next week's deposit and never say a word to anyone about this."

Reluctantly, he took the check from my hands.

"Why would ye do this for me?"

"I'm doing it because you're a good man, even if you are stupid. You came to my defense once even if you don't realize it, and I want to do the same for you now. Just promise me one thing."

"Anything."

"If there is ever a time when Margaret asks you to keep a secret for her, promise me that you won't do it. Promise me you'll tell Kamden."

His wiry brows pulled together.

"What do ye mean?"

"It doesn't matter. Just promise."

"Aye. I promise. Thank ye, lass."

I stood and wrapped my arms around him in a big hug.

"You're welcome. Merry Christmas, Henderson."

I breathed easily on my walk back to the castle. At least now we had a safety net. While things were pleasant now, Kamden and I were both opinionated, fiery people. It was still very possible everything would be shot to hell by the time the week was over.

If so, and everything ended up just how it had the time before, at least Kamden would be able to find his way back to me.

Whether Margaret wished him to or not.

An hour away from her was absolute torture after such a teasing statement. What did Harper expect him to do for that long? He started by getting two empty suitcases from his closet and filling them with random clothes, shoes, and blankets before placing them by the door. They would need to be heavy enough to not raise suspicion.

Once that was done, Kamden took to pacing the room with Sileas by his side. He couldn't wait for her to return. How many times had he dreamed of making love to her over the last five years? Countless times. But each one only left him wanting her more. She couldn't possibly understand the hunger he had for her now.

She would find out soon enough.

I knew what awaited me on the other side of Kamden's bedroom door. I could sense him from all the way out in the hallway. The intensity of it halted me in my tracks. I wanted to weep for how badly I wanted to feel him inside me, but that need didn't mean I wasn't freaking terrified.

So much time had passed. What if things were different between us? Even though kissing him was enough to turn me into mush, what if our real sexual chemistry was gone? Or what if I was just so rusty that he found himself questioning if his memories of our past were accurate? Either outcome horrified me and left me paralyzed outside the door.

I must've done something to make Kamden aware of my presence, for just as I was about to turn around and flee, the door opened and he pulled me inside.

"What are ye doing standing out in the hallway?"

"Deciding whether or not to run and make an excuse for it later."

He tilted his head to the side in question.

"Run? Why would ye do that?"

Kamden's green eyes were as lusty as I'd ever seen them. His gaze traveled down my neck as I spoke and locked on the dip between my breasts just as my breathing escalated in response.

"I..." His hands slipped beneath my shirt and slowly slid upward as he bent to kiss my neck. I could hardly breathe. "Do you want me to be honest?"

He answered as he trailed his lips along my collarbone.

"Always."

"Kamden, I'm terrified."

He stopped his act of delicious torture and lifted his head to look at me seriously.

"Terrified of the stone or of me?"

Our plan for that evening had nothing to do with my fear.

"I'm not worried about tonight, and it's not that I'm scared of you, exactly. I'm afraid of this. It...it's been so long, Kamden. What if I'm really bad at it now? What if it isn't good?"

He smiled and gently lifted my hand so that he could kiss the inside of my palm. The sweetness warmed me through.

"Lass, I'll not have ye worried about a thing whilst in my bed. Memories of yer skill in matters such as this are seared into my memory forever."

I groaned and retreated until my back hit the wall.

"I know. That's what I'm afraid of."

"Harper." He stepped toward me, his expression desperate and needy. "I've never wanted anything as bad as I want ye right now. 'Twas always our love for each other—even unspoken as it was—that allowed for such wondrous lovemaking between us. That hasn't gone away. If anything, it has grown stronger with every night I spent apart from ye."

His hands were on me again, slowly tugging and lifting my shirt until my arms lifted to assist him. On impulse, I reached to remove his. In moments, all our clothes were scattered on the floor. He lifted me with ease, and my legs wound around him as he walked me over to the bed.

"'Tis like riding a bike. Let me show ye how little ye have to be afraid of."

I lost myself in the sensation of loving him. As he entered me, I cried out his name. We moved together in a familiar rhythm that only comes with the most seasoned lovers.

"I love you." The words tumbled out of my mouth for the first time in five years. This time, I wasn't met with cold silence.

"I dinna know what love was until I found ye, Harper. And I'll never know such love again."

We reached our peaks in a shattering unison that left us both trembling and gasping for air.

I didn't remember ever being so happy before.

By the time Kamden and I drove away from the castle, with the entire staff looking on, it was nearly two hours later than originally planned. Margaret was in a tizzy about it. Which honestly—petty person that I am—gave me an immense sense of satisfaction.

"At least we won't have to wait in Margaret's barn until dark to make the walk back up here."

"Aye, 'tis the only reason I wished to tup ye the third and fourth times."

I laughed and reached for his hand as he drove us down the long pathway away from the castle. The pond stretched out to our left, and a sudden horrifying possibility entered my mind.

"Hey Kamden, did you by any chance see where Mitsy landed in the past after seeing her disappear in your dream? I mean, did she just wake up on the side of the pond or on the castle footsteps?"

"No, I dinna see anything past her vanishing before me. Why do ye ask?"

"I'm just wondering if this will work the same way as our wishes. We made them right before falling asleep, and we woke with them granted. If you throw the rock in the water, will we end up in the water, as well? We will both get sick if we end up in there tonight."

He dismissed my worry right away.

"Surely, it canna work that way. Why a person might drown being shocked in such a way. I doona think ye have anything to worry about."

I didn't feel the same optimism, but I said nothing.

It was a short drive to Margaret's home. As Kamden expected, her shed was empty and the car fit easily inside. Closing our coats, Kamden grabbed the rock, and we made the short hike back to McMillan Castle.

***

*L*ights still shone brightly through the windows of the castle as we approached it from behind, but no one seemed to be outside. With any luck, we would be able to skip the stone without anyone taking notice.

Kamden moved quickly, and I hurried to keep up with him.

"Don't throw that thing until I'm over there next to you and hanging on. I'm afraid if you throw it when we aren't touching, you'll leave me here."

He paused and extended his hand in my direction.

"Ye certainly have a lot of theories about how this wee rock will work."

"I have theories about everything. I'm a woman. I think. That's what we do."

He ignored my short-handed insult and continued to walk with me until we met the water's edge.

"Are ye ready?"

All I could think of was how cold that water must be at this time of night.

"I suppose I'll have to be."

With the eagerness of an over-excited child, Kamden pulled the rock from his pocket and skillfully sent it skipping across the water.

Everything whirled around us quickly, and the first thing I felt on the other side of consciousness was water.

Damn that Morna straight to hell.

CHAPTER 21

*M*cMillan Castle—1650

Strong arms pulled me from the freezing water as I sputtered and cursed. The water was so cold, it felt like knives on my skin. From the sounds coming from Kamden, the tumble into the water was just as painful for him.

"I told you. Gah, I could've at least put on some thermals or something."

Kamden said nothing.

I should've been much more worried about the reactions of those surrounding us. What if they weren't accustomed to people landing in the pond from a different time? While Kamden believed it had happened once before, there was no reason for us to believe they were expecting us now. At least, that's what I assumed until the big, burly, dark-haired god that pulled me from the water spoke. His voice was deep, velvety, and sexy as hell.

"Lass, 'twill be easier for us to warm ye if ye stay still. I'm Baodan. We've been expecting ye for over a day now."

Baodan—I knew the name and the face now that I looked at it. His portrait hung with all the others in the great hall of McMillan Castle. This man served as laird here.

Seeing sense in his plea, I stopped flinging about and allowed the woman beside him to drape a thick, wool blanket around my shoulders. She had the most gorgeous red hair I'd ever seen.

"The first time I landed in that water, I nearly drowned. You would think Morna would come up with a better way for people to get back and forth from here. Truthfully, I think she does it for her own amusement."

It was one thing to think about the possibility that all of this could be true. It was another thing entirely to have people I'd read about in this castle's histories standing and speaking in front of me—especially when half of them were quite obviously not born of this time. Now that I was on solid ground and wrapped in something warm, I could pick them out easily—their modern vocabulary and American accents gave them away.

The woman next to me, along with three other equally stunning women, two men, and a young boy, all seemed to have traveled the same way we had at one point or another.

Kamden addressed the group despite the chatter in his teeth.

"H...how ddddd...did ye know we...we were coming?"

The little boy, who looked as excited as Kamden had before throwing the rock, raised a small pocket watch in the air and spoke.

"Morna told us. We're so glad you're here. It's been awhile since we've had anybody new come back."

A maternal-looking blonde stepped forward. I guessed by the way the young boy looked at her that she was his mother. "Cooper, let's get them inside and in dry clothes before we discuss anything further."

Everyone filed inside quickly, and before Kamden and I could say two words to each other, we were taken in different directions

—the women off with me towards one area of the castle and Kamden off with the men in another.

It was the strangest thing to walk inside a place that had basically been my home for the better part of several years and see it through the eyes of those that owned it first. Their belongings and décor lined the halls and filled the rooms. I always felt so at home in McMillan Castle before, but I didn't feel that way at all now. It felt like all of our memories were somehow wiped away in this time. Knowing all that was yet to happen, and the castle didn't yet hold our memories broke my heart in a way I never expected.

"You don't look so good. Are you okay?"

They led me to what Kamden used as his study. In this time, the room was a small bedchamber for what appeared to be one of the castle's live-in staff.

I turned toward the second blonde. She was younger than the first and far more blunt.

"I'm fine."

I could tell she didn't quite believe me, but thankfully, she didn't press further. I didn't know how to explain to her how I felt. I truly expected to find it so interesting to see the castle in this time. Instead, I just found it immensely unsettling.

The nameless woman smiled gently at me then turned to address the rest of the group.

"Why don't you guys go and check on the boys? I'll help her find something to wear, and we'll meet up with you in a bit."

No one opposed the woman's suggestion. I thought perhaps they could all see that I felt overwhelmed. Once we were alone, she faced me once again and extended her hand.

"I'm Jane. I'm a part-time resident of the castle. My husband and I split our time between here and Cagair Castle. It's a long story."

That explained why I didn't know who she was. They weren't McMillans so their portraits wouldn't have hung in the hall.

"I'm Harper. It's nice to meet you."

"There's a selection of dresses laid out for you just over there. I'll step out while you change. If you need some help, just holler. Some of it's sort of complicated."

Even as badly as I wanted out of my own wet clothes, the last thing I wanted to do was put on a garment from this time. My visceral reaction to all of this baffled me. Where had my adventurous spirit gone?

Then I thought of Kamden, and deep down I knew.

Kamden loved me, but I knew the one thing his heart always longed for the most.

Family.

He would love it here. He would never want to leave.

And I could never stay.

Kamden never dreamed he came from such kind and conversational men. With only his grandfather as reference, he expected to be welcomed by a cold and stern group of duds. Nothing could've been more opposite of how these men were. They were kind, funny, and welcoming. Conversation flowed easily among them. Their knowledge of modern times—no doubt thanks to their modern women—made no topic too difficult to discuss.

He changed quickly. By the time he joined the men in the dining hall, they had ale and food ready and waiting for him. If he'd only known all of this was available to him as a child, he would've run away here instead of to Margaret's.

Hours passed this way. When Harper and the other women didn't join them, he assumed they were off somewhere enjoying conversation just as much as the men were. Only when all the ladies save Harper entered the dining hall did Kamden realize something was wrong.

"Where is Harper?"

Jane—he knew her name only because she moved to kiss

Adwen before approaching him—walked to his side and grabbed onto his arm.

"She's gone to bed. Can I talk to you for a minute?"

Worry gripped him, and he hurried into the hallway with Jane so they could speak alone.

"Is she okay?"

"Yes, she is. Listen, I don't really know either of you. I know it's not really my place, but I just wanted to give you a heads up. Will you take some advice from someone who's been in a similar situation?"

He would take any advice he could get. If more of it had been offered to him throughout his life, perhaps he wouldn't have messed things up with Harper the first time.

"O'course I will. What's happened?"

"Harper and I had a nice long talk earlier. She didn't really open up very easily. It took some prying, and I only did so because I recognized her doe-eyed sense of dread the moment she walked into the castle. I remember feeling exactly the same way the first time I came through."

Kamden could see that Jane struggled with whether or not to say just what she wanted to. She shifted from foot to foot as she stood in front of him.

"'Tis fine, lass. My feelings are not easily hurt. Tell me what ye think I must hear."

"I'll be frank then. Honestly, I don't really know how to be anything but frank, but I was struggling to see if I could think of a way to say this more gently."

"Ye needn't be gentle."

Jane smiled before delivering her blow.

"Good. The two of you can't stay here."

As much as he loved it here, the thought never crossed his mind. Harper was his priority now. She would never want to live here.

"O'course. We wouldna wish to intrude on yer lives at all."

Jane laughed and shook her head.

"No, it's not that at all. We've got the room, and you wouldn't be intruding. It's Harper. She isn't meant to be in this time."

"I know that."

Jane continued to explain her rationale to him, pausing midway through when she realized what he'd said.

"I recognize myself in Harper, Kamden. I'm not meant to be in this time, either. She...what did you say? Did you say you know that?"

He nodded calmly.

"Aye. Harper would never want to stay in this time. From now on, where she goes, I go."

His new friend looked equal parts surprised and relieved.

"Oh. Well, good. That's really good. Why does she not seem sure of that, then?"

It saddened him to know that all was not yet healed in her heart.

"While Harper may have forgiven me for my folly of five years ago, that doesna mean the pain from those years has healed completely. Part of her still canna believe that I truly love her the way I do."

"Sounds to me like you need to make a grand gesture."

Kamden smiled. He had just the thing in mind.

"Aye, though I'll need some help, and if ye have access to it, a bit of magic, as well."

CHAPTER 23

"Good morning, love. I need ye to wake up. I've got something to show ye."

Sad and conflicted, I had fallen asleep with a heavy heart and spent all night in a tormented state that kept me tossing and turning. Despite that, I never heard Kamden come into the room. If he had any sense at all, he would've noticed that my absence from the group was a sign that something bothered me. If anything, I expected him to wake me so he could ask me about it, not to use sweet kisses down the side of my face to pull me from sleep.

Something about the soft touch of his lips against my skin prevented me from waking in the same mood I went to bed in.

I turned toward him and allowed his kiss as I spoke against his mouth.

"What is it?"

"Ye have to get up to see. I think ye'll like it."

"Is it outside?"

"No."

"Good. Give me five minutes. I'll meet you out in the hallway."

I would have to tell him today that I wouldn't be staying here. If he wished to, I wouldn't begrudge him for it, but he needed to know I wouldn't be joining him. But as I watched him leave the room, he radiated such excitement that I knew I couldn't tell him until after I enjoyed whatever it was he wanted to show me.

It took me more than five minutes to dress. Jane was right—these dresses were rather complicated, but eventually I managed.

I looked ridiculous.

"Whatever this is, it better be wor..." I stopped midsentence as I swung open the bedroom door to see Kamden down on one knee. I swallowed hard as flashbacks of that dreadful day five years ago passed through my mind.

"Harper, I see the look in yer eyes, and I beg ye not to panic. Hear me out. 'Twill not be the same."

I closed my eyes and gathered myself. I could do this if I just kept breathing and remembered all of the other things that were already so very different this time around.

"Okay. Speak."

He smiled, gathered my shaking hands in his, and kissed my knuckles before looking into my eyes.

"I love ye, Harper. I love the way yer hands show me what's in yer heart. I love the way ye love others. I love so many things about ye, but do ye know what I love most? I love that ye respected yerself enough to deny me when I dinna give ye what ye deserve. Ye taught me more that night than anyone has in my life. I'll not spend another day without ye."

He could see that I was about to interrupt him and hurried to continue so that I could not.

"This trip here has been the Christmas miracle I've waited for all my life. I've always wanted to know my family, but my home lies with ye. Marry me, Harper. Marry me and run McMillan Castle as ye always wished to. I will stand dutifully at yer side and let ye make all the decisions. Yer judgement is far better than mine. Without yer guidance in those early days, I would've given up and sold the castle to the highest bidder. Ye saved it. Ye saved me. Now let me save ye from yer own fear, for I already know what ye are thinking."

Tears streamed down my face as I listened to him. I could no longer stand and look down at him. I dropped to my knees and wrapped my arms around him.

"Oh yeah? What's that?"

"Ye are worried that I feel I'm giving something up by not staying here. Ye couldna be more wrong. Besides, I've arranged a way for us to have both. One last bit of magic to make all our Christmas wishes come true."

"What do you mean?"

"'Tis true that I doona wish to leave these people and never see them again, but I also have no wish for us to take any more swims in the middle of the night while the rest of my staff is not around.

"We canna live the past five years over again but we can change their outcome. On Christmas Eve, we will return to the year we left the first time—to the snowstorm—to 2016. We have just a few days to change what happened between us last time. Let us return to 2011 tonight so we can make peace with Margaret and enjoy the days until we return to our own time together."

It wasn't only my hands that shook as I lifted myself off the ground. My knees could barely support my trembling frame as I waited for him to say the words once more.

"Ask me again."

"I love ye, Harper. I'll never love another. Will ye marry me?"

My "yes" was met with resounding applause. As he slipped the ring on my finger and gathered me into his arms, I looked down the hallway to see every resident of McMillan Castle cheering us on.

Christmas was always my favorite time of the year. I loved the snow, the songs, the family gatherings, but most of all I loved the sense of magic that hung in the air. I never dared to believe that such magic really existed and that Christmas miracles could be true until now.

After five years and two very strange time jumps, I was finally home, held tightly in Kamden's arms once again.

cMillan Castle—December 24, 2016

amden and I married in the castle's great hall in the middle of a blizzard, on the day we returned to the present. To the castle staff and my family, it seemed like the longest engagement ever, but for us, it was just a few days. It took some work, but with the help of our new magical friend, we managed to get all of the castle's staff, the McMillans from 1650, and my grandparents to the castle so they could attend. Even Morna and her husband, Jerry, made the trip.

My grandfather officiated the ceremony. As Kamden and I sealed our vows with a kiss, I knew there would never be a Christmas as wonderful as this one. I didn't care if the storm never ended. It allowed us to bask in the love, joy, and family that surrounded us.

"Well, it seems that yer meddling has worked once again. Not only that, but ye managed to drag me out into the cold once more. Are ye pleased with yerself?"

Morna laughed and leaned into her husband as they stood with the other guests to celebrate the happy couple as they walked down the aisle as husband and wife.

"Aye, I'm verra pleased. I love Christmas."

She expected Jerry to huff in objection, but she could feel him smile against her cheek.

"I do, too."

Laughing, she turned into him and kissed him until he blushed.

"Did ye just admit to loving Christmas?"

Her husband cleared his throat and looked down at the ground.

"'Tis the season for miracles, is it not?"

She smiled and took his hand. It was time for them to return home. Her work here was done.

"Aye, and through love, all things are possible."

<hr>

MORNA'S MAGIC & MISTLETOE

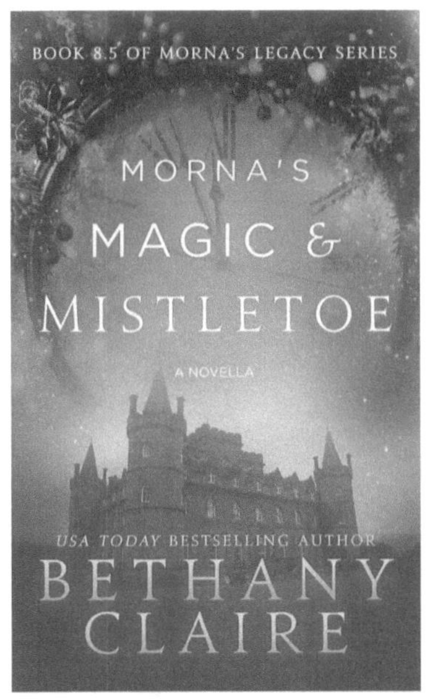

CHAPTER 1

M cMillan Castle, Scotland—December of 1651

Mitsy is watching me again. She isn't normally awake so early, but with Baodan away for a fortnight to assist our friends at Cagair Castle, she's allowed young Rodric to sleep in her bed, and the child kicks in his sleep like an angry mule. For the past three nights she's slipped out of her bed the moment her son fell asleep and retreated to his bed. Rodric believes he's getting the special treat of snuggling with his mother while his father is away, but both of them end up getting a good night's sleep. Unlike many of my other grandchildren, I'm not certain a flock of geese flying straight through Rodric's bedchamber would wake him. Come morning, the wee babe is none the wiser to his mother's trickery.

The only complication comes in when I wake up at my usual time each morning. My bedchamber sits right next to Rodric's and as is normal for all mothers of young children, the slightest unexpected noise wakes Mitsy. Try as I might to move silently out of my room, she hears me each and every morning. So now, at least until my son returns home, I have a companion joining me for my quiet morning hours of precious solitude.

I allowed her in the sitting room under one very strict condition: that she say nothing to me during our time in the room together. She's kept her word, but I may have to be the one to break our agreement. I'm not sure I can stand to sit across from her much longer. Not knowing what she's thinking while she looks at me is driving me mad.

She thinks I'm so enthralled by the snowfall outside that I'm unaware of the look in her eyes. She's wrong. I've lived in Scotland my entire life. More specifically, I've lived in this part of Scotland —this very castle—since I was fourteen. It snows almost every day in this part of the country during winter, so I've seen my fair share of snow. While it is quite stunning with the way it falls around the pond and slowly turns the water to a frozen blanket of ice, beauty isn't the reason I sit in my favorite chair, by my favorite fireplace at the same time every day to look through the frosted window. I sit here because if I situate myself early enough, just as the sun begins to come up, I get to listen to the castle come awake. To hear my many grandchildren begin to stir, to hear their tired mothers and spoiled fathers start their day fills my heart with gratitude.

There was a time—a long time—after Niall died that I wasn't sure I would ever be capable of feeling any positive emotion ever again.

While I was now on the other side of such pain, it had been the battle of my life surviving it. The confusion and guilt I'd felt almost killed me, for how can a mother reconcile knowing that her son is a murderer? But the moment I watched another of my beloved sons leave to fight for his own life centuries ahead of me, I knew that giving in to my grief wasn't an option. There was still purpose to my life, still people that needed me, still love to be found. While Eoghanan was away, I'd barricaded myself away and fought—fought through the emotions, fought through the anger, fought through the soul-crushing grief.

Those closest to me allowed me the space I needed to rant and rage and live like a vagabond near my son's grave. I spent weeks wading through the hurt. There were days I was sure it would never end, that I would drown in a pool of my own tears, that my heart would quite literally break in two. Some days I even begged for it to, for then the pain would truly be over. But it didn't. And with time, I found peace.

There was nothing I could've done in the raising of my son or in my loving of him that could've prevented his actions. While I raised two sons that are better men than I could've ever dreamed they would be, there was never anything to be done for Niall. His actions weren't my fault. I couldn't have saved Baodan's first wife. I couldn't have saved my sister. I bore no responsibility for Niall's acts of murder.

Of course, it took me a long time to see the evil inside him. It took me even longer to acknowledge it. Mothers love their children beyond all reason—we will fight for them, die for them, and we almost always believe the best of them.

It was the darkest time of my life, but now I was truly afraid of nothing. The worst had already happened to me, and I survived. If there was a blessing to be found in anything that happened, that was it.

Mitsy coughed quietly to my left and I turned to see her still staring in my direction. I truly couldn't stand it any longer.

"Mitsy, I said ye couldna speak to me if ye sat in here, but yer eyes have been screaming at me for days. What is it?"

She blinked for what seemed like the first time in hours as her cheeks flushed a red that nearly matched the shade of her hair.

"I don't know what you mean. I wasn't staring at you—just through you. I think I was half-asleep."

Crossing my legs and pulling the blanket that lay across my lap up a little higher, I shook my head in denial.

"What is that foul phrase that ye and Jane are so fond of—bullshit? Aye, that is it. Ye are full of it, Mitsy. Ye are wide awake. What is it ye've been wishing to say to me for days?"

"You need more, Kenna."

"More?" While I always found much of what Mitsy said to be perplexing—her twenty-first century phrasing and language often conflicted with my seventeenth century language—I hadn't the slightest idea what she meant this time. "More? Lass, look around. I live in one of the finest castles in Scotland. I've not known a day of poverty in my life. I doona know what it feels like to go hungry. I know few who are as fortunate."

Mitsy said nothing as she stood and lifted her chair. Carrying it until it sat right beside my own, she returned to her seat, faced me, and reached forward to gather my hands in hers.

"You're right. Most people would be perfectly content to have the life that you do, but you're not most people. You know as well as I do that you can both be grateful for what you have and still want more. If you didn't believe that, you wouldn't constantly be encouraging everyone around you to go after the things they want. You're bored here, Kenna. You need some adventure."

"Adventure?" I laughed as imaginings of me crawling aboard a ship and sailing to new land crossed my mind. I'd be so seasick in a day that I'd want to throw myself overboard. I was too old for adventure. "Mitsy, lassies as old as me doona wish for adventure. All we want are quiet mornings, early dinners, and a good night's sleep."

Mitsy withdrew her hands and crossed her arms defiantly.

"Bullshit. Bullshit on all counts."

"There ye go with that language again. Is it truly necessary?"

"Ha. That's rich, Kenna. You've a filthier mouth than the old man who owns the tavern in the village. You just curse in Gaelic rather than English so it sounds more pleasant."

Guiltily, I glanced down. She was right. "Ach, mayhap so. It doesna matter. Get on with it."

Mitsy smiled and held up one finger. "First of all, you aren't old. You're barely past fifty." She lifted one more finger. "Second, I feel quite sure a huge portion of people in their fifties would be quite offended by your little statement of what 'people your age' want. I know you, Kenna. You would love for your days to be a little less predictable, you would love to get to experience firsthand just a little bit of the magic so many of your family members now take for granted."

I'd never said any such thing out loud, but I couldn't deny that she was right. Magic surrounded my family. Magic had been the single force that had helped both of my sons find the women they loved—magic, and the meddling witch, Morna. I was grateful to her for all she'd done for my family but so far I'd experienced little such magic myself. I was more than a little curious to see what it would be like to spend some time in another century.

When I said nothing, Mitsy continued.

"I think you should get out of town for a little bit—go with Cooper when he leaves at the end of the weekend. He'd love to have you along, and I'm sure Morna wouldn't mind the extra house guest."

"No." I dismissed her suggestion immediately. December was the busiest time of year at McMillan Castle. There were celebrations to prepare for, villagers to assist during the cold weather, and grandchildren that expected me to uphold our annual Christmas traditions.

"No?" The enthusiasm waned from Mitsy's voice. She'd not expected such a firm refusal. "You don't want to at least discuss the idea a little bit?"

Smiling, I softened my expression and leaned forward to pat her knee.

"I know ye mean well, Mitsy, but there's no need to discuss this. It wouldna be a good idea."

"And why exactly is that? I guarantee you that for every reason you give me as to why you shouldn't do this, I can give you ten reasons why you should. Come on then, give me your first excuse."

Aggravated, I stood and stepped closer to the fire as I reached up and placed one hand on the mantle.

"I doona need many excuses. My first is good enough. While young Cooper may be able to survive a quick dip in the freezing pond at this time of year, I would surely fall ill and die."

I could never make any sense of Morna's method of time travel here at McMillan Castle. Everyone who traveled forward or backward through time ended up splashing around in the castle pond upon arrival in their new time. It was an unnecessarily rough entry after a very long trip.

Mitsy laughed and moved to stand next to me by the fireplace.

"Nice try. You know as well as I do that she's changed that."

I was entirely unaware of the change. "I can assure ye, I've heard of no such thing."

"What? You experienced it yourself. The way we all went forward for Kamden and Harper's wedding—via the West tower of the castle—it's as simple as that now. No more rock throwing, no more swimming in the lake. Cooper's getting a little older now, and she wanted to make it easier for him to make the trip on his own."

The wedding of my twenty-first century descendent was the only time I'd traveled into the future. I'd seen many wondrous things, but much to my dismay, I'd had no time to explore them— I'd not even had the time to travel beyond the castle grounds.

"Oh. I assumed the witch only made an exception the one time since there were so many of us going forward at once."

Mitsy shook her head and smiled. "Nope. What's your next excuse?"

"I..." I hesitated. I wasn't sure, but I knew there must be some other reason I couldn't go—even as much as I might secretly want to. "I'll not deny that I'm tempted by yer suggestion, Mitsy, but I would make an awful fool of myself in yer time. I've nothing to wear, I doona know how things work, and Cooper shouldna spend his time with Morna explaining every little thing to me."

Little footsteps approached the doorway and Mitsy and I both turned to see early-riser Cooper burst through the door.

"Did you ask her yet? What'd she say?"

Winking at me, Mitsy faced Cooper.

"She's undecided. I think she needs you to convince her."

He ran toward me as quickly as his little feet would carry him, and I opened my arms to catch him as he jumped up and into my arms. He was growing quickly. I wouldn't be able to pick him up much longer. Until that sad day came, I would hold him anytime he wished me too.

"Come on, Nana. Anything that you're worried about, we've got a plan for. I promise. I know you're nervous, but it would be so much fun. I'd love for you to come with me."

Excitement like I'd not felt in years blossomed within me as I gave myself permission to do something unexpected.

"Are ye sure, Cooper? I know ye enjoy yer time with Morna. I wouldna wish to intrude."

"Are you kidding? Morna would love it. And so would I. Please, Nana. Come with me."

Mitsy reached her hand up to tussle the top of Cooper's wavy curls. She'd known all along that the moment Cooper was in on the plan, I wouldn't be able to say no.

"Kenna, if I can promise you that we'll get you everything you need, that we will prepare you in every way, will you do it?"

"If ye will make certain I willna make a fool of myself, then aye, I'll go."

Cooper squirmed out of my arms and grabbed onto Mitsy's hand to pull her out of the room. Turning to look back at me over his shoulder, he smiled at me as they left.

"Don't you worry, Nana. We've got everything under control."

That was exactly what I was worried about.

CHAPTER 2

Chicago – Present Day

Malcolm Warren looked forward to the last day of school before Christmas break every year. It meant two full weeks with his daughter and granddaughter as they enjoyed their annual trip to Scotland to visit his brother and sister-in-law. This year would be especially festive, for at fifty-eight years young, he was an uncle for the very first time.

Rosalind was excited, too. With his window rolled down so he could wave to her from in front of the school, she started talking to him before she even got in the car.

"Will the baby be walking yet? Do you think Emilia will let me hold him?"

"Hello to you too, kiddo. Get in the car before you freeze to death. I think it's colder here in Chicago than it will be in Scotland."

Once Rosalind was safely inside the car with her seatbelt

fastened, Malcolm answered his granddaughter's insistent questions.

"The baby won't be walking, though I expect he will be crawling all over the place. And of course Emilia will let you hold him. You'll be a big help to her. How was the last day of school?"

Rolling her eyes, the young girl huffed and shook her head.

"It was a total waste of time. This whole week was. It was all parties and Christmas crafts. What am I doing in school if not to do some real learning? I would've been better off just leaving for Scotland a week early."

Malcolm smiled to himself as he drove the short distance to the home they all shared.

"You know, most kids like the days when there's less school work."

She glanced over at him, giving him a smile identical to her mother's, and Malcolm's heart squeezed. His girls were his world. They would never know how much either of them meant to him.

"Pops, have I ever been like most kids?"

"No, and that's one of your best qualities. Most kids drive me crazy."

Rosalind laughed as he pulled into the driveway.

"I know you try to seem grumpier than you are, but nobody buys it. You like everybody."

It was true. While his stature might be intimidating, Malcolm knew his heart was softer than most men he knew. He was an incurable sap.

"Some people buy it. I can be grumpy when I need to be."

Rosalind ignored him as she opened the car door and stepped outside. He knew immediately from the way her eyes darted over to the tightly shut garage door she'd just noticed what he'd already seen—her mother still wasn't home.

"She's not here, Pops. I knew this was going to happen. I just knew it."

Malcolm hurried to place a reassuring hand on his

granddaughter's shoulder as he guided her up the front steps to their home.

"Don't worry yet, Rosie. She could just be stuck in traffic. We don't know that she had to work late."

Shoulders slumped, head down, the young girl leaned into him as he worked to open the front door.

"She always has to work late. We're going to miss our flight."

"Don't you worry about that—we still have an hour or so before we have to be at the airport. We are not going to miss our flight. I'll call the hospital right now. Why don't you go and pack the last of your things and bring your bag downstairs? We can get the car loaded while we wait on her."

Waiting until Rosalind disappeared at the top of the stairs, Malcolm closed the door and made his way into the kitchen. Pulling out his phone, he saw the notification he dreaded might be there—a voicemail from his daughter.

Turning the volume down low so Rosie wouldn't hear it—he could hear her lingering on the stairs—he pressed play and held the phone up to his ear.

"Hey Dad. Look, I know you guys aren't going to be happy with me, and I really hate to do this, but I simply can't leave the hospital right now. Half the nursing staff is trying to take off, and I have too many patients who need me. You guys go ahead and leave for Scotland. I'll catch a flight out sometime next week. I'll definitely be there by Christmas. Tell Rosie that I love her. I love you too, Dad. Oh, and Dad. Don't call the hospital. I don't have time to discuss this with either of you. Just leave and have a great first day in Edinburgh. I'll meet you guys there soon. Bye."

Rosalind entered the kitchen before he had time to call for her.

"I guess I shouldn't bring Mom's bags down? I can tell by your face that she isn't coming."

"I'm so sorry, sweetheart. She's just too swamped..."

"No!" Rosalind's angry voice interrupted him as tears began to swell in her eyes. Her knees wobbled as she gripped the doorway.

"Don't make excuses for her. Not anymore. She always acts like she has a good reason, but there's no good reason for this."

Malcolm couldn't argue with her. He knew the pain his daughter was in all too well, but it didn't give her permission to abandon her daughter. For the better part of two years, she'd closed herself off from all life outside the hospital, and it was Rosalind who suffered for it.

Moving across the room, Malcolm dropped to his knees and reached to wrap his arms around Rosie. She buried her head in his neck and cried.

"You're right. I won't. I know there have been lots of times that she hasn't been there for you since your father passed away, but this time she's gone too far. This isn't right or fair. I'm as angry with her as I've ever been. But this is Christmas, and I refuse to let her ruin it for you."

Ripping herself away from him, Rosalind picked up her bag and stormed through the front door of the house.

"She already has. Now, let's get this stupid show on the road."

Anger always caused Rosie to lash out at those around her. Only in the car for a few seconds, she began to honk the horn at him, fire in her eyes as he dragged his own bag outside and locked the front door.

The young girl was heartbroken and angry, and he would pay the price for it.

Malcolm could sense with every fiber of his being that his beloved granddaughter would give him hell during every second of their trip to Scotland.

cMillan Castle – 1651

"You've no reason to be nervous, Kenna. From the first moment I met you, I knew you were a woman far ahead of your time. Much like Mitsy and Grace were born in another time but belong in this one, I've always wondered if perhaps you belonged in theirs."

I turned toward Bebop in surprise as we continued our morning walk. It was a ritual we started almost immediately after his arrival in the seventeenth century. Each morning, shortly after breakfast, we would meet in the castle's garden where, no matter the weather, we would walk for over an hour. It was good exercise for us both, and over the years we'd become the best of friends.

"Why would ye say that? I've never felt that way myself."

"Well, for starters, you don't think like most people born and raised in this time. Kenna, you are as open-minded as they come. And perhaps you've never felt that way yourself because you've never spent time in another century. I won't be surprised if you have no desire to come back after a few weeks away."

"I'll want to come back. There are far too many people here who I love to stay away."

Bebop reached over to squeeze my shoulder. "And that, my dear, is the only reason I believe you will come back"

"Do ye truly believe I'll love it so much?"

"I do. This isn't exactly related to the subject at hand, but would you like a good laugh?"

I would never say no to that.

"O'course, I do."

"We both know Cooper regularly asks interesting questions. There is nothing the young boy won't say or ask, but this question surprised even me, and I'm rarely surprised by anything."

My curiosity piqued, I took one step closer to him as we walked.

"What did he ask ye?"

"He asked when the two of us were going to get married."

"Wha...what...whatever gave him that idea?" I felt like the air had suddenly been kicked from my chest. It was the most ridiculous suggestion I'd ever heard.

Bebop shook his head as he chuckled softly.

"I haven't the slightest idea. I guess he just assumed that since we are both his grandparents now and both of our spouses are gone that we should naturally be together."

"Oh. Well, I suppose if I were seven years old, I might think as he does. What did ye say to him?"

"Firstly, I explained to him that despite my youthful appearance." He paused to chuckle at himself. "I was significantly older than you. Then, I went on to tell him that anyone who knows my real name and still calls me 'Bebop,' probably doesn't have any romantic inclinations for me."

"And do ye have them for me? I know that ye doona."

"I would be lucky to have you, Kenna, but no, you are the

dearest friend I have here, and I wouldn't want to do anything to ruin that."

"Good." I pointed up ahead where our anticipated guests were approaching the castle. "They're here."

Mitsy's closest friend, Bri, her husband, and their children, along with Bri's mother, Adelle and her husband, Hew, were coming to stay with us for Christmas. Adelle, as I'd learned shortly after Cooper's warning that they had a plan for everything, had already been assigned to help me prepare for my time in the future.

Bebop picked up his pace and reached his hand behind to wave me forward.

"We best hurry then. I've not been around Adelle too much, but I know she has a penchant for talking. You and Cooper leave this evening and I expect she will have a week's worth of information to tell you. Best you get started soon."

Nerves and excitement gathered in equal measure in my chest as I marched toward my first lesson on how to survive in the twenty-first century.

I had just fastened myself into my first-ever bra when both my daughters-in-law, Grace and Mitsy, burst into the room where Adelle and I were picking modern outfits for me to pack from her wide selection.

Mitsy gazed unabashedly at my chest for a matter of seconds and then turned to address Adelle.

"Nice. You're a little bit taller, Adelle, but other than that, you two are just about the same size."

"We are. Lucky thing too since much to my dismay the rest of you girls have let your collection of modern clothes dwindle over the years."

Grace laughed and passed a white button-down blouse in my direction.

"We don't really need them anymore. Why go to the hassle of keeping things that we don't wear handy?"

"You girls must be more evolved than I am. Don't get me wrong. I love my life here, but the fashion of this time doesn't suit my tastes at all. I don't really wear them anymore, but sometimes just looking at my old clothes makes me happy. I'm thrilled they will finally be getting some use."

The buttons on the blouse felt strange beneath my fingers. While the clothes were undoubtedly more comfortable, I felt uncomfortable in them—exposed and wholly unlike myself.

Grace came to stand behind me in the mirror and leaned in close while Adelle and Mitsy began discussing what they missed most about life in the twenty-first century. They were split between hot baths and microwavable popcorn.

"It will take some getting used to, but once you do, you'll love this way of dressing. And if it makes you feel any better now, you look absolutely gorgeous. How does the makeup feel? Do you think you can manage it yourself?"

"Thank ye, Grace." I reached up to gently brush at my newly blackened lashes. "It feels less odd than I expected. Aye, I think I can manage. Adelle took her time showing me how to apply it, though I refused much of what she offered me." Adelle had shoved an entire satchel full of makeup toward me but I only ended up setting aside four items to pack—all of which were entirely new to me: a light powder, eyeliner, mascara, and a burgundy-colored lipstick.

"What you have on is perfect. You don't need much. You're stunning without anything on. I can hear my youngest screaming in the other room so I can't stay away long, but I wanted to come in here and tell you something while it was on my mind. I know that you're going *with* Cooper but I don't want you to feel like you are going to *care for* Cooper. He's stayed alone with Morna and Jerry many times. I trust them with my son completely. What I'm saying is, don't use Cooper as an excuse not to get out and explore while you're there. I want you to soak up everything there is to see, to seize every opportunity that comes your way. You deserve this. You deserve some time away. You deserve some fun. Okay? Promise me you won't feel the need to stay with Cooper every second."

Turning away from the mirror to face her, I reached my arms around Grace to hug her close.

"Thank ye. Having ye tell me that yerself will certainly make me more likely to do so. Are ye coming to see the two of us off?"

McMillan Castle's youngest babe let out an ear-piercing scream and Grace stiffened in my arms.

"Yes, of course. I want to squeeze both of you before you go. Now, however, I must go see to that. Eoghanan is good for many, many things but comforting crying babies isn't one of them."

Grace left, followed shortly by Mitsy, leaving Adelle and me to pack up the rest of my borrowed belongings alone.

"Grace is right, you know. You need to take full advantage of your time there. With Morna involved, it's bound to be a wonderful time for you. Do you mind if I give you my own piece of advice—one grandmother to another?"

Cooper and I would leave within the hour. Everything was real now, and I could no longer hide my apprehension.

"I consider myself to be a rather strong woman, but the closer I get to leaving, the more nauseous I feel. I'll take any advice ye can give me, Adelle."

"Great. And just so you know, I'm only saying something because Grace told me how you sent her to Eoghanan's room before they were married, so I know you're secretly a modern-minded lady like myself. Otherwise, I wouldn't risk offending you."

I laughed and reached to squeeze Adelle's hand. "I canna remember the last time I was offended by anything."

"That's really good. Okay, I can tell by your complexion that it's been a really long time since you've had a good lay. If I know Morna at all, she will see to it that the opportunity arises while you are with her to fix that. Do it. Forget about all of the rules of propriety that apply to things here. Things are very different in the twenty-first century. Have the sex. Eat the cake. Drink the extra glass of wine. Let your hair down a bit."

Whatever I'd expected her to say, it hadn't been that.

"Ye can tell by my complexion?" The thought horrified me.

She shrugged. "What can I say? It's always been my superpower. Now, let's get you to Cooper so the two of you can head out."

Laughing, I lifted the handle of my modern roller bag and then leaned playfully into Adelle.

"Do ye know what, Adelle? I know that I doona know ye verra well, but I already know that I like ye verra much."

Smiling, she wrapped her arm around my shoulder as we left the room.

"I like you too, Kenna. I'm totally serious, though. When you guys return in two weeks, I expect your face to be glowing. Glowing from all the sex."

"Aye, I understood what ye meant by glowing from yer first reference to my ruddy complexion."

She nodded. "Just driving the point home."

"I believe ye did. I shall endeavor to return home all aglow."

Laughing like lassies half our age, we made our way to the castle's west tower together.

CHAPTER 4

On The Road to Conall Castle, Scotland – Present Day

If Rosalind sighed any louder, the tourists in the very back of the bus would be able to hear her. It was now three days into their trip and with no word from Rosie's mother, the young girl's mood continued to decline.

Listening to the young girl cry herself to sleep had been the deciding factor for Malcolm. Staying in his brother's home where they all had so many shared memories of Christmases together only seemed to make matters worse for his granddaughter. It only reminded her that during a time of year when both of her parents should be there, neither of them were.

There was no need for them to stay in Edinburgh for the entire trip. Perhaps it would do Rosalind some good to get out of the house and explore the country a bit. They could travel for a few days and then return to Edinburgh for the real Christmas celebrations.

Unable to sleep from the soft sounds of Rosie crying inside

her room, Malcolm had arranged a weekend getaway in which they would explore a bit of the Highlands. And now, only twelve hours after the decision was made, they were aboard a bus, enjoying the three-hour scenic drive from Edinburgh to the first stop on their trip—Conall Castle.

At least he was enjoying the drive. So far, the diversion wasn't working for Rosie.

"This is the castle you wanted to see, isn't it? I was almost certain this was the one you mentioned to me before."

Rosalind didn't face him as she answered. Instead, she kept her gaze focused out the bus window to her left.

"Mom and I planned to see it together. We can just add this to the long list of things she's missed."

"We can always come and visit it again when she gets here."

Rosalind turned slowly toward him, her eyes red and teary. Her eyes and nose were beginning to look raw from all the crying. Malcolm needed to find some way to make the child smile.

"Don't you know it by now, Pops? She isn't coming. Last Christmas was just too hard on her. I know she hasn't said it yet, but I know her. She won't be here for Christmas."

Malcolm worried that his granddaughter was right. Tim had loved Christmas so much. His daughter seemed incapable of celebrating the holiday now that he was gone.

"It won't always be this way, Rosie. Sometimes, grief takes a very long time to work through. She will find her way back to you."

Taking a deep breath in through her nose, Rosalind turned away from him and stared out the window once more. He could see Conall Castle in the distance through the front window of the bus. They were almost there.

"Let's not talk about your mother anymore today. Let's just try and enjoy this time together."

As the bus pulled to a stop and the castle's guide stepped aboard the bus to welcome them, Malcolm turned his attention to the tour. One by one they got off the bus and followed the perky and knowledgeable guide along the short trail leading up to the castle's main doors.

While he was certain Rosalind had followed him off the bus, he turned to whisper to her halfway through the tour and found her no longer behind him. Frantically, his gaze tore through their group. She was gone. Rosalind was nowhere to be found.

McMillan Castle – Present Day

"Ach, Cooper, does it always hurt so much?" I gripped my head painfully as we slowly moved down the tower stairwell into the twenty-first century version of my home.

The method of travel was simple enough. All we needed was for Cooper to open his magical pocket watch, ask Morna to bring us forward, and in a flash we disappeared, only to reappear in the exact same location seconds later, centuries ahead of the time we left. As simple as it was, the magic's effects on my body could be felt all over. I was disoriented, and while my body ached everywhere, nothing hurt as badly as my head.

"Don't worry, Nana. Harper keeps some ibuprofen handy. She'll have it waiting for you."

I was mildly aware of modern medicines. My daughters-in-law kept several pills and tinctures hidden away for times when illness befell anyone in the castle that a simple herbal mixture wouldn't cure.

"Only for me? Does yer head not hurt?"

The young boy shrugged and bounded down the stairs ahead of me.

"Nope. The more you do it, the easier it gets. Plus, you're old so that probably has something to do with why you feel so bad."

Shaking my head, I met up with him as he waited at the bottom of the stairs for me.

"I believe we need to have a discussion about my actual age. Several instances as of late have given me reason to believe ye think me far more ancient than I am."

Cooper smiled and let out a quick giggle.

"I'm only teasing you, Nana. You're not old. You don't look it anyway."

"Thank ye. Now, where is this ibuprofen?"

"It's right here."

I looked up to see Harper, the wife of my descendent and the true leader of McMillan Castle in the twenty-first century. She was energetic, organized, and without her my home would've fallen into disrepair long ago. I gratefully accepted the pills and glass of water she extended in my direction.

"Neither of you look too worse for wear. You'll be pleased to know that Jerry is already here. He's got the car all warmed up for you."

"He's here already?" Cooper's voice couldn't have sounded any more excited. "We left our bags in the tower. Let me go and get them so we can get to Morna's."

Harper reached out a hand to stop him.

"Don't worry about that. Kamden will gather up your bags. I told Sileas you were coming this morning, and he's been wagging his tail all morning with excitement. Why don't you go and say hello to him and leave your things to my husband?"

The castle dog, Sileas, was almost taller than Cooper when standing on all fours, but the sweet beast collapsed on the ground and rolled over onto his back like a small puppy the moment Cooper neared him.

With Cooper occupied, Harper hooked her arm with my own and walked with me outside to the car.

"I'm glad you decided to come, Kenna. It will be good for you."

Still nervous, my voice was much more shaky than I wished it to be as I answered her. "That's what everyone keeps saying. I hope all of ye are right."

"We are." She leaned in to hug me and kiss my cheek as Jerry stepped out of the car to greet me. "Christmas is the most magical time of year. I can't wait to see what happens to you over the next few weeks."

My first car ride was thrilling. While Cooper slept restfully in the back seat of Jerry's very tiny car, I happily sat next to Jerry in the front as I delighted in the swirl of scenery that changed every second.

"Ye are going to be fun for all of us, lass. I can tell."

I knew smiling for hours was a bit much, but I truly couldn't stop. Everything outside the car window was amazing. With all of the means of travel I was accustomed to, it would've taken days to see what we'd seen in three hours of driving.

"What do ye mean?"

"Yer excitement is contagious. 'Tis always a joy to watch another experience something for the first time. It has been far too long since we've enjoyed the company of a newbie to this time."

While I could discern the meaning of the word *newbie* by its context well enough, it was a word I'd never heard before in my life.

"How far away are we?"

Cooper's sleepy voice spoke to us from behind and I twisted to look at him.

"I doona care if it takes us all night to get there. I never expected a ride in a car to be so pleasurable."

Out of the corner of my eye, I could see Jerry lift one hand from the wheel and point ahead of him.

"We are nearly there now. I'm turning onto the dirt road which leads to Conall Castle and our inn as we speak."

I faced the front to see the faint outline of the castle in the distance, but there was something else along the road ahead, a faint outline of a creature or a person walking along the road's outer edge.

"Look, guys—it's a girl!"

I leaned forward and strained to make out the form Cooper pointed at. Sure enough, a girl who couldn't be more than a few years older than Cooper, walked all alone ahead of us.

I liked the strange girl instantly, despite her rather unfriendly demeanor. I recognized the look in her eyes —the grief and the anger that was so potently felt, she no longer tried to hide it at all. Not so long ago, I'd been there myself. She also had a defiantly independent nature that I appreciated in any woman, but most especially in someone so young. Despite having so much growth ahead of her, she already knew herself more than many women ever do.

"Look, sir, I appreciate you offering me a ride, but I don't know you. There's no way I'm getting into that car with you."

Jerry, accustomed to willful women, was unbothered by the young girl's refusal. He remained patient, calm, and insistent as he tried to reason with her. Cooper and I watched on in silence, enjoying the exchange.

"Lassie, 'twould be improper for me to leave a child stranded along a dirt road. 'Tis at least a mile back to the castle. I'll not do it. If ye willna get in this car, I shall follow along beside ye until either whoever ye are with finds ye or yer legs give out from exhaustion. 'Tis snowing and ye are near soaked through. Ye've no hat on yer head, no muffs on yer ears, and no gloves that I can see. When we do find whoever ye are with, I shall scold them for allowing ye out of doors without anything to keep ye warm."

"Watch it, old man." There was fire in the girl's tone. Something that Jerry had said made her immediately defensive. "You'll say nothing to my grandfather. It's not his fault that I ignored him."

Jerry smiled and cast me a quick glance.

"Ah. Thank ye, lass. We are finally making some progress. At least I now know who ye are with. Is yer grandfather back at the castle? If so, why doona ye get in the back with Cooper and we will drive ye to him?"

The young girl pointed to Cooper in the back seat who responded by waving at her. She rolled her eyes in response.

"How do I know that you didn't kidnap that little boy in the back and now you want to kidnap me, too?"

Cooper quickly protested by rolling down his window and sticking his head outside to speak to the girl directly.

"I am *not* that little. And Jerry hasn't kidnapped me. I'd like to see someone try to take me if I didn't want to go."

Quietly, so the girl outside couldn't hear him, Jerry leaned back and whispered over his shoulder to Cooper.

"I'm not sure if I'd be so confident about that, lad. It did already happen once before if ye doona remember?"

On impulse, I reached out and hit Jerry softly on the arm. The very memory of the old witch who'd taken Cooper from us once before made my blood boil. I tried my best to block it from my memory. I was certain Cooper tried to do the same.

The girl laughed and crossed her arms, leaning back onto her heels.

"Only someone really little would feel the need to tell me how 'not little' they are."

Cooper's face flushed red as he sank back inside the car.

Jerry laughed and attempted to divert the conversation back toward him.

"There. Cooper has told ye himself that he is not kidnapped. If ye truly doona wish to get in this car, then fine, turn yerself around and walk back toward the castle. I'll follow behind ye to make certain ye get there safely."

I could see by the flash in the young girl's eyes that she saw this as a victory. Without a word she turned and marched off in front of the car.

I leaned over and spoke softly to Jerry—not that she could hear me from outside the car anyway.

"Ye really are going to have to follow her all the way. She's strong-willed. She doesna wish to give in to ye."

Jerry nodded and pressed on the brake as he turned to address Cooper.

"Aye, I know. Cooper, what should we do? Ye know women well."

I wasn't all together sure how true that was, but I could see by the way Cooper lifted in his seat that Jerry's confidence in him was just what he needed after the girl's insult. It wouldn't hurt to let Cooper think of an idea to try.

Cooper smiled and unbuckled his seatbelt. "I know just the thing, guys. Just give me some space, okay?"

We both nodded and allowed Cooper to get out of the car. Rolling down my own window, I urged Jerry to do the same.

"Open all the windows and pull up beside them rather than behind. I wish to hear what they are saying to one another."

Jerry obeyed without question.

"What are you doing? I don't know you either, little boy. You need to get back in your car and leave me alone."

Cooper carried himself tall and didn't shrink at the girl's cold welcome. Instead, he moved to block her path and extended his hand.

"You could at least say hello to me. My name's Cooper, what's your name?"

Forced to stop, the young girl eyed him suspiciously. Cautiously, she extended her hand.

"Rosalind." She hesitated and then added, "but most people call me Rosie."

I smiled as Cooper shook her hand and moved out of her way, falling in step beside her as she continued her march back toward the castle. The name suited her. Significantly taller than Cooper, the girl was slender and pale with very short strawberry-blonde hair that fell much more in the realm of strawberry than blonde. Her eyes were jade green, and the smattering of freckles across her face would, one day when she was older, be stunning.

It was unusual in my time to see a female with such short hair, but I quite liked it. It fit the young girl's personality perfectly. Eager to see what Cooper would do next, I watched on.

"It's really cold out here, ya know?"

Rosie nodded but didn't look over at Cooper as she walked.

"Yes, I do know. Maybe you should get back in the car with the old man and the woman who keeps staring at me."

I shrunk slightly back in my seat but didn't look away at her words.

Cooper shook his head.

"Nope. As long as you're walking, I'm going to walk next to you. And, as you said, I'm little and it's very, very cold out here. I might get sick."

To emphasize this, Cooper coughed rather dramatically into his arm.

Rosalind stopped cold, crossed her arms as she'd done before and looked at him.

"You people are crazy. I don't like any of you one bit."

Cooper grinned. He could see that he was succeeding.

"We're just trying to help you."

Turning, she stomped away from him and opened the car door before crawling inside.

"I don't need anybody's help. The second we get back to the castle and I find my grandfather, I don't want to see any of you guys ever again."

Jerry laughed and sped up as we barreled toward the castle.

"Verra well, lass, but see ye to yer grandfather, we shall."

When Malcolm saw the old, rickety car pull up to the front of Conall Castle, the terror that had gripped him for the better part of an hour melted away in a rush. He could see Rosalind's red hair through the window, and his knees nearly gave way as relief washed over him. While he'd known she couldn't have gone far—there was only one road leading to the castle—he'd been terrified.

Running outside to meet her, he gathered her up in his arms and dropped to his knees.

"Where on earth did you go?"

Rosalind was stiff in his grip. With a muffled voice, she spoke into the front of his shirt.

"You've got to let go of me, Pops. I can't breathe. I didn't go anywhere. I was just bored to death on the tour and thought I'd walk around a little while. I was just walking down the road."

It was only when he released her and stood that he took notice of the old man standing on the other side of the car. While it took him a moment to recognize him—it had been at least five years since he'd seen him—he knew as soon as he heard the man's voice that it was Jerry.

"Malcolm! Why, I dinna know Rosie was yer granddaughter. Had I known, I wouldna have been so patient with her. How are ye, man? 'Tis been far too long since ye visited these parts."

The snow now fell in a heavy blanket over them. As he leaned forward to hug Jerry, he could see Rosie trembling beside them from the cold. She was wet all the way through.

"I'm much better now. Thank you for picking her up."

"O'course. I was on my way back home when we spotted her. I dinna know who she belonged to, but I couldna verra well leave her out in the snow."

Noticing the castle's tour guide a few yards away, Malcolm reached for Rosie's hand.

"Jerry, it's good to see you, but I'm afraid we must both get back to the group. Rosie delayed everyone long enough by wandering off and the entire group has been searching for her. I need to let them know she's back."

Just as he began to step away, Jerry reached and grabbed his arm.

"By all means, let them know the lass is safe but then why doona the two of ye gather yer bags from the bus and come with me back to the inn for the night? Morna would never forgive me if she found out that I bumped into ye and then dinna bring ye back to the house so she could see ye."

Malcolm couldn't deny the appeal of Jerry's suggestion. Rosalind needed to get dry, and Morna and Jerry's inn was undoubtedly closer than the tour group's next stop.

"We wouldn't be intruding?"

Jerry waved a dismissive hand.

"Not at all. I promise ye, my wife would insist on it if she were here so I must do so on her behalf. Rosie can wait in the car for ye while ye gather yer things."

Seeing his granddaughter inside the car, he leaned in close to whisper in her ear before leaving to retrieve their things.

"When we get to the inn, we will discuss this further."

hile she said nothing, it was evident that Rosalind was near tears as she waited for her grandfather. Her breathing was tight, and I could see her reddened cheeks from the mirror outside my window.

Jerry and Cooper could sense the tension in the young girl, as well, and we remained quiet as we waited for the man I now knew was named Malcolm to return with their belongings.

When he began his walk back toward the car, I was able to get a clear view of him for the first time.

He was one of the most handsome men I'd ever seen. As tall as both of my sons, I would be dwarfed in size if I stood next to him. His hair was very dark and thick, slightly unruly, and much like my own, it had begun to gray in mixed places throughout. His blue eyes stood out from amongst his mass of black hair, and he had the sort of scruffy facial hair that made it look as if he were in the beginning stages of trying to grow it out. Although, I expected that with all of the fascinating tools I knew existed in the twenty-first century, that he kept it trimmed that way all the time.

I didn't realize he'd stopped walking and that we were both staring at one another until his knuckles lightly rapped on my closed window. Startled, I jerked back as my cheeks warmed in embarrassment. I was certain they were now as red as Rosie's.

"I'm so sorry to ask you this," Malcolm straightened and swept his hand downward in a motion meant to emphasize the length of his legs. "I don't think I'll fit in the back seat. Would you mind switching with me?"

There was no question that if he attempted to sit in the back, he would be forced to sit in a terribly uncomfortable position, if he could manage to fit in the back at all.

"Oh. Aye, o'course." Fumbling with the door handle, I

eventually managed to clumsily step outside. When I righted myself, Malcolm extended me his hand.

"I hate to have you move. I'm Malcolm, but you can call me Mac, most people do."

He had quite possibly the largest hands I'd ever seen. I found them to be wildly attractive.

Strong yet gentle, his fingers were long and masculine. The touch of them against my own as he slid his hand around mine made my knees wobbly in a way that both shocked and horrified me.

"'Tis no trouble at all, I assure ye. I...I'm Kenna. Ye may call me Kenna." It was a ridiculous thing to say, and the smile that spread across his face at my words made me want to disappear into the snow.

"Very well. It's a pleasure to meet you, Kenna. Here, let me open the door for you."

As he ushered me into the back seat of the car next to a wet and freezing Rosie who was forced to slide over into the middle, his hand touched my back and I gasped. Thankfully, Cooper was the only one who noticed my quick intake of breath, but the oddly perceptive child immediately turned his head away from me to giggle.

The drive back to Morna and Jerry's was short, and as expected, Morna stood outside her home awaiting our arrival.

I was the first one to climb out of the car, and before I managed to say one word of greeting to her, Morna pulled me to her in a tight embrace.

"Ach, lassie. I'm so pleased ye decided to join Cooper." And then, lowering her voice so that no one save me could hear her, she pressed her lips against my ear and whispered. "Our other guests doona know about any of the magic. Best we not tell them."

Raising her voice once more, she pushed me away and moved to gather up Cooper, most assuredly to give him the same warning. Not that it was needed. Everyone who'd ever fallen prey to Morna's meddling magic quickly became accustomed to keeping secrets. Cooper would know not to say anything.

"Cooper, lad. I've missed ye more than ye know. Get yerself over here and give me a hug."

I gathered our belongings as Morna and Cooper hugged. Then I walked over to Jerry so he could direct me.

He attempted to reach for the bags, but I quickly spun them away from him.

"No, thank ye. I can manage both bags just fine, Jerry. Where would ye like me to place them?"

Smiling, Jerry pointed to the top of the stairs.

"Straight up and to yer right there are three rooms. Cooper prefers the room nearest the staircase. Why doona ye take the middle room? Rosie can have the room at the far end."

Nodding, I stepped away. "I'll just place these in our rooms then I'll come downstairs to visit. Thank ye both for letting me stay."

"We are so happy to have ye here, Kenna. We will have plenty of time for conversation. Ye must be exhausted from the journey. If ye get to yer room and feel like resting for a bit, please do so."

By the time I reached my room, my arms ached from fingertip to shoulder from the weight of Cooper's book bag.

The bed looked so inviting.

Surely, a short rest would do no harm.

I woke to the familiar sound of knuckles lightly rapping. For a few moments upon opening my eyes, I forgot where I was. It was only when I noticed the glow of electric lighting from the side table to my right and the strong smell of food from the kitchen below that everything came flooding back. I was at Morna's—some three hundred plus years ahead of the time I'd been born in.

Pulling myself from the bed, I stood and stretched then nearly fell backwards on the bed once again when I cast a glance out the window to see that the sky was now pitch black. I'd slept for the rest of the day.

The light knock returned. I ran a quick hand through my undoubtedly messy hair and moved to answer it. Expecting Cooper—although, if I were honest with myself, it would've surprised me if he'd actually knocked—I jumped back at the sight of Malcolm standing tall in the doorway.

"Did I wake you? I just saw that the light was on so I thought maybe you weren't sleeping. Forgive me, Kenna. It can wait until morning."

Still drowsy and confused at his presence, I yawned and held up a hand to keep him from leaving.

"No, no. 'Tis fine. I shouldna have slept so long. How far into evening is it?"

He pulled his lips to one side as if he were reluctant to tell me.

"It's close to midnight now. I'm the only one up. I should've assumed that you'd just fallen asleep with the light on, but I saw it and thought perhaps you'd awakened. Now that you're up, are you hungry?"

I found myself unable to remember the last time I'd eaten. The day leading up to my departure had been so filled with preparation and activity, I didn't think I'd stopped once to eat and with all of the traveling today, I knew I'd eaten nothing.

"I'm famished."

"Good. I know I saw Morna stash some leftovers in the fridge. I'll go and warm it up."

Smiling, I nodded and reached for the door.

"Thank ye. Just give me a few moments to fully wake myself and I'll join ye downstairs."

I waited until he disappeared from view before I tip-toed from my room over to the bathroom at the end of the hall. I'd used only one modern toilet in all of my life and to my everlasting embarrassment had been forced to call Mitsy into the room to help me figure out how to work it. To avoid such mortification this time—I'd sooner die than have to call my grandson into the bathroom to educate me on twenty-first century waste removal— I had Adelle give me a thorough lesson on all the new objects I would find in Morna's home.

A mirror hung on the back of the bathroom door, and as I sat down to relieve myself, I caught a glimpse of my reflection. I'd never looked so frightening in all my life. Dark smeared circles surrounded my eyes from smeared mascara. My hair was ratted and smashed drastically to one side. And—worst of all—the top four buttons on the white blouse I was wearing had opened while

I slept. If not for the bra underneath, my breasts would have been totally exposed.

Still, even with the bra, Malcolm had just seen more of my bare chest than any man in the last fifteen years.

---

*E*ven unkempt from sleep, with eyes as dark as raccoons from her makeup, Kenna was stunning. And by God her breasts were perfect. Not that he intentionally looked at her breasts. They'd just been so there, so evident with the way her blouse lay open. He was certain she'd not known. She would be embarrassed when she noticed. Of course, he would say nothing of it. It was best to let her believe that he'd seen nothing below her chin.

The food was already warm and laid out by the time she entered the kitchen. As he expected, her face was now bare, her hair pulled back, and her blouse firmly closed.

"I haven't the slightest idea what this is, but it is delicious. Morna asked me before she went to bed to direct you to the food if you were to wake up hungry during the night."

Kenna's brows pulled together as she sat down in the chair opposite him.

"Why would she tell ye to do that? Does she not expect ye to sleep, as well?"

Malcolm realized that she must've not seen his pallet in the middle of the living room floor on her way to the kitchen.

"She only asked because I'm sleeping in the living room. I suppose she suspected I would wake if anyone came downstairs. Though, she's wrong about that. It always takes me awhile to go to sleep, but once I do, I'm out like a light."

Kenna lifted the fork he'd laid out for her, smiling as she took her first bite of food.

"'Tis shepherd's pie. Quite a delicious one." Speaking between bites of food, she continued. "Malcolm, ye needn't sleep on the floor. I can move my belongings over to Cooper's room and sleep with him."

Malcolm had seen clearly enough the young boy's desire to appear older than he was to his granddaughter. It wouldn't do to have the boy's grandmother sleep with him.

"I wouldn't dream of it. I believe Cooper has taken a bit of a fancy to Rosie. And she already wounded his confidence enough tonight. If she saw that you were sleeping in his room..." he paused and shook his head, "well, I'm not quite sure what this new version of my granddaughter would say to him, but she'd ridicule him for it. The floor suits me just fine. The mattress Morna placed there is honestly quite comfortable."

Malcolm watched as concern crossed Kenna's face. She loved the young boy dearly, and he could see why. Despite Rosie's harsh words, Cooper had been nothing but a delight during their meal. And while he knew Rosie's words must have hurt him, the child had hidden it well.

"What do ye mean? What happened?"

Standing, he went to retrieve a fork for himself before joining in on the other side of the pie.

"That's actually why I came to your room. I just wanted to apologize on behalf of Rosie. She'll be apologizing to Cooper in the morning, I've made sure of that, but I just wanted you to know that how she's behaved since you all met her...well, it's not typical."

Kenna's face softened somewhat and she surprised him by reaching forward to gently lay her hand on top of his. He stilled underneath her touch.

"'Twas Mac ye said I should call ye, aye?"

He nodded.

"Mac, I raised three children and am surrounded by grandchildren almost every day. I know all too well that to judge any child by one day's ill-tempered mood is folly. 'Twas clear to me the moment I saw Rosalind that something had upset her greatly. We all lash out when we are angry. What did she say to him?"

"She asked him if he wanted her to cut up his food since you were sleeping. That surely someone so young couldn't manage by himself."

Kenna's eyes grew wide and Malcolm noticed that he immediately missed her touch as she pulled her hand away and crossed her arms. She didn't look angry at all. If anything, she appeared amused.

"And how did he answer her?"

Malcolm smiled thinking back on the youngster's words.

"He carefully lifted his knife and cut the perfect bite of pie before placing it in his mouth like a gentleman three times his age. Then he looked directly at her and said, 'I think I can manage, but if you have any trouble with your piece, I'll be happy to help you, Rosie. And just so you know, I may look younger than I am now, but it won't be that way forever.'"

Kenna smiled wide and nodded slowly.

"That sounds like Cooper. I doona think there is need for Rosie to apologize come morning. I verra much doubt that Rosie's words wounded him at all."

If Kenna was correct, the boy was indeed much more grown-up than he appeared. Malcolm knew that at such an age, to be called small by a girl he liked would've been crushing.

"She will apologize whether Cooper needs the apology or not. No matter how upset Rosie is at her own situation, it gives her no right to intentionally try to hurt others."

Kenna resumed picking at the edges around the pie.

"Aye, fine. 'Tis o'course yer choice what ye have her do. I only meant that I doona want ye to worry for Cooper's feelings. His whole life he's dealt with people underestimating him, and he always handles it with grace. He's been a grown man trapped inside a child's body since the day I first met him."

Setting her fork to the side, Kenna pushed the pie toward him and Malcolm stood to clean up the table.

Discarding the few scraps that remained and placing the dish in the sink to wash later, Malcolm returned to his seat.

"I've no doubt of that. Since the day you met him?"

"Aye. Cooper is not my grandson by birth, though I love him no differently than those who are. His mother married my son only a few years ago."

"Ah. And how do you know Morna and Jerry? Cooper seems quite close with them."

Malcolm watched as Kenna hesitated a long moment and he couldn't help but wonder what about the question gave her pause.

"She's a distant relative of mine through marriage. My husband was her cousin. Morna and Cooper took to one another the moment they met. I suppose she and Jerry are in some way grandparents to him, as well, now. The child has many."

"He is blessed then. I'm the only grandparent Rosie has left."

The confession slipped from Malcolm without thought, and he immediately felt strange. He hated nothing more than other people's sympathy, and it took much for him to open up. Why then, had he spoken so easily of something so delicate with this stranger?

Thankfully, Kenna gave little in the way of sympathy.

"'Tis always difficult when children lose those they love at a young age. Is yer wife recently passed? Is that what wounds the girl now?"

Malcolm looked into Kenna's eyes and saw no pity. She didn't avoid his gaze, didn't smile softly to make him comfortable. It endeared her to him even more. And somehow, it made it easier to speak of things he rarely ever did.

"No. Rosie is named after her grandmother though she never knew her. My Rosalind has been gone seventeen years now. Rosie's father passed away two years ago this next week, and while she still grieves for him, her anger is now directed at her mother.

She was supposed to be on this trip with us. She claims she is swamped with work, but Rosie knows better. I don't blame her for her anger. I'm angry, as well. She does not, however, have reason to make everyone else around her—most especially strangers—miserable."

"Not a one of us is miserable, Mac. Allow the girl her anger. She will come around in a few days. If I know Morna, she will see to it that Rosie's mood lifts sooner rather than later. Now," Kenna stood and stretched just slightly before turning away from him, "while I can scarcely believe it myself, I feel as if I could sleep even more. Thank ye for the food. I should go back to bed."

"You're very welcome. Sleep well." He hesitated to do so as she climbed the stairs, but couldn't keep from calling out to her once more as she reached the top. "Kenna?"

She turned toward him with a smile. "Aye?"

"Thank you."

"For what?"

"I didn't leave that conversation feeling sorry for Rosie or myself. I don't remember the last time I felt that way after speaking to anyone about our losses."

Her voice was quiet, but her tone was sad as she answered him.

"Doona thank me. My lack of sympathy wasna intentional, I assure ye. Perhaps my own dealings with grief have hardened me more than I knew. Goodnight, Mac. Rosie is lucky to have ye."

As Malcolm waited for her bedroom door to close, he knew he wouldn't sleep a wink tonight for wondering about what had pained his beautiful new friend so much.

CHAPTER 8

Despite my insistence that I was indeed still sleepy after my many hours long nap, I didn't sleep a minute after returning to my room. Instead, I lay awake thinking of Malcolm—of how easy it was to speak to him, of how polite he'd been not to mention my appearance earlier in the night, of how handsome he looked dressed so casually for sleep. It was the first time in well over a decade that such thoughts of a man had occupied my mind.

Eventually, just past five when I knew Cooper would be awake. I tiptoed over to his room and slipped inside.

As expected, he sat propped up in his bed with a mound of pillows, a book on his lap. He lay his book down beside him and smiled at me as I entered.

"What are you doing up so early, Nana?"

"'Twas the nap I took last evening. I slept far longer than I should have. Cooper, I'm sorry for not tending to ye last night. I quite abandoned ye."

He shook his head and scooted over so I could sit down beside him.

"You didn't abandon me. I'm used to being with Morna and

Jerry all by myself. I didn't think anything about it, I promise. Do you feel more rested?"

I suspected my sleeping patterns would be turned around for days, but for now, I did feel quite rested.

"Aye, I do. What of ye, Cooper, did ye sleep well?"

Gently laying his head against my shoulder, Cooper answered.

"Yes. I always sleep well. Maybe it's 'cause I know Morna has magic, but I always feel completely safe here. I don't worry about anything."

"Do ye not usually feel safe at home?"

"I do, but magic just sort of brings a whole other level of safety to it, ya know?"

I laughed and gently rested my own head against the top of his.

"Aye, I suppose ye are right. Cooper, Malcolm came to see me last night. He wished to apologize on behalf of Rosie."

The child lifted his head and twisted to face me. His brows pulled toward his nose in confusion.

"What for?"

"He was worried that she might have wounded yer feelings over dinner."

Cooper smiled widely. While the light was low in the room, I thought I saw a slight blush in his cheeks.

"She didn't hurt my feelings."

"No? What she said to ye wasna verra kind."

"No it wasn't, but she's not really upset with me. I know that. I think she's *wonderful*."

I had to swallow the giggle that rose up in my throat at the sound of complete awe in Cooper's voice as he called Rosie wonderful. It seemed that Malcolm was right—Cooper fancied the lass.

"Wonderful...how so?"

Cooper hesitated and crossed his arms as he pursed his lips.

"I wish I had a better answer, but the truth is, I just don't know her that well yet. It's just a feeling I have. Rosie is something special. Don't worry though—I'll get to know her. She may not think much of me now, but someday I'll grow. Then she will like me so much, it will drive her crazy."

The thought seemed to delight Cooper.

"So ye think ye will know Rosalind for a long time, then? Ye doona believe that once she and her grandfather leave that ye willna see her again?"

Cooper smiled and turned his head to look up under his lashes at me with an expression that was meant to tell me that I should've already known the answer.

"Nana, don't you know how Morna works by now? She hasn't admitted it yet, even though I tried to get her to, but I know Morna's magic has something to do with them being here. I have no doubt that Mac and Rosie will be in our lives for a very long time. Do you doubt it, Nana?"

It truly hadn't crossed my mind until now. Everything about the situation seemed entirely coincidental, but perhaps Cooper was right. If he was, did her plans only relate to Cooper and Rosie, or did it all have something to do with me and Mac, as well?

"I see that ye did find yer way to the kitchen after the rest of us were abed. I'm glad for it, lass. It dinna please me to go to bed without seeing ye fed, but I dinna wish to wake ye, either. Did Mac help ye heat everything?"

Entering the kitchen after my first glorious experience with a shower, I moved to where Morna worked over a flame to see what she was cooking.

"Aye, he did. Do ye need help with anything?"

Morna quickly waved me away.

"No, lass. 'Tis only eggs, and the toast and coffee are nearly ready. I've also some haggis and black pudding for ye and Jerry. No one else will eat it."

"Not even ye?" Morna was as Scottish as I. It surprised me that she would dislike food she'd undoubtedly been raised on.

"No, I've not touched either food since the age of ten when I learned what each item was made of. If my brother or father were still here, they'd think it traitorous of me to say so, but I canna stomach it."

I'd never given the making of either food much thought. I had no intention of doing so now. Eager to change the subject, I quickly peeked inside the living room to make certain that Malcolm still slept soundly on the floor.

With his soft snores audible from the bottom of the stairway, I knew it was safe to ask my question.

"Morna, how do ye and Jerry know Malcolm and Rosalind?"

Extending a mug in my direction, Morna carried her own over to the small table and motioned for me to sit next to her.

"Well, we dinna know Rosalind until last night, and it has been many a year since we've seen Malcolm. As for how we know him, in truth, 'tis his brother, Kraig, that we knew first. We met Kraig at the hospital in Edinburgh when Jerry had his knee replaced over a decade ago. He was his surgeon, and despite Jerry being the most cantankerous patient the poor doctor ever had, the two of them took to each other. We've been friends with the young lad ever since. In fact, I introduced Kraig to his wife, Emilia. We met Malcolm at their wedding."

Smiling, I shook my head.

"It shouldna surprise me to hear that, Morna, but for some reason, it does. Have ye ever met a singleton whose love life ye havena decided to meddle in?"

I knew the moment I saw her mischievous grin what I'd walked into.

"Ye are still single, Kenna. I've yet to meddle in yer life."

"Cooper is none too sure of that. He told me this morning he believes Malcolm and Rosie's appearance here is yer doing. And I'm not certain that being widowed is the same as being single."

Morna laughed and reached over to pat my hand.

"Mayhap for the first few years after such a loss, such an answer is acceptable. While ye are widowed, ye are free to love again. It has been fifteen years, Kenna. Ye are verra, verra single."

"So..." I took a sip of my coffee to listen for Malcolm's snoring. It still reverberated through the hallway. "Is Cooper right, Morna? Have ye decided to meddle in my life next?"

Morna scooted her chair right next to mine and leaned in to whisper.

"Believe it or not, lass, my magic is not the only force in this world which conspires to bring those that are meant to be together, together. While I know Cooper dinna believe me, I had no hand in this. I canna begin to tell ye how surprised I was when I saw Jerry pull up with two extra guests."

I leaned away from her. "Why are ye whispering, Morna?"

Grinning, she leaned in even closer and kept her voice low.

"Kenna, Mac has been feigning sleep since ye came down those stairs. There is no need for him to hear what I'm telling ye. Now, while I promise ye I had nothing to do with ye all finding Rosie yesterday, that doesna mean that there is no reason for his arrival. The two of ye would make a fair match, 'tis plain to see. And while I'll not use magic in this instance, I would be lying if I said I had no intention of meddling. I intend to clear the path for the two of ye just a bit, just to allow ye to see where things might lead. I would advise ye not to get in my way."

Before I could protest or even respond, Morna stood, winked at me, and then screamed out for everyone in the house to hear, "Breakfast is ready. All of ye best wake and come to the kitchen before it cools."

By mid-morning, Morna began to execute her "light meddling." Over breakfast she all but begged Malcolm and Rosalind to stay one more day so they could help us decorate the inn for Christmas. With Rosie quite reluctant to return to Edinburgh, Malcolm agreed.

With Morna, Jerry, Cooper, and Rosie pulling down boxes from the attic, the nosy and insistent witch sent Malcolm and me out on a task to find the perfect Christmas tree from a farm a half hour away.

Knowing that Morna believed us to be a good match changed the dynamic between us. While Malcolm hadn't been able to hear our conversation, it had shifted something in my own mind, which made me nervous and awkward in his presence. I couldn't look at him without wondering "what if?", without thinking through a thousand different scenarios, without questioning whether or not my feelings were a result of actually liking him or simply the result of being on my own for so many years. Back home, I'd quickly ended any possibility of a relationship with anyone else—I'd never been interested in the slightest. Now, for some reason completely beyond me, I was.

Was it the trip? Had being away from home and in a time so unfamiliar simply overexcited me so much that I was seeing possibility, that I was seeing attraction, where it wasn't? I found this the most likely cause of my feelings and did my best to silence the endless chatter of thoughts in my mind as we pulled away from the inn.

"Don't you find it odd that the kids didn't want to come pick out a tree?"

Laughing, I remembered both children's faces when they'd told us that they wanted to stay and help Morna and Jerry get the decorations down. It was evident in their glee that Morna had somehow offered them something that appealed to them even more.

"I suspect we will return to find both of them so sick from whatever sweet treats Morna has bribed them with that 'twill be clear why they wished to stay."

"Why would she bribe them?" Malcolm's tone was genuinely curious, and I realized once more that he truly hadn't been able to hear Morna's whisperings to me.

A younger woman would've lied—would've made some excuse that kept awkwardness at bay—but sometime during my forties, my worries over what others thought of me had blessedly diminished. Being relieved of that torture was entirely worth the cost of the wrinkles such a decade had brought me. If this man was meant to like me, he would. If not, he wouldn't. Bringing up Morna's thoughts on the matter wouldn't change things one way or the other.

"Morna sent us on this errand so that we would be alone. She believes we would make a good couple."

I expected him to make light of such a statement. He did anything but.

"Does she? Well, I don't know you well enough yet to know if she's right, but I'll not go so far as to disagree with the old woman either. She said the same of my brother once, and she couldn't have been more right."

His use of the word *yet* warmed me from naval to nose. I could fool no one. While I might not care what the average stranger thought, I very much wanted this man to like me. For with each new thing he said, I found myself liking him just a little bit more.

---

*L*ord only knew how they would get the tree Kenna picked back to Morna and Jerry's. The car was small, the tree large, but Malcolm couldn't find it in himself to deny her. She was right anyway—the tree was perfect. It would fill the window in Morna and Jerry's inn, and once it was lit and decorated, it would be visible from the road to all who passed by.

"I can tell by the way ye are staring at it, ye doona think we can get it back. 'Tis fine, Mac. While this one is beautiful, I doona mind if we find one a bit smaller. No one else will mind, either."

"No, no." He reached out and placed his hand on her back to reassure her. "They will help get it situated on top of the car. We have plenty of straps to get it secured. I just...you may have to help direct me when turning corners and such. I suspect it will hang down a bit over the windshield. It's going to block part of my view."

"Oh. Well, aye, I can certainly try to do so."

"Great. Let's go pay for it."

They walked side by side to the station where they could pay for the tree and await some assistance. As they passed the car, Kenna stepped away and called back to him.

"I'll meet ye there. I left the money Morna gave us in the car."

"No need. The least I can do for her allowing Rosie and me to stay is buy them a tree. I'll pay for it myself, and I'll leave the extra money with Jerry, for I know Morna won't take it back if I try to give it to her."

Malcolm waited for Kenna to return to his side before approaching the young woman taking payment for the trees.

As he reached into his wallet for his credit card, Kenna leaned into him, her voice shy.

"What is that?"

He didn't have any idea what she referred to.

"What is what?"

She pointed to the card in his hand, and he struggled to keep confusion from etching his face.

"Oh, it's my credit card. I spent the last of my pounds at the Conall Castle gift shop. I need to find another ATM once Rosie and I return to Edinburgh. I doubt there's another one close."

Kenna continued to look at the square piece of plastic quizzically.

"'Tis money?"

He nodded and slowly handed the card to the young woman in front of them who unabashedly looked at Kenna with the confusion he was trying so hard to hide.

"Yes. In a sense. Don't you have one?"

Kenna shook her head. Malcolm had visited Scotland many, many times. The entire country was entirely modernized. Even isles that only had access to larger stores if they traveled by ferry had their own small shops that accepted credit cards. How did anyone in today's society not know what a credit card was?

"Kenna, what part of Scotland did you say you were from?"

Malcolm watched as her face changed, shielding her curiosity as she righted herself and smiled at him.

"I dinna say. Doona worry. I can see well enough what it does. I believe I'll wait in the car."

He didn't know if he'd ever been so baffled in his life. Clearly, while Kenna could see that the card had served its purpose to pay for the tree, she had no idea how it worked. And her quick dismissal of her curiosity once she realized he found it odd confused him even more.

Something was strange about this woman. He very much wanted to find out what it was.

The ease with which I was able to speak with Malcolm had lowered my guard. I was accustomed to being around twenty-first century people who knew precisely from which time I came and had no problem explaining to me all the things I didn't know. What had happened with Malcolm was exactly what I'd feared most when Mitsy had suggested such a trip. I looked like a fool, and I couldn't begin to tell him why.

I said nothing on the ride back to Morna's, save for the occasional direction I would give by leaning my head out of the car window to make sure that the road was clear. Thankfully, Malcolm said nothing of the incident at the Christmas tree farm. For the second time of me embarrassing myself in front of him, he proved himself to be a gentleman. There was at least some comfort in that.

When we returned to the inn, everyone was delighted at our choice of tree, as I knew they would be. The boxes of decorations were down, and everything was dusted and laid out for us to decorate.

We all had a wonderful time, and as the day went on and Malcolm didn't treat me like a mad woman, my worry abated. We all visited, laughed, decorated, and drank more than our fair share of hot chocolate as we worked together to make Morna and Jerry's home one of the most splendidly beautiful Christmas homes I'd ever seen.

By the time night fell, we were all exhausted and happy.

"It has been some years since Jerry and I had the energy to place so many lovely decorations out ourselves. Most years we just settle for a simple tree and a few strands of lights. This year's display makes my heart happier than any of ye can know. Thank ye for yer help. Now, let us sit down and enjoy one last meal together before Mac and Rosie leave us for Edinburgh tomorrow."

I'd known they were leaving. They weren't even supposed to be here today, but somehow through the day's festivities I'd forgotten, and the reminder that our new friends would be gone saddened me more than I wished to admit.

What would I do for the next two weeks without Malcolm here? While I'd never expected to meet him, suddenly the next days at the inn with only Cooper, Morna, and Jerry to occupy me, left me feeling rather empty.

It seemed that I wasn't the only one with such emotion, for over dinner, few words were exchanged—not until dessert was being finished and a hesitant Rosie glanced over at Morna for courage before addressing her grandfather.

"Pops, I have a question for you."

We all watched on as Malcolm lay his fork on his plate and looked over at Rosalind.

"You do? What is it?"

"Do we have to go back to Edinburgh? We always do the same things there. You visit with Uncle Kraig and Aunt Emilia, and I get stuck playing solitaire. Then you guys drag me around to fancy restaurants I don't even like until the real fun begins on Christmas Eve. Can't we stay here until then and then go back to Edinburgh in time for actual Christmas?"

If that was indeed what the young girl's Christmases in Edinburgh looked like, I didn't blame her at all for wanting to stay with Morna. Hope fluttered inside me as I watched Mac contemplate Rosie's plea.

"There's part of me that wishes we could, but I have tickets to the symphony tomorrow night. They were expensive and difficult to get. Plus, Kraig and Emilia would be very disappointed. I'm sorry, Rosie. We need to go back tomorrow."

"I have an idea."

Horrified, I looked over at Cooper and shook my head as I tried to stop him.

"No, Coop. We doona intrude on other people's business. Malcolm has given his answer. Ye doona need to suggest any ideas."

While not normally one to disobey, Cooper unabashedly argued with me.

"Why not? It's a good idea. I think Malcolm would like to hear it."

Just as I meant to speak more harshly to him, Malcolm stepped in to rescue Cooper.

"It's okay, Kenna. What's your idea, Cooper?"

Now that he was allowed to speak, Cooper hesitated.

"What...what if Rosie stayed here and you went to Edinburgh with Nana? I know she would like to see the city at Christmastime, and I doubt that we would make the trip there on our own. She's more likely to enjoy the stuff that Rosie wouldn't."

Before I had a moment to object or Malcolm had a moment to answer, Morna smiled and stood from the table as she started to gather dishes.

"Why Cooper, 'tis a splendid idea. Malcolm, ye know we would take great care of Rosie. The lassie expressed a desire to learn how to bake this afternoon while ye and Kenna were away. If I had a few days with her, I could teach her much."

Rosie quickly chimed in, her voice filled with anticipation.

"Oh, please let me, Pops. This school break has been rotten so far. If Mom's not going to be here for Christmas, you could at least let me do something I want to do for a few days. Please let me stay. Go and do the things you have to do in Edinburgh and then come back and get me in a few days. Please. I would love you forever, Pops, if you'd let me."

I saw the exact moment Malcolm surrendered. Smiling, he nodded.

"Okay, okay. Fine. If you want to stay here a few days, that's fine, Rosie. I have no doubt you'd have more fun here with Cooper than you would in Edinburgh. But you've all made quite the assumption by assuming that Kenna would even want to accompany me."

Speaking with as much enthusiasm as the children, I interrupted him as Grace's insistence that I not concern myself with Cooper while here crossed my mind.

"I do want to. I really, really do."

There was an excitement in Malcolm's eyes as he looked at me that caused the hairs on the back of my neck to stand on end.

"I'm pleased to hear it. We'll leave first thing in the morning."

The drive to Edinburgh the following morning in the car Morna had "delivered" for us during the night, was long, but nowhere near the length of time it would've taken me to travel there in my own time. I was in a constant state of amazement in this century, but I promised myself before leaving the inn with Malcolm that I would not make the same mistake I'd made the day before. If something confused or surprised me, I would keep my reaction to myself and make a special note to ask Cooper about whatever I saw once I returned to get him in three days' time.

Pulling into the city required me to stifle all sorts of emotions. While Edinburgh's grand castle still sat on top of the city center, so much else had changed. The lights, the cars, the noise—I wasn't sure I was a good enough actress to hide my utter amazement.

"I called my brother last night after everything was decided. They're expecting you. No need to be nervous."

Perhaps that's how my excitement looked to him with the way I was all but bouncing in my seat with my eyes peeled outside the window, but in truth, I wasn't nervous at all. I was delighted at the opportunity to explore this time period. While I'd listened to everyone's insistence that I enjoy this time and see as much as I could while here, I'd not really expected such an opportunity to arise.

The city was beautiful at Christmas—covered in snow, with garland and lights strung up over many buildings and doorways.

I didn't realize I'd not replied to him until Malcolm spoke up again.

"Are you all right, Kenna? You've hardly said anything since we left Morna and Jerry's."

Reluctant to look away from the window on the chance that I might miss something wonderful, I turned my head and smiled at him. He was right—I'd been quite rude.

"Ach, I'm sorry, Malcolm. 'Tis only that I canna remember the last time I was so excited about anything. I've simply been enjoying the view."

He smiled a crooked smile, and my heart sped up in response. The view outside was wonderful, but I couldn't have been missing anything that looked better than looking at him.

"You don't get to Edinburgh very often, then?"

I answered honestly. "The last time I was in Edinburgh, I was fifteen years old."

He looked as if he didn't believe me.

"Truly? Have you lived in Scotland all your life, or did you leave here for a while?"

"Aye, and all of my life."

Malcolm slowed the car and turned the corner onto a street lined with tall, connected buildings with doorways lining the front and steps leading up to each one. They looked like homes, though I'd never known homes to be connected in such a way.

"In what part of Scotland do you live, Kenna? I still haven't gotten an answer from you."

I wasn't sure how to answer him. I didn't know just how familiar he was with Scotland's geography. If he was familiar at all, it wouldn't be difficult for him to catch me in a lie. Most especially since I had no way of knowing if areas that were once remote, still were today. I decided it best to lie as little as possible.

"I live with my...my nephew at McMillan Castle. McMillan is my last name. He and his wife run the castle and keep it open to visitors. I assist in managing the staff."

It was an answer that was only about halfway true, but I saw no way for him to be able to discern that I lied.

His face lit up, as if my words had suddenly solved a great mystery.

"Ah! Well, that explains it, then. I'm sure you have people that bring whatever you need to the castle. If so, there wouldn't be much need for you to leave the area or to do your own shopping."

While I didn't quite appreciate the insinuation that others did everything for me, I couldn't argue the point. In truth, there was much that was taken care of for me. I was a remarkably blessed woman in any century.

Slightly embarrassed, I nodded.

"Aye. Though 'tis not as if I couldna do any of those things myself if I needed to."

His hand reached across the space between us and squeezed my hand as the car slowed to a stop in front of one of the doorways.

"I wasn't suggesting that you couldn't. That just explains your reaction to my credit card at the Christmas tree farm yesterday. Hey, McMillan Castle is the one with all of the extraordinary Christmas decorations, isn't it? Rosie has wanted to see it for years. Perhaps, you could arrange a special tour for us?"

I nodded and then pointed to the woman who had just appeared in the doorway closest to the car.

"Aye. O'course I can. Is that Emilia?"

I knew her name from Rosie's mention of them yesterday. The

moment a man cradling a baby appeared next to her, I knew I was right.

"Yes, it is. She will be thrilled to meet you. Don't worry about your bag. I'll get them after we say hello."

The moment I stepped outside the car, the woman called to me.

"Kenna, lass, if ye wish to see Edinburgh at Christmas, ye have come to the right place. While he may not be Scottish himself, Malcolm knows the city better than even I do. 'Tis a shame, but it seems that it often happens in such a way. Locals doona appreciate the uniqueness of a city the same way that visitors do, so we doona get out and see as much."

Emilia talked quickly and without end as she wrapped one arm around my shoulder and led me inside their home.

While quite small, the home was beautiful and welcoming. I'd been unable to keep up with Emilia's chattering. Just as I worried that I wouldn't be able to answer her should she ask me a question, I was rescued by a hand at my back and turned to greet Malcolm's brother.

The man, while shorter than Malcolm, still stood far above the top of my head. He strongly resembled his brother with the same thick dark hair and brows. But where Malcolm had blue eyes, Kraig had brown, and his face was clean-shaven. He also had no gray in his hair. As I examined his face, I looked over his smooth unweathered skin and saw a man not much older than my sons. Kraig Warren looked all of twenty years younger than his elder brother.

"Welcome to Edinburgh. You must be Rosie's new favorite person. By agreeing to come with Malcolm, she got to stay away. I know we were boring her to tears."

Kraig pulled me in tight with one arm while still holding the baby in his other arm. Once he released me, I reached out and placed my palm gently on top of the babe's head.

"And this must be Robbie, aye?"

Kraig nodded, and the glimmer in his eyes as he looked at his son nearly brought tears to my eyes.

"Yes. I don't imagine he will sleep too much longer, though. Soon he will bid you a proper hello by screaming at the top of his lungs."

I grinned as he walked away and Malcolm came up behind me. He must've read my mind for he leaned in close to answer the question I'd not yet asked him.

"Kraig was the surprise of my mother's life. She had him when I was twenty-eight years old, at the age of forty-four. Our father was forty-eight. My mother and my wife were pregnant at the same time." He laughed. "It was a very strange time in my life."

Eyes wide, I looked up at him.

"Ach, God bless her. Kraig would've been seven years old when yer mother was my age. I canna imagine it. My grandchildren are work enough. Did she..." I hesitated. "Did she live long enough to raise him?"

Malcolm smiled and pointed to a photo on the small table to my left.

"Oh, yes. She's still very much alive. You'd never guess she's as old as she is. She lives in Scotland now, just across the street actually. I'm sure you will meet her either tonight or tomorrow." He paused and his brows pulled in. "Which I suppose means that I lied to you before, though I didn't mean to. My mother is technically a grandparent to Rosie, but she's lived in Scotland since Rosie was born. They're not very close."

I'd thought nothing of it.

"It takes more than blood to form a bond, Malcolm. Look at wee Cooper. I am not his blood, but I am no less his grandmother for it. In the same way, blood doesna necessarily make someone a grandparent. Ye dinna lie."

"Oh look at the two of ye. Look where ye are standing."

Emilia stood in the kitchen but pointed to us. She looked thrilled. We both looked blankly back at her.

"Ye are under the mistletoe. Come now, Malcolm. Ye must kiss her. 'Tis bad luck if ye doona do so."

I'd not been kissed in fifteen years. My entire body seized up with nerves at the thought of being kissed now. Surely, I'd forgotten how. Surely, I would do it all wrong.

I had little time to think on it as Malcolm's hand slipped to my lower back and he pulled me gently against him, his head quickly bending to my ear.

"You heard her. We can't have bad luck following you around."

I'd always thought the notion of women swooning in response to a man's touch lacking in realism. I was a level-headed woman—ahead of my time is what my daughters-in-law always called me—but as Malcolm's lips brushed against my own, I knew that if not for his steady hand holding me tight, I would've dropped to the floor like a sack of flour.

It was that wonderfully, deliciously good.

CHAPTER 12

"Are you awake? I was surprised to see the fire still burning when I woke to relieve Emilia for a little while."

Malcolm stood from his makeshift bed on the couch and waved his brother downstairs to join him.

"Yes, wide awake. Here, why don't you hand me Robbie. I'll bounce him until he goes back to sleep. You can go back to bed if you wish."

While his brother didn't hesitate to hand him the baby, he didn't turn around and head back upstairs.

"I'm awake now, too. I'll stay up and visit with you. I haven't had a chance to visit with you alone yet."

Malcolm knew well enough what his brother would ask him, and he had no answers to give him.

Whether it was the touch of someone new or just the fact that Malcolm was so warm from laying near the fire, young Robbie relaxed instantly as Malcolm cradled him in his arms. He continued to bounce the child gently as he walked around the room.

"It's been a long time since I've held a baby—not since Rosie was one."

Kicking Malcolm's pillow onto the floor, his brother collapsed onto the couch and propped his feet up on the coffee table.

"You've always been good with them, but I don't want to talk to you about babies."

Keeping his voice low so Robbie would continue to drift to sleep, Malcolm walked over behind the couch.

"I know what you want to talk about, but there's not anything for me to say."

"Sure there is. You didn't tell me anything on the phone yesterday when you called to tell me she was coming with you. Who is she?"

Malcolm still knew so little about her. Just as he'd begun to believe that her strange behavior at the Christmas tree farm had been explained away, her behavior at the symphony had raised new questions in his mind.

He couldn't recall a single melody the symphony played. He'd spent the entire two hours watching her take in the spectacle.

She looked on with the wonder of a small child. As the lights changed around the stage, her eyes darted around to watch them as if looking for the source. When the conductor stepped up to the microphone and his voice boomed out over the audience, she'd nearly fallen out of her chair. It was the strangest thing he'd ever seen. It was incredibly enchanting. Wonder was something he'd not felt in decades. That Kenna could still be so surprised and fascinated by anything at their age was one of her many attractive qualities, but it still made no sense.

"I've only known her a few days. She's related to Morna and Jerry. She and her grandson were visiting them when Rosie and I intruded on their trip. The rest is exactly what you've heard. Rosie wanted to stay and Kenna wanted to see Edinburgh at Christmas. So here we are."

His brother twisted in his seat on the couch and looked back at him.

"And that's it then. She's just your friend?"

Kenna had given him no indication that she was interested in anything more than his friendship. While he hoped that would change, he couldn't claim that they were more than that now.

He nodded and his brother stood from the chair and reached for Robbie as he shook his head.

"I wonder what Emilia would say if I kissed one of my female friends under the mistletoe like that? I can't imagine that she would be very pleased."

I woke sometime in the early hours of the morning, just past midnight, with my bladder so full I thought it might burst. While I knew it probable that there was a restroom somewhere on the top floor, I had no desire to start opening doors in the dark, and I knew with certainty that there was one just past the front door on the bottom floor.

With Malcolm sleeping on the living room couch, I opened the bedroom door quietly, intending to sneak through the house unnoticed. Instead, as I opened it, I could hear voices from down below, and the staircase was illuminated by the fire that still burned.

"And that's it then. She's just your friend?"

It was Kraig's voice. I knew I should back up into the room and close the door and hold it until morning—Malcolm's answer to his brother's question was not something he intended me to hear, but I desperately wanted to know his answer. Instead, I moved just a little closer to the staircase and listened.

Nothing. Malcolm gave no answer. Before I could move away, Kraig was moving toward the staircase with the baby in his arms, calling back over his shoulder something about kissing his friends under the mistletoe.

Knowing that I could do nothing to keep from being seen, I spoke out to try and avoid the uncomfortable interaction that was headed my way.

"Kraig, is the baby awake? I was just going down to the restroom but if ye'd like me to take him for ye, I'd be happy to."

Kraig smiled at me and reached a hand out to gently squeeze my arm in thanks.

"No need now. Malcolm got him to sleep. I hope we didn't wake you."

Perhaps too dramatically, I dismissed him with a wave of my hand.

"No, ye dinna at all. I dinna even know ye were down here until I saw ye coming toward me on the stairs. Goodnight, Kraig."

Hopeful that I'd covered up my eavesdropping well enough, I made my way downstairs to where Malcolm stood behind the couch.

"Ye should be asleep, Mac. Ye promised me a full day of sightseeing tomorrow, and I'll not let ye out of it even if ye are tired."

He laughed and looked down at me. I suddenly felt very self-conscious in Adelle's robe.

"I think my anticipation for tomorrow is precisely why I can't sleep. Don't worry. I won't back out on you."

Leaving him to return to bed, I went to the restroom and came out with every intention of sneaking back upstairs. Instead, I walked past the living room to find Malcolm sitting on the couch as he faced the fire.

"Do ye not wish to at least attempt some sleep?"

Using his head to wave me over, he didn't face me as he spoke.

"Why don't you come and sit by me a minute? Maybe after some conversation, I'll feel like sleeping."

I knew he'd not meant anything unkind, but I didn't hesitate to point out what his words had suggested.

"Well, thank ye. I'm so pleased to hear that speaking with me is an effective way to put ye to sleep."

He laughed, his voice deep. Knowing that I would now sleep little myself, I went to join him. He sat at one end of the couch with both the middle and its other end unoccupied. I began to retreat to the couch's other end, but the warmth of him was too alluring. Cautiously, I slid closer toward the middle.

"You know I didn't mean it that way. Kenna..." he hesitated as I turned to look at him. The glow from the fire made his eyes look even more blue than usual. With the memory of his lips against mine still fresh in my mind, I couldn't keep my eyes from drifting toward his mouth.

"Aye?"

"May I ask you a question?"

"Ye may."

He reached for my hands. I adored how strong and warm his grip was. His hands completely enveloped my own.

"What are we doing? I'm past the age where games suit me. Shall we be friends or is it possible that we might be something more?"

I could hear my heart beating in my ears. There was only one thing I wanted to do in answer to his question.

With my hands still clasped in his, I closed the space between us and leaned in to kiss him.

The urging of all the twenty-first century women in my life sounding in my mind, I allowed myself to stop thinking as I moved against him, opening to his tongue as his hands pulled away and moved to the sides of my face. We kissed until my body shook all over from need. Recognizing where this would lead if I didn't stop soon, I pulled away.

"Was that your answer? If so, I'm very much in agreement with it."

Malcolm's own breath was shaky, and the need in his eyes made it difficult for me to breathe. I scooted away to give myself the space to gather my composure.

"In a way, though 'twas not all of my answer. I wish to tell ye something."

While I was here, I wanted Malcolm. I wanted to feel alive, to dust off some of the neglected parts of my soul and body, but I needed him to understand that I could promise nothing beyond the next few days. It wouldn't be fair to either of us to enter into something that was bound to cause us eventual pain without knowing exactly what would come.

"Tell me. I would listen to you say anything."

Hesitantly, my voice unsteady as the effects of his kiss continued to course through me, I told him everything that was on my mind.

"Mac, I was fourteen when I married my husband—still a child. And while I did love him in my own way—I never would've chosen him for myself. He was two verra different people, and I kept my distance from him because of it. He was a remarkable father to his children—fair and gentle with them all his life. But William was far too serious and harsh with me. He never laughed when we were together, and I only saw him smile in the presence of his sons. Our marriage cost me much of my childhood, but for him, our marriage cost him the woman he truly wanted to marry. While I played no hand in our betrothal, I doona think he ever forgave me for it."

I could see the question in Malcolm's eyes and paused to give him time to ask it.

"It was an arranged marriage? At fourteen? That's outrageous, Kenna."

Ignoring most of his questions, I continued.

"Aye, 'twas arranged from the time of my birth. If there is a blessing to come from it, 'tis that William vowed to never force his own children into such an agreement. Despite our lack of passion for one another, we lived easily together as husband and wife.

"William has been gone for fifteen years now, and there's been no one since then. I only tell ye this so that ye may understand why I'm about to propose something that may not be acceptable to ye. If 'tis not, I willna blame ye for it."

I waited for him to say something, but instead he just nodded, urging me onward.

"I've never known what 'tis like to explore a relationship of my wanting. If I were wiser, I would stifle what I feel for ye now and accept yer friendship. But Malcolm, for once in my life, I wish to be selfish. I wish to be selfish even knowing that in a few days, we will go back to Morna and Jerry's where ye will collect Rosie and I will most likely never see ye again. We live in verra different worlds, we canna pretend otherwise. So..." I was shaking all over again, but no longer from need. I'd never felt so vulnerable, so open to rejection. "To answer yer question after a verra long explanation—aye—I wish to be more than friends with ye, but I canna promise ye that anything shall last past the next few days. Can ye accept that and not think me the most selfish of women?"

Malcolm looked at me for a long moment, the need still evident in his gaze. He smiled slowly. As he pulled me against him, he whispered in my ear.

"Kenna, I will take you any way I can get you for as long as you'll allow me. I've never been one to worry too much about the future. All we have is now."

As his lips began to nip at the length of my neck, I allowed myself to drown in the sensation of his touch, quickly silencing the small voice in my mind that insisted I'd just asked him to agree to something I would never be able to uphold myself.

Malcolm stayed true to his promise. Despite the fact that we both were sleep deprived after spending most of the night visiting, cuddling, and aye, occasionally kissing by the fire, he was up and ready for our day in the city before I was.

I found twenty-first century clothing so much more difficult to assemble. In my own time, I owned only four dresses save for the two I reserved for only the most special of occasions. There was nothing to think about when getting dressed—no decisions to make and no make-up to fuss with. With the assortment of items Adelle packed for me, I was left confused each and every morning as I tried to piece together items of clothing that would look nice together.

Since it was freezing outside and snowing on and off almost every day, I chose a pair of tight jeans, boots that went over them almost up to my knee, and a thick wine-colored sweater. After throwing on a hat, a scarf, some gloves, and my coat, I was ready to go.

I was determined not to apologize for making him wait on me.

It was known across all time periods and countries that women take longer.

"So, what do ye have planned for the day?"

Seeing that I was already bundled up for outside, Malcolm reached for his own coat and scarf, donning them as he spoke to me.

"Lots. I'll drive us closer to the city center. Then I thought we could get a ticket for the double-decker buses. I'm sure being Scottish, you'll find them very touristy, but they really aren't a bad way to get from place to place, and it helps you get a layout of the whole city."

I was only familiar with the word *bus* because of the bus Malcolm and Rosie had been on at Conall Castle. I hadn't the slightest idea what a double-decker bus could be.

"I will find nothing too touristy, Mac, I assure ye. I've never been on a double-decker bus."

Surprise framed his features. It was an expression he wore often around me, and try as I might to not give away how out of sorts I was in this time, it was impossible to always say just the right thing.

"Well, good. Then you won't mind it. Here's a summary of the itinerary I have planned for us. If there's anything you don't want to do, just tell me, and we'll find something else."

When I nodded, he looked down at his list and began to read.

"First, after taking the whole bus loop, I thought we could grab breakfast at Emilia's favorite café. She used to work there as a teenager. They have the best coffee in Edinburgh."

I smiled as I glanced over to see Emilia nodding enthusiastically.

"Sounds perfect."

"Next, I thought we would go over to the German Christmas Market. They have some of the prettiest trinkets and toys you've ever seen, and there's a big ferris wheel that will give us a spectacular view of the city."

Again, I had no idea what a ferris wheel was, but I said nothing.

"Afterwards, I thought we could go to The Dome for lunch in the tea room and to see their unbelievable decorations."

He paused and looked up at me and I knew he was wanting some sort of confirmation that all his plans were okay with me.

"I canna wait, Malcolm."

He let out a big breath of relief and grinned with pride as he looked back down at the list. The gesture made him look two decades younger—slightly nervous and even a little shy.

"Okay, after lunch, I thought we could explore the Scottish Market for a bit and then go on a tour of Edinburgh Castle."

"Oh, aye, let's. I would love to see the castle." Edinburgh Castle was the one thing he'd mentioned that I knew. I'd been there once as a child. It was where I'd first been introduced to William. It would be fascinating to see how much had changed.

"Then we most certainly shall. And lastly, I have us booked for an early dinner reservation at The Witchery. It's an Edinburgh tradition, and I know you'll enjoy it. Is there anything you want to change?"

I wished to do everything he mentioned, but I hated the idea of him repeating activities he'd already experienced many times for my sake.

"No, though I do have a question for ye. Have ye done all of these things before?"

He nodded and stuffed the list into his pocket before buttoning up his coat.

"Yes, but I enjoy doing them every year, so don't worry about that."

"There must be something ye wish to do in Edinburgh that ye havena done before. Whatever 'tis, let's do it after dinner."

"I know exactly what he needs to do." Emilia's voice interrupted as she made her way over to me. "Malcolm desperately needs an education in real Scotch. I've taught Kraig everything I know, but I've never had the opportunity to do the same with Malcolm. I know just the place the two of ye can go. They stay open late, and they offer tours that give ye more to taste than the wee sips most distilleries do. He'd love it."

I didn't even look up at Malcolm as I answered her.

"Aye, 'tis perfect. Every foreigner needs a proper introduction to Scottish whisky. Can ye arrange it for us?"

She gave me a quick nod and turned to address her brother-in-law.

"Malcolm, I'll text ye the address and time I've booked ye for in a while. Now, get out of here and have a grand time. I'm sure the two of ye will be out late. We will see ye tomorrow morning."

With his head already starting to ache and his feet far less steady than he liked, Malcolm had only two questions.

First—why couldn't they have gone on a basic whisky tasting tour—one where they only got to taste the smallest sip of each whisky? Such a tour would've sufficed just fine. Second—how the hell was Kenna still standing? She'd drunk just as much as he had and showed no signs of intoxication. She was one of the daintiest women he'd ever seen. Short of stature, slender, all of her features were petite. How then, was she drinking him under the table?

Thankfully, as their host reached for their glasses to pour yet another dram of whisky, Kenna reached out a hand to stop him. Malcolm simply couldn't drink another drop.

"Thank ye, sir, but I believe my companion here has had all he can manage." She leaned over the counter playfully and whispered below her breath as she giggled. "He's American."

Perhaps, she was more affected by the tasting than he originally thought. Still, she was holding her liquor far better than he was.

"Kenna." He spoke slowly and with intention. He'd be damned before he slurred his words in front of her. He was a grown man and one that didn't drink often. He'd not have himself looking like a lush. "We can't drive back. The car is safe where I parked it this morning. Do you want to step outside and hail us a taxi while I pay for the bottle we are bringing back to Emilia and Kraig?"

Confusion and something resembling panic crossed Kenna's rosy cheeks, but before he could inquire into her concern, their tour host stepped in.

"No need. We've cars waiting out front. 'Tis customary on this specific tour. Rarely do we have a guest that is fit to drive afterwards."

Had this been Emilia's intention? Malcolm couldn't help but think that it must've been.

Kenna held tightly onto his arm as she stood from the barstool and waited for him.

"Shall we go then? Ye doona look so good, Malcolm."

He didn't feel so good.

"Yes, I think we should."

Just as their guide had promised, a car awaited them outside the distillery. With Kenna snuggled warmly into him on the ride back to his brother's house, he found it difficult to stay awake. Just as the car pulled up to the front of the house, Kenna leaned up to kiss his cheek.

"I had the best time tonight, Mac. Truly, I dinna ever want today to end."

Paying the driver, he stepped outside and took Kenna's hand. Emilia had left the outside light on for them. Walking up to the front door, he paused and leaned in to kiss her. She melted against him instantly. It was all he could do to remain of sound mind. He wanted to be with her more than he'd wanted anything in his life —but not tonight, not when both of them were exhausted from their day in the city and more than a little tipsy.

"I'm not sure I've ever had more fun with anyone, Kenna.

Now..." Pulling away while he still had the wits to do so, he turned to insert the key into the lock. "I must bid you goodnight the moment we step inside. Otherwise, I'll ask you to come to bed with me."

He expected her to reprimand him. Instead, as they stepped inside, she took his hand and led him over to the couch where his bed was all set up.

"I doona mean to offend ye, Mac, but even if I did join ye here this evening, I believe ye would be asleep before ye could undress me."

Perhaps she was right. His lids did feel very heavy. Gently, she guided him down to the couch, pushing his shoulders back until he was lying down. She moved to pull off his shoes. He didn't want to fall asleep until she was gone. He wanted to see her every moment he could.

"Kenna, what surprised you most about today?"

Setting his shoes next to the couch, she moved to sit next to him, gently brushing the hair from his face as she leaned in to gently kiss him goodnight. After a quick peck on his lips, she stood and answered him as she made her way upstairs.

"Besides learning that ye canna hold yer whisky, ye mean? I think perhaps 'twas Edinburgh Castle. It truly hasna changed all that much in the last three hundred some odd years."

By the time her words made their way through his whisky-doused brain and he realized the oddity of them, she was gone.

He fell asleep dreaming of the castle and what Kenna could've possibly meant by such a strange statement.

Several nights of sleep deprivation and a day filled with a flurry of activity seemed to have caught up with Malcolm when I woke the next morning. I slept pretty late myself and took my time getting ready before wandering downstairs. When I finally did make my way downstairs, Malcolm still slept soundly on the couch, despite the noise from Kraig, Emilia, and little Robbie in the kitchen.

It made me feel better to see him sleeping. The foolish mistake I'd made came to me in the middle of the night, causing me to sit up in bed in such a panic that it had taken well over an hour for me to calm myself and go back to sleep. My last words to Malcolm before going to bed—while clearly a result of too much whisky—could've been disastrous had he not been so altered by drink himself. The fact that he still slept gave me some hope that he wouldn't remember my words when he did wake.

"Good morning, Kenna. Ye look better than I expected ye to. I doona believe I'll be able to say the same for Mac when he wakes."

I gratefully took the cup of tea Emilia extended in my

direction and moved to sit by Robbie who was strapped into the most ingenious invention—a seat and a table in one that kept him upright and able to sit at the kitchen table with everyone else without being held.

"I believe ye are right. The poor man doesna drink often, 'twas plain to see." I paused as I reached out to take little Robbie's hand, smiling as his chubby fingers wrapped around mine. "Why, Robbie looks fine and happy this morning in his...his..." I stalled on purpose, hoping that Emilia would simply believe that I'd forgotten the word and would answer my question that way. She didn't disappoint me.

"His highchair."

"Aye, highchair. The word slipped my mind for a moment."

She laughed and set a plate of breakfast down in front of me.

"whisky will do that to ye. Did the two of ye have a good time yesterday?"

I waited until she and Kraig were both seated with their food before I began to eat.

"Aye, there wasna a single activity that I dinna love. He couldna have planned a better day out."

"I'm so glad the two of ye had a good time. I canna remember the last time Kraig and I had a day out just the two of us. I wouldna trade Robbie for the world, but he has changed my life in every way. Sometimes, I canna remember the woman that I was before him."

Emilia sighed in a dreamy way that caused me to really study her for the first time. While fatigue couldn't fade the young woman's beauty, the sleep deprivation that comes to any parent of a small child had left its mark. Small bags hung under her eyes. I doubted she'd taken any time for herself in months.

I had an idea, although I knew I couldn't manage it by myself.

"Emilia, do ye have a phone I could borrow and perhaps a computer I could use? I'd like to check on some things and call my grandson."

I only knew what a computer was from seeing it at Morna's and only knew how to operate a phone because of the detailed instructions Cooper had given me before I left, including the number to Morna's so I could reach him.

Emilia stood without hesitation, and I momentarily regretted interrupting her meal.

"O'course. I'm sure the lad will be glad to hear from ye. Follow me into Kraig's office. 'Tis just off the kitchen. There is a phone in there, and ye can use the computer for whatever ye like. Ye can even bring yer breakfast with ye if ye wish. Kraig eats in there all the time."

Lifting my plate with one hand and holding my tea with the other, I followed her, the surprise taking form in my mind as we went.

"For the love of God, Emilia, please tell me you have some aspirin."

Squinting, Malcolm trudged into the kitchen. He couldn't remember the last time he'd slept so late or felt so rotten.

"Look there."

His gaze traveled to the place on the table where his sister-in-law pointed.

"I've already set some aspirin next to yer breakfast. Along with some coffee and a secret mixture that will taste awful but will have ye feeling just like yerself by lunch."

Malcolm sat at the table, popped the painkillers, and looked squeamishly at the glass of gray liquid sitting next to his coffee.

"What's in it?"

"Dinna ye hear what I said? 'Tis a secret. Just drink it. I promise, ye will be glad ye did."

Pinching his nose to keep from smelling the vile concoction, he chugged it in two swift gulps. As soon as it was down, he reached for his coffee and drank. He didn't care if it was hot enough to burn him, he needed the taste of the previous liquid out of his mouth immediately.

"That was the worst thing I've ever tasted. Where's Kenna? Did you make her drink that?"

Emilia laughed and leaned against the kitchen island.

"Kenna dinna need it. And she's in Kraig's office. She said she wished to call her grandson and needed to take care of a few things on the computer."

Hoping that Kenna would still be on the phone and that perhaps he would be able to say hello to Rosie, Malcolm scarfed down his food and stood to head to the office.

He knocked lightly, but when there was no answer he stepped quietly inside, standing back while Kenna spoke.

"What is the name of the place that Jane always says she misses, Cooper?"

There was a short pause, and then Kenna answered the boy, excitement in her voice.

"Aye, a spa. And how do I find and plan a spa?"

Another short pause as Malcolm watched on in amazement. Could she really not know about all of the things Cooper was explaining to her?

"What is a 'google'? Can I call this google? Oh...I must type it on the computer."

He continued to watch with amusement as Kenna typed one finger at a time on the keyboard.

"Cooper, if I arrange this, should I just give Emilia the cash to pay for it?"

Malcolm could barely hear the boy's voice, but it was just mumbling from so far away.

"Oh, I see. I need one of those credit cards. I doona have one."

He couldn't keep quiet any longer. She was clearly struggling, and he could see by the way she held one hand up to the side of her face that overwhelm was setting in. With the mention of a credit card, he saw his opening.

"I have one. What is it that you're trying to do, Kenna?"

Turning toward him, Kenna smiled. The relief on her face was evident.

"Ah, Cooper, never mind, lad. Mac is awake now. I believe I can get him to help me."

Now that he stood right next to her, he could hear the boy clearly.

"Oh, good. I was about to have to hand the phone to Morna. You were getting into stuff I don't know anything about."

Kenna laughed and held the phone away from her so he could hear better.

"Aye, well ye needn't bother Morna now. Are ye having a good time, Cooper? How is Rosie doing?"

"Oh, I'm having the best time, though I still haven't been able to get Rosie to warm to me. Not to worry though, she'll crack eventually. And Rosie's having a good time, too, I think. She and Morna have been spending so much time in the kitchen baking up all sorts of yummy goodies. I think by the time you and Malcolm get back, Jerry might be as fat as Santa Claus."

Malcolm always loved the way Kenna laughed, but when laughing in response to her grandson, there was a special joy in her voice that caused his heart to skip just a little. He knew the kind of love she felt when speaking to him. The love of a grandparent for a grandchild surpassed anything he'd felt in his life.

"I'm so glad, Cooper. Is Rosie around? I'm sure Mac would like to speak to her."

"Actually..." Cooper's voice sounded regretful. "She and Morna went into town to get some more baking stuff. There's no telling what they will make next."

Malcolm lowered his head and spoke into the phone to calm Cooper's worries.

"It's okay, Cooper, I'm sure Rosie is enjoying having some space away from me for a bit. I'll see her tomorrow when we return."

"Sounds good. I miss both of you guys. Good luck planning your surprise."

Malcolm waited to speak again until Kenna said her goodbyes and hung up the phone.

"So...what is it you are trying to do? Why would you need to give Emilia cash?"

Malcolm listened to Kenna intently. As she laid out her plan to give Kraig and Emilia a day and evening away, he knew that what he'd been trying to silence inside of himself for the better part of two days was true. He was in love with Kenna McMillan. He might not know her well, but he knew enough. She was kind, funny, and thoughtful. She loved her grandson deeply and said whatever was on her mind. He knew what he'd told her before, but it was no longer true. He was fairly certain that it hadn't been true then. He wouldn't be able to let her go tomorrow. He wasn't sure that he would ever be able to.

"Did ye...did ye hear me? Ye doona look as if ye heard a word I said. Will ye help me? Do ye mind if we stay here this evening and watch the babe for them?"

Shaking himself from his thoughts, he smiled and bent to kiss her.

"I heard every word. Of course, I'll help you. I can't think of anything else Emilia would want more this Christmas. Scoot over. I'll get everything set while you go and tell them to pack a bag for the night."

Kenna stood without a word and all but skipped away from him in excitement.

He called out to her just before she left the room.

"And Kenna...don't let Emilia turn this offer down. She will try to."

"Oh, doona ye worry about that, Malcolm. I always get my way. I doona know what 'tis exactly, but people have always had a difficult time telling me no."

He knew precisely what it was. The woman contained magic, surely, and he was entirely under her spell.

While I hadn't noticed the black dress until after I arrived in the twenty-first century—for I surely would've had Adelle remove it immediately if I had—I was grateful it was there as I readied myself for the evening while Malcolm worked at preparing dinner for the two of us in the kitchen.

I felt naked in the dress with the bottom hem hitting just at my knees. I'd never worn anything that showed so much of my legs. And the cut at the top was even more scandalous. I was now showing even more than I'd revealed to Malcolm the day my blouse had burst open during my nap. Still, I thought I looked quite beautiful in the dress. I hoped Malcolm would think so, too.

If I didn't wake with the dewy skin Adelle was so sure I needed after wearing this tonight, there was nothing that would get Malcolm to sleep with me.

Slipping on the pair of heels, which were another twenty-first century invention I could see no sense in, I reached for the lipstick I'd yet to wear and carefully applied it before heading downstairs.

I spent the better part of two hours feeding, changing, and

bouncing the child before he finally fell asleep. I very much hoped he would at least give us a handful of hours of alone time before he woke up in need of some attention.

"Kenna..." Malcolm's tone was nearly breathless. "You are the most beautiful woman I've ever seen."

I felt almost ill at how quickly my body warmed in response to his words. He looked rather handsome himself, though he wasn't dressed up as I was.

"That canna be true, but I'll accept the compliment. Thank ye. What are ye making?"

"Braised beef in a cherry sauce with crisped onions and asparagus. It's the only dish I know how to make well."

"I'm sure 'twill be delicious."

I walked over to wrap my arms around him, but he quickly stepped out of my way.

"It's nearly ready. Let me step into the bathroom and change. You look so nice. I don't want to look like a slob next to you."

I grabbed his hand and pulled him back toward me.

"No, doona change. No one will see us. I only wore this for ye and I think ye look handsome dressed just as ye are."

His response was immediate. A low, guttural noise escaped from deep within his throat. Pulling me against him, he kissed me greedily, allowing his hands to roam my body in a way he never had before.

I gasped and moaned in response, pressing one of my breasts into his palm as his hand slipped down my chest while his other hand roamed down to cup my bottom.

"Mom?"

Thinking that I'd just found the fault in him I'd been waiting for, I stilled and pulled away. I should've realized by the inflection in his tone, but it took me far too long to catch on.

"Malcolm, while I am a mother, I am not yer mother and the thought of ye referring to me as 'Mom' makes my skin crawl all over. Perhaps we should cease this and just eat."

Malcolm's expression looked horrified.

"God, no, Kenna. I would sooner die than call you Mom. It's my actual mother. She's here."

An unsettling mixture of relief and embarrassment rushed over me as I turned to see an astonishingly beautiful elderly woman standing no more than ten steps from us. As I locked eyes with her, she lifted her hand and waved before giving me the biggest smile I'd ever seen in my life.

CHAPTER 16

"Excuse me. I believe I hear Robbie upstairs. I best go and check on him."

Malcolm waited until Kenna was out of view to address his mother. The moment he turned toward her, his mother pursed her lips guiltily.

"I am so sorry, Malcolm. Kraig told me that you had a lady friend here tonight, but it truly never crossed my mind that she was anything more than a friend."

He'd known that Kenna was bound to meet his mother sometime during her stay in Edinburgh. He only wished his mother's timing was better.

"Why would you assume that?"

She lifted her brows and looked up at him knowingly.

"Well, it's been a very long time, son. Forgive me if that isn't where my mind went right away. I am sorry for intruding though. If there's anything I can do to make it up to you, just say the word."

As if on cue, Robbie let out a bloodcurdling scream that reverberated down the stairway. He didn't even have to ask the question before his mother stood and brushed off her lap.

"Absolutely. It's been months since Emilia has allowed me to take Robbie overnight. I believe she feels guilty asking me because she knows that I raised babies much later in life than most. As if that is her fault, of all things. I'll go and take the child from Kenna now. Start cleaning the kitchen. It will increase your chances greatly. Nothing turns a woman on more than the sight of a man doing dishes."

Thankful that his mother's shocking remarks had lost their effect on him ages ago, he did as instructed. He loved his mother, but he'd never been so ready for her to be out of his sight.

I'd rocked and bounced my fair share of babies, but never had I seen one so upset. Robbie screamed endlessly. With each new wail, I knew my hopes for what this night could be were now squandered.

"There is nothing wrong with his lungs, is there?"

I half-smiled, half-grimaced as Malcolm's mother, Nel, stepped into the nursery and closed the door behind her.

"Aye, I doona believe the wee lad is accustomed to being away from his mother."

"Oh no, not at all. It won't last forever, of course. I think it's something that most first-time mothers go through, but Emilia rarely wants to be separated from him for more than a few hours. The fact that she agreed to let you and Malcolm watch him overnight is proof of just how exhausted she must be."

"I've not heard her complain once since I've been here, but aye, I do believe fatigue was beginning to take its toll."

I stood from my seat and cradled the baby as I began to swing him side to side. Slowly, his wails began to subside.

"How many grandchildren do you have?"

I couldn't help but smile when thinking about each and every one of them.

"Five."

"And how many children do you have?"

"Three." The sharp, familiar pang that always coursed through me at the thought of Niall ran its way up and down my body. "But one of my sons passed away a few years ago."

Nel's expression was immediately sympathetic. "I'm so sorry."

She glanced down in the way that people often did at hearing such news and shifted from foot to foot for a moment as she looked for a way to transition to a more pleasant conversation. Eventually, she spoke again.

"I am sorry for interrupting your evening. To make up for the intrusion, I've decided to take Robbie with me back to my place across the street. I believe you two probably need some alone time."

The embarrassment I felt at knowing that Malcolm's mother knew what we were up to caused me to immediately regret every instant I'd been so straightforward about such matters with my own sons' significant others. I was always so blunt with them—it couldn't have been very comfortable for them to hear me speak of such things. I certainly wasn't comfortable now.

I fumbled over my words as I tried to respond to her.

"Oh...um...that 'tisn't necessary. Truly."

She reached forward and pulled Robbie from my arms, sending him into a fit of screams, once again.

"I believe it is. Kenna, it was wonderful to meet you. I haven't seen my son so happy in a very long time. Please don't hurt him."

My heart squeezed familiarly in response to her plea. I knew precisely what it felt like to worry over the well being of a child's heart.

"I doona wish to hurt him." I paused, unsure of why I felt compelled to explain anything to her. "But, we are from verra different worlds. I'm not sure there is anything either of us can do about that."

"There is always something to be done. You only have to decide whether or not you want to put forth the effort."

Turning before I could respond, she turned and fled the room, leaving me to think on all she'd said.

I wanted to be with Malcolm this night—I wouldn't deny myself that—but deep down I knew sleeping with him could only have two possible results. Tomorrow I would either wake happy and full of clarity, or I would wake utterly and completely miserable with confusion.

I took my time before joining Malcolm downstairs. I needed a few moments to reset my mood—to open myself up to the possibility of intimacy once again. After taking a quick glance in the mirror, I nervously made my way to the staircase. Malcolm stood in the living room, in front of the fireplace as he stoked away at the logs he'd just added to the fire.

"I wasn't sure at first, but it turns out her surprise visit wasn't such a terrible thing after all, was it."

He must've heard my footsteps for he didn't turn and look at me as I approached. Hesitantly, I wrapped my arms around him from behind and pressed myself against him for warmth.

He sighed, hung the fire poker back on its hook, and turned into me, winding his hands through my hair as he did so.

"It must be near morning now. It felt as if she was here forever."

Laughing, I leaned back to bare my neck to him as he bent to kiss it.

"I doona believe she even stayed an hour. We still have the whole night."

Malcolm ceased his soft touches up and down my neck as he pulled away and regarded me sternly.

"Thank God for that. For, Kenna, I plan to spend the rest of the night exploring and tasting every last inch of you. That is..." He hesitated, and I didn't miss how his lower lip trembled just slightly. "If you'll allow me."

I wanted to be with him in every way that I possibly could.

Smiling, I nodded and reached for the collar of his shirt.

"I want ye to make love to me, Malcolm. Over and over again until I am too blissfully weary to do anything other than sleep."

In answer, he gently spun me away from him, and gently pulled down the zipper at the back of my dress. It hung loosely at my shoulders, and he moved his lips to my cheek kissing it softly before dragging his tongue down the arch of my neck. I shivered at the sensation as his hands slipped through the opening in the back of my dress, sliding against my bare skin.

I gasped as his hands cupped my breasts. When he moved to gently tug at my nipple with his fingers, I moaned and leaned into him.

He shifted and my dress began to slip. Instinctively, my arms jerked upward to prevent its fall.

"Wait."

Malcolm stilled immediately, quickly withdrawing his hands before stepping away from me.

"What is it? Do you want me to stop?"

With arms crossed over my front to keep the dress up, I faced him.

"No. The verra last thing I want ye to do is stop. 'Tis only that I'm frightened, Mac. I havena...'tis been a verra long time since anyone saw me naked."

Relief washed over Malcolm's face as he smiled and stepped close to me, wrapping his arms around me in an embrace that helped to melt away my fears.

"Come here, Kenna."

He turned and walked to the couch, leaving me to follow him as I continued to cling to the front of my dress.

Once I was seated next to him, he placed his hands on the sides of my face and kissed me until I was warm and tingling all over. When he pulled away, his voice was strained with need. "I don't think any man enjoys vulnerability, Kenna, but for you I will lay myself bare. I am frightened too. So frightened that if I weren't pressing my legs into the ground right this second, I'm afraid my legs might tremble. It's been a very long time for both of us. There is no need for us to rush tonight. I will take as much time as you wish me to."

Knowing that I wasn't alone in my nerves was all I needed to hear. Rising, I allowed the dress to fall down to my waist as I crawled into his lap and began to kiss him.

True to his word, and ever the gentleman, he did take his time, undressing himself before pulling the dress off me completely and laying me backwards on the makeshift bed. We explored and tasted one another slowly. When we finally did come together, it was all I could do to keep from weeping at the pleasure that rolled over and through me as we rocked together in unison.

I'd heard whisperings of what lovemaking could be between a man and a woman—the feelings one could experience when two people came together as one.

Until now, I'd never experienced it for myself.

I would never, ever be the same.

---

*T*horoughly sated, deliriously happy, and now rather hungry, Malcolm sat across from Kenna by the fire where they both sat draped in sheets as they munched on a bag of microwave popcorn and sipped on glasses of wine. While he didn't believe that either of them had ever held much back from another, their shared intimacy had opened them both up in a way that had them sharing with each other like never before. He could scarcely believe his ears now.

"You can't be serious. Ever?"

Kenna smiled, laughed, and popped a handful of kernels in her mouth. He loved that she didn't wait to finish eating to answer him. She spoke as she munched, and it made him feel even closer to her.

"Aye, I am verra serious. I always knew it was supposed to be possible, but my late husband was never overly concerned with how pleasurable the experience might be for me. Sex was for creating our children, little more."

Malcolm shook his head in disbelief. What sort of a fool could show her such little care?

"The man sounds like a damned moron."

Kenna reached for a log behind her and tossed it into the fire as she laughed.

"I'll not speak ill of my sons' father, but I willna disagree with ye, either. Do ye know, Malcolm, thinking on the young girl I'd once been, I believe I know the sort of man I would've chosen for myself had I been given the choice. I believe it would've been someone like ye—someone who knew how to show strength and gentleness in equal measure, someone who showed kindness in all things, and who knew how to laugh. Someone who made me feel wanted."

He was certain he'd never been given such a kind compliment. He hardly saw himself in such a good light.

"I wish I had known you then, Kenna. Or, at the very least, I wish I'd met you ten years ago, when we were both far enough past the loss of our spouses to be open to new love. It would've given us so much more time than we can ever have now."

A sadness crossed Kenna's face, and the melancholy feeling quickly spread through Malcolm, as well.

"Kenna..." He paused, not wanting to ruin the evening but knowing they couldn't avoid the conversation forever. "Did you mean what you told me before? Do you really intend for this to end when I drop you off at Morna and Jerry's tomorrow?"

She scooted near him and leaned into his chest.

"I doona want it to be over, but I must see first. There is someone I must speak to, to see what might be possible."

Who besides the two of them would need to have any say in how things progressed? Malcolm couldn't imagine, but he knew better than to question her too much.

"I want you to know, Kenna, I will want you for as long as you want me. Whatever happens from here on out is entirely up to you."

And he meant it. If she would have him, he was hers. He would do anything he needed to do to make it work.

He only hoped she would give him the chance.

The drive from Edinburgh to Morna and Jerry's the next morning was an awkward one. We were both exhausted, and the great joy of the night before seemed to put a damper on our feelings of today. Neither of us knew for sure where our relationship would go from here and the uncertainty had us both out of sorts.

I'd already decided that I wanted Malcolm in my life for much longer than the end of today, but until I spoke with Morna, I couldn't know for sure if my hopes were foolish. How many families could Morna safely expose her magic to? Our relationship would put her most at risk. I would say nothing to Malcolm until I spoke to her.

I rode for the first hour thinking about all of the possibilities— all of the ways Morna might respond to my request. Thankfully, Malcolm eventually spoke, breaking the silence and providing me with a distraction from my nervous thoughts.

"Kenna, do you remember how when we got to Edinburgh, you mentioned that you could arrange a tour of McMillan Castle for Rosie and me?"

I'd forgotten, but I'd most assuredly meant every word. Kamden and Harper would both be thrilled to show them around.

"Aye, were ye thinking about taking Rosie there on yer way back? 'Tis out of the way, but 'tis worth the trip."

He smiled at me and reached over to squeeze my hand. The simple contact seemed to ease the tension inside the car—as if his touch broke through an invisible barrier between us.

"Yes, that's what I was thinking. I know she won't be happy to leave. I hoped that if I could tempt her with the promise of something I know she's wanted to see for a while, she might make it a little easier on me."

"Aye, I think it could be just the thing to make leaving easier for her. I'll call them as soon as we get to Morna's."

"Thank you." He lifted my left hand and kissed it. I leaned toward him as much as the barrier in between our seats would allow.

"'Tis no trouble at all."

"Kenna..." He paused the way he often did before asking me a question. It seemed to be a habit of his. I found it rather endearing.

"Aye?"

"There's a question that has been on my mind since the first night I met you, but there hasn't really been an appropriate time to ask it. I'm afraid it will make you sad, but I'd very much like to know."

He had to know that after such a statement, any female would be too curious to discourage whatever his question might be. Whatever could he ask me that would make me sad?

"Being sad shall hardly kill me. Ask whatever 'tis."

"That first night we met, when I thanked you for not showing me pity, you said you'd experienced your own share of grief. I know you lost your husband, but after all you've said of him, I think you must've meant something more."

Knowing that I intended to share more of my life with him meant that I wanted him to truly know me—to know and understand my wounds as well as my joys.

"Aye, I did. The grief I referred to...a few years ago I lost a son."

I'd never spoken of Niall to anyone outside of my family, and I hardly knew how to do so now.

"My son wasna a good man. He had an evil in him that I was blind to for far too long. While I refuse to take responsibility for his actions, I do sometimes wonder." My voice caught as the inevitable lump rose in the back of my throat. Turning away, I allowed the tears to fall as I continued. "I...I sometimes wonder if I had I seen who he really was sooner, perhaps I could have done something to prevent everything that happened."

Without a word, the car slowed as Malcolm pulled to a stop on the side of the road. He waited until I faced him to speak.

"I will show you the same courtesy that you showed me. I will give you no pity, but I don't believe this is the sort of discussion one should have while driving. I want you to know that I hear you and that I recognize the strength it must've taken for you to get through something so horrible. I am sorry, Kenna. You only have to tell me what you wish to."

It was right of him to recognize that I would be as reluctant to someone's pity as he was, and I appreciated the space he created for me to tell him the story. I did so for the better part of an hour. Sobbing, I told him things that I didn't even know I needed to say out loud—things I could never say to my family, for they were too intimately connected to all that had happened. Having someone outside of the situation made it so much easier.

"I think what pains me the most is the undeniable truth that I still love him. I shouldna love such a monster. But even years since his passing, even knowing that he murdered my first daughter-in-law, knowing that he murdered my sister and tried to kill his brother and me, I still love him fiercely. 'Tis why it took me so long to see the truth—we mothers always believe the best of our children. Perhaps, 'tis what it means to be a mother—no matter the joy it can bring, it can also be the most painful thing in the world."

Malcolm had tears in his eyes, too, but not tears of pity—his gaze made that clear. They were the tears of empathy. While one separates, the other binds. I'd not thought it possible for me to feel closer to him than I had last night, but in some way this story was even more personal than sharing my body with him. I'd never felt so close to anyone.

"Of course you still love him. Love, once truly given, doesn't ever go away. And there is no truer love than that of a parent for their child."

He brushed the hair from my face and stroked my cheek as I drew in shaky breaths.

I knew I needed no one's permission to love Niall, but just hearing Malcolm acknowledge that it was okay made me feel so much less alone. I felt free for the first time in years, as if some poison within me had finally been flushed away.

"I've never cried in front of anyone the way I just cried in front of ye, but now I'm quite ready to stop. Do ye know any good jokes, Malcolm?"

He chuckled just a little and raised his brows mischievously.

"Not a one, but I think I know of something that might put a smile back on that beautiful face of yours."

I was open to anything.

"What?"

He grinned and reached to open the door on his side of the car.

"Get out for a minute. I'll show you."

No sooner did I step out of the vehicle than I was smacked directly in the middle of my chest with a giant snowball.

Chaos ensued as we played and wrestled in a giant field of snow just off the road in the middle of nowhere.

We arrived at Morna and Jerry's two hours later than expected, soaked through, looking utterly a mess, and blissfully happy by each other's side.

Our late arrival at the inn changed everyone's plans—not that anyone minded. Rather than head to McMillan Castle for their tour today, Malcolm and Rosie would leave tomorrow. The extra time together gave me hope that I would be able to speak with Morna before they left, and one way or another I would be able to tell Malcolm how things could move forward.

While the days spent together had made Cooper tolerable to Rosie, it was evident that it would still take much convincing for her to consider him a friend. Ever the determined young lad, Cooper wasn't worried in the least.

"Nana, I think I'm in love."

"Really?" Smiling at him as he entered my room, I patted the bed so he would come and sit down. I'd just finished drying my hair from the snow fight and was carefully applying just a little bit of make-up so I would look presentable for dinner. "What makes you think so?"

"Do you remember when Dad was falling in love with Kathleen?"

I nodded, laid the lipstick down, and faced my grandson. "Aye."

"He was so grumpy and strange, but he still wanted to be around her. That's how I feel now, Nana. I shouldn't want to be around someone that dislikes me so much, but..." he held up both palms and shrugged as he shook his head, "for some reason, I kinda like it that she's so mean to me."

Laughing, I moved to pull him into a hug.

"'Tis something I will never understand, but it seems to be common amongst men, Cooper. Perhaps, ye are right. Ye may have gotten yer first taste of love."

He pulled away and grinned up at me with excited eyes.

"Should I tell her?"

Panic ran through me as I dropped to my knees to discourage him.

"Ach, no lad, I wouldna do that if I were ye. I doona think Rosie would take to it well, and while those first feelings of love can be verra powerful and they come on verra fast, they also often pass just as quickly."

Thankfully, Cooper didn't seem bothered by my dissuasion. He nodded as if he understood and moved toward the doorway.

"Okay, good thinkin', Nana. I'll wait."

"Good, I truly think that best, Cooper. Are ye headed downstairs?"

He nodded and reached for the doorknob.

"If Morna isna busy, will you ask her to come up here? I'd really like to speak to her."

"Sure thing, Nana. She's not busy. She's just watching Rosie cook. She's gonna make the whole thing by herself tonight."

There was such admiration in Cooper's voice when he spoke of Rosie. There was no question—my grandson had found his very first crush.

The smells coming from the kitchen were wonderful. Situating his bag next to his pallet on the living room floor, a freshly showered and dry Malcolm called out to Morna to see if he could offer some help.

"Morna, that smells fantastic. Is there anything I can do to help you?"

Rosie's voice answered him.

"It's me, Pops. Morna's not in here."

He stepped into the kitchen to see his granddaughter smiling the first true smile he'd seen on her since arriving in Scotland. Standing proud in front of the stove, she wore an apron that hung just a little too long. It didn't matter that she had to stand on her tiptoes to look down at the food, she appeared to know exactly what she was doing.

"Are you making all of this yourself?"

She reached for a spoon, dipped it into the pot she worked over, then carefully balanced it over her hand as she walked over to him.

"Yes. Morna watched me for a little while just to make sure I didn't have any questions, but when she saw I had it mastered, she went to go see Kenna. She's letting me do everything on my own tonight. Here, taste it."

Taking a brief second to blow on the stew, he placed the spoonful in his mouth.

"It's delicious."

Rosie regarded him skeptically.

"Really? You don't have to lie to me."

"Really, Rosie. It's wonderful. I can't believe you learned so much in just a few days."

Malcolm would be forever grateful to Morna for the way she'd turned this holiday around for his granddaughter. It seemed the old woman had known just what Rosie needed.

"Morna is a great teacher, Pops. She even taught me how to

read UK recipes. They use measurements that are pretty different than how we do things back home, but it didn't take me long to get the hang of it. It actually makes more sense than what we use. Pops..." Rosie laid down the spoon and surprised him by wrapping her arms around his waist. "Thank you for letting me stay. I know I wasn't very nice to you. I'm sorry. I was just...I was just sad."

He bent to kiss the top of her head. If he loved the child any more than he already did, he worried his heart would burst from it.

"I know, kiddo. It's okay to be sad. Just a few more days and then your Mom should be here."

"I hope so, Pops. I really, really do. But even if she doesn't come, this has already been one of my favorite Christmases ever."

"Well, it sounds like you need to thank Morna for that, Rosie."

"No, Pops. It's not Morna that made this great. It was you. If you hadn't tried to cheer me up by booking that tour to Conall Castle, we would've never stayed here."

The decision had been so last minute. All he'd wanted was to get Rosie out of the house in the hopes of making her smile. How could he have possibly known that such an outing would change so much for both of them?

Even if things didn't turn out how he hoped, he would treasure his time spent with Kenna for the rest of his life.

"You know what, Rosie? This has already been one of my favorite Christmases, too."

"*D*id ye really believe for a moment that I would say ye couldna tell him, Kenna?"

I didn't know Morna as well as many of the members of my family. While I knew she often allowed matters of the heart to direct her decisions, in my mind, it was still entirely possible that she could reject my suggestion.

"I dinna know."

Morna patted my knee in a motherly fashion.

"Lass, 'twas I who encouraged ye to see if the two of ye had something together. It pleases me more than ye know that ye do. I thought on this quite a lot while ye were in Edinburgh. As ye know, there have been many I've had to share my magic with over the years, and if one thing is for certain, 'tis rarely knowledge they accept easily. I think I know of a way that might make him more accepting."

I'd seen first hand what a difficult time Grace's sister, Jane, in particular, had with learning of time travel and the magic that surrounded pretty much all who knew Morna. If the old witch had any idea as to how to make it easier for Malcolm to accept, I would allow her to direct our next steps.

"Morna, ye have done this many more times than I. Whatever ye wish me to do, I shall do it."

"Good. Pack yer bags and tell Cooper to do the same. When Malcolm and Rosie leave in the morning, we are going to McMillan Castle with them."

"Are ye so ready to be rid of us, Morna? Ye do know that Cooper and I were meant to stay with ye for another week, aye?"

"Aye, I know 'twas the original plan, but it no longer fits with what needs to be done. Ye need to be at McMillan Castle with Malcolm. If ye and Cooper will be headed there anyway, ye may as well go home afterward."

While Cooper was normally very sympathetic to the needs of others, he wouldn't be so forgiving of anyone who shortened his time with Morna.

"I canna do that to Cooper, Morna. He's looked forward to his time here for so long."

Morna stood, quickly dismissing my concern.

"Doona worry about that, lass. Much as I loathe to admit it, I lost a bet with the lad, and my loss has caused me to do something that I've sworn more than once I wouldna do again."

I knew from experience that it was never a good idea to make bets with Cooper. He never forgave a debt, and I knew of only one thing that Morna had vocally promised to never do again.

"Ye canna mean...?"

"Aye. I hope the wee lad knows how much I love him, for he is the only one that could get me to agree to go back once again. It seems Jerry and I will be spending Christmas in the year 1651."

"Oh, Morna!" I stood and threw my arms around her as she laughed. "I've not heard such good news in a verra long time. Everyone at the castle will be so excited. We must send word to everyone—all of the relatives—and have them come stay, too. It will be a grand reunion. We are long overdue for one anyway."

Morna sniffled, and I pulled back with shock to see that she was crying.

"Well, if I shall be there anyway, then I would verra much love to see everyone."

Gripping her shoulders, I gave them a reassuring squeeze.

"Then we shall make certain that ye do. Now, tell me. Just how should I explain everything to Malcolm once we get to McMillan Castle?"

The nerves I felt standing nearly naked before Malcolm were nothing compared to the nerves I felt walking into the grand room of McMillan Castle. Morna was right—it was the perfect place to tell him the truth. My likeness hung in the room, right in line with the dozens of portraits of my ancestors and the descendants that would come after me. It would be a sure way to get him curious for the portrait looked exactly like me. Only in the McMillan Castle of today, the woman in the portrait should've been dead for hundreds of years.

While it would help raise the question in his mind, he would still believe me mad. Any sane person would. Thankfully, McMillan Castle provided quick access back to my own time where I could show him in person. Morna, Kamden, and Harper were in on the plan, too. They would keep Cooper and Rosie occupied and away from this part of the castle for the next few hours—plenty of time for me to tell him what I must and also to take a quick trip back into the past to prove that all I said was true.

After that, it would be up to him. If it turned out to be too much, he and Rosie could leave, and I would officially let go of the dream of being with Malcolm.

"Where did everyone else run off to?"

"I believe they are ice skating on the pond. Then they plan to go on a carriage ride through the grounds."

His expression was quizzical.

"Are we not joining them?"

"No, Malcolm. I need to speak with ye."

"Do you intend to put me out of my misery? Please say that you are. I don't think I can stand another moment of wondering. Rosie and I leave this afternoon. I made myself very clear to you in Edinburgh. I want you. I want to be with you, and if all continues to go as well as it has the past few days, I want to enjoy the next forty years of my life with you at my side. But I need to know, Kenna...do you want me, too? Did you find whatever answers you needed—speak to whomever you needed to speak to?"

"Aye, Malcolm." I hurried to his side, reaching up to kiss him as his nearness helped my fears fade. "I want ye. I want ye more than anything I've wanted in my entire life. And aye, I spoke to whom I needed to. But there is something I must tell ye. It may change the way ye feel about our future together."

Reassuringly, he took my hands and kissed them.

"I don't think there is anything you could tell me that would do that."

Pulling one of my hands from his grip, I pointed to my portrait behind him.

"I want ye to look at that painting, Malcolm."

He turned and stared at my likeness for a long moment before speaking.

"Wow. I knew you were a McMillan, but you're a McMillan by marriage, correct? How could a McMillan ancestor resemble you so much?"

"'Tis not an ancestor. The woman in that painting is me."

Malcolm's brows pulled together in confusion, and his mouth opened and closed several times without a word.

Just as he started to speak, his phone rang.

Instinctively, I knew the call was not good news.

cMillan Castle – December of 1651
Three Days Later

I didn't cry upon returning home to my own century. It wasn't as if Malcolm had broken my heart or disbelieved my story. In truth, I'd not given him the chance to do either of those things. Malcolm's phone call from his daughter had made the absurdity of my dream for us clear.

The lives of his daughter and granddaughter were in America. Even if he loved me—which I knew he did—he would no sooner ask them to uproot their lives than I would ask my family to uproot theirs. Even if I told him about the magic, it would bring our worlds no closer together.

"Your skin looks better, but other than that, you look worse than I've ever seen you. It's been three days, Kenna. I know that you and I aren't very close, but you have to tell someone what happened while you were away. I'm nosy enough to hound you about it even though I can see you're hurting, so it might as well be me. Now spill."

It didn't surprise me in the least that Adelle would enter my room without knocking. She wouldn't leave me alone until I told her something. I would tell her only what was absolutely true. Not a word more.

"I fell in love. As foolish as it sounds, I fell in love with a great man in a matter of only a few days, but it couldna ever work. I'll not upend his world by telling him the where and how I live when our love is doomed from the start. He's gone. Back to America with his granddaughter, which is exactly where he should be. I'll not speak of this again. 'Tis too painful and I'll not be sad at Christmas for 'twould only spoil the season for everyone else. Please leave me, Adelle, and doona ask me anything else."

She must've recognized just how much my heart was aching, for in a move quite out of character for her, she turned and left me without another word.

I did cry then. It was well into the night before I fell asleep, my pillow soaked with tears.

Chicago

Malcolm was angry—angrier than he'd ever been. It made no sense. None of it. Just minutes after telling him that she wanted him more than anything she'd wanted in her life, Kenna ended things with a coldness that nearly knocked him over.

All he'd done was announce that he and Rosie would have to fly back to America before Christmas. It had been Madeline on the phone with the news he'd hoped wouldn't come, but expected anyway. She'd decided not to come to Edinburgh for Christmas, after all. Despite the fact that his daughter had insisted that he and Rosie stay to enjoy Christmas in Scotland, he knew in that instant what they must do. For his daughter to believe it was acceptable for her to choose not to spend Christmas with Rosie, well, that was a line he simply wouldn't allow her to cross. His daughter needed a reality check. If that meant he would have to cut their trip short to give it to her, he would gladly do so.

He never expected such an announcement to incite such a shocking reaction from Kenna. She had children—children she loved more than life itself. He'd been so certain she would understand.

Instead, even as he tried to explain to her, to tell her that while he must go back to Chicago now, he would come back to Edinburgh for the new year so they could work things out and decide best how to make their relationship work, she'd had none of it. She ended things quickly, bidding him farewell as if he were little more than a stranger.

He still couldn't wrap his mind around the fact that it was truly over. What had happened to change her mind? And what had she been about to tell him? Her nonsense about the portrait was still a mystery. It was almost as perplexing as what she'd said to him about Edinburgh Castle on the night of the whisky tasting.

There'd been so much anticipation, so much excitement, and then in seconds, it was all gone. His heart hurt in a way he didn't know was possible.

"Dad?" His daughter's voice stirred him from his thoughts as she spoke to him from the chair next to his in the living room of their home. "Where are you? It's definitely not here."

He answered her unthinkingly. "You of all people have no right to speak to me of being away."

His daughter jerked back as if he'd slapped her. "What is that supposed to mean?

While Malcolm regretted the abrupt nature of his words, such a conversation with his daughter was long overdue. While it was always best to speak when not angry, he doubted he would feel a sense of calm ever again. And what he needed to say to Madeline was too important. If she didn't wake up from her selfishness soon, her relationship with Rosie would be irreparable.

"Madeline, you know exactly what I mean. I know that losing Tim was difficult for you and I have tried to give you the space you needed to grieve, but this has gone far beyond that. You're punishing your daughter for something that isn't her fault—you're avoiding her because she looks like him. She sees you pulling away. And as much as it breaks her heart to do so, she's pulling away from you, too. She knows that she must in order to protect herself."

Madeline's face was red and angry and tears pooled in her eyes as she answered him, her voice shaky.

"You don't know what you're talking about. I'm not punishing her. It's just...it's too hard, Dad."

His own voice rose with his anger.

"Tough. Life's hard. If you think you're the only one that has ever gone through something, then you need to pull your head out of your ass. You lost your mother when you were Rosie's age. What would it have done to you if I'd treated you the way you treat Rosie? You'd think you'd see that. It's exactly the same thing. You look just like your mother. It was hard for me, too, but I wasn't as selfish. I'm not sure I've ever known anyone as selfish as you, and I won't put up with it anymore."

"Put up with it?"

Madeline was screaming at him now, and Malcolm knew Rosie would hear them. Maybe that was okay. He wanted his granddaughter to know that he was willing to fight for her.

"Yes, Madeline. I won't put up with it."

"Put up with it?" His daughter repeated herself, the octave of her voice high and filled with venom. She was shaking all over. "This is my house, Dad. Did I ask you to move in here? No, I did not. You did it after Tim died because you insisted that I needed you. Perhaps for a time, you were right, but I don't need you anymore. Pack your things and get out. You are no longer welcome in my home."

For the second time in the span of a week, Malcolm's world collapsed.

hristmas Day

A knock on his hotel room door woke him just past nine in the morning, Christmas Day. He hoped to spend the day sleeping. Perhaps then, he would pass the holiday without reflecting on the fact that it was his first Christmas spent alone.

Losing Kenna was difficult enough, but being away from his granddaughter on her favorite day of the year was unbearable.

"Room service. I've got your breakfast here."

The voice was strange, oddly high for anyone old enough to be working in a hotel.

Flipping the lamp on next to the bed, he called out in answer. "I didn't order any room service. You must have the wrong room."

There was a slight pause, and then, "It...It's free on Christmas Day."

Hope coursed through Malcolm's body. It almost sounded like Rosie, but of course, that couldn't be so.

"I'm not hungry."

"Oh, come on, Pops. You're really making it hard for me to surprise you. I've been up since five waiting to come and get you, but Mom made me wait until the sun was up."

Tears filled Malcolm's eyes as he stood from the bed, threw on his sweats and a shirt and ran to the door to pull his granddaughter into a hug.

"What are you doing here?"

She squirmed until he released her.

"I already told you, Pops. Mom and I have a big surprise for you. She's in the car downstairs. You gotta hurry."

Reaching for his coat, he left his other belongings in the room. Everything that he needed was right in front of him.

*

Inside Madeline and Rosie's home—he was no longer sure he could call it his own—Malcolm walked into a living room filled with wrapping paper. Open packages lay sprawled out all over the floor. Only one unwrapped present remained under the tree.

"What can the surprise be? You two already did the fun part without me."

"Oh, no we didn't. This wasn't nearly as exciting as your present. Mom just let me open these so I would stop bugging her about going to get you so early."

He didn't think he'd ever seen Rosie so excited about anything.

"Ah. Well, I can't imagine what it could be. Do you want me to sit?"

"You better, Pops. Otherwise, I think you might fall over."

Madeline walked up behind him and wrapped one arm around his waist, pulling him into a hug.

"Rosie, you're going to give it away if you're not careful. Why don't you grab it and bring it over here?"

As Rosie walked to the tree, Madeline turned to look up at him. "I'm so sorry. You were right about everything. That's the only reason I got so mad. I knew you were right even as I was screaming at you. I just couldn't stand what I'd done. I love you, Dad. "

"Oh, Madeline." He kissed the top of her head as if she were a small child. To him, she always would be. "I love you more than you will ever know. I'm sorry for how harsh I was. I should've gone about it another way."

"No, Dad. I don't think I would've been able to really hear it if you had. It was the first time in my life I think I saw you really, truly angry, and I believe it may have saved my life. It woke me from a fog I was in for far too long."

Rosie was back by their side, pulling at his arm to try to get him to the couch. "Come on, come on. You gotta open it now."

As soon as he sat down, Rosie placed the package in his lap. He carefully began to unwrap the paper. Rosie was bouncing up and down in her seat as he opened the box. As he looked down at the contents, all he could feel was confusion.

Packing tape, labels, and a business card for a Chicago realtor lay inside.

"Is this a polite way of telling me that you've found me a house of my own?"

Rosie leaned across him to shoot her mother a disapproving look.

"I told Mom that it wasn't nice to trick you that way. Lift that stuff up, there's something else underneath."

At the bottom of the box were two envelopes.

"Open the one on the left first, Dad."

Following his daughter's directive, he picked up the envelope on the left and carefully broke its seal. Pulling its contents free, he unfolded the papers, and read aloud, "Dear Mr. Kilmer, I would like to inform you that I am resigning my position at Mercy General Hospital effective January 7th."

He stopped and looked over at his daughter in bewilderment. "Madeline, is this real or another part of the joke?"

Rosie answered. "It's real, Pops. I went with her when she delivered it. Now, open the other one. It's the best one."

His curiosity caused him to be less careful with the opening of the second letter. Turning the contents over so they would spill onto his lap, he stared at the tickets as he struggled to comprehend what all of this could mean.

"It's three one-way tickets to Scotland, Pops!"

"I see that, Rosie. You were right. I'm glad you told me to sit down. Now will the two of you please tell me what's going on before I lose my mind?"

Rosie pointed at her mother. "Take it away, Mom. This part's all you."

Twisting, Malcolm directed all of his attention to Madeline, his confusion giving way to curiosity and a glimmer of hope that frightened him more than he wished to admit.

"Come on, Madeline. What is this?"

"I didn't sleep for the first twenty-four hours after you left. I want you to know that I've thought through all of this. It isn't some knee-jerk decision. Rosie and I have discussed this extensively and she is one hundred percent on board."

"I sure am!"

Malcolm turned to wink at Rosie before waving his hand toward Madeline so she would continue.

"Chicago has too many memories—too much pain—for all of us. We all need a fresh start. All of our family is in Scotland now anyway. It's the only place that makes sense for us to move to. Plus, I need a slower pace of life, and the job that I've been offered sounds like just the thing that will give me that."

Malcolm could scarcely believe how quickly his worst nightmare was turning into his greatest joy.

"You already have a job?"

"Yes. As you know, Emilia's mother is the director of a home health agency that oversees a large portion of Scotland. They have need of a new nurse on the Isle of Skye, and she's offered me the job. Grandma Nel has agreed to let us all live with her in Edinburgh until Rosie and I can find the perfect place."

"Just you and Rosie?"

"Yes, Dad, just me and Rosie. Skye isn't that close to Edinburgh, but it's not all that far from McMillan Castle. Rosie told me about Kenna. That's where you need to be. It's time that I learn to stand on my own two feet. You'll still be able to see us all the time."

Sadness filled him at the mention of Kenna's name.

"Kenna doesn't want me. She made that very clear."

Rosie rose from the couch and moved to stand in front of him, blocking the space between him and Madeline.

"Don't be stupid, Pops. Of course she wants you. She just got scared is all. You gave up on that *way* too easy."

Madeline's head appeared beside Rosie's as she leaned over to speak to him.

"I don't know this Kenna, but I bet Rosie is right, so here's the plan, Dad. We will enjoy Christmas Day here together. I have a breakfast casserole and some coffee cake in the oven now. Then, you'll start packing, because your flight leaves tomorrow. Rosie and I will meet you over there after the New Year. Go and get her, Dad. It's way past time for you to be happy again."

McMillan Castle – 1651

Christmas Day was over, but the celebrations at McMillan Castle would last until after New Year's Day. With Morna and Jerry visiting us in the seventeenth century, it had taken no convincing to get all of our distant family and friends from all over Scotland to join us at the castle. The Conalls—those who had remained at their home when Bri and Adelle came—made the trip over, and all of those at Cagair Castle made the journey, as well. McMillan Castle was bursting at the seams with guests, but not one person complained. We were all thrilled to spend the holidays with those we loved most in the world.

The one downside to the large number of guests, however, was that it was nearly impossible to find a single blessed moment for one's self. I was a woman who required solitude more than just about anything. It was why my early morning hours were so precious. Even those were no longer possible—guests were staying in the room in which I always lit my morning fires.

The day after Christmas, in the late afternoon while all of the children were occupied or sleeping and their parents were outside enjoying a sleigh ride around the castle grounds, I saw my opportunity to escape to my bedchamber for just a little while.

I'd looked forward to the quiet all day, but rather than finding my room empty, I stepped inside to see what could only possibly be a ghost or a delusion.

Malcolm, dressed in clothing not suited to this time, stood a few arm lengths away.

"Wha...How?"

I stuttered as he faced me.

"Morna led me to your room. Kenna, this has been one of the longest days of my life. My head aches, and it isn't just from the time travel. Please get over here and kiss me so I will know I wasn't a fool to come all this way for you."

I nearly fell over from the shock of seeing him here. Even as I crossed the short distance between us and allowed him to take me in his arms, I couldn't make sense of it. I allowed the kiss to go on until he pulled away.

"Is this why you panicked, Kenna? You didn't want to tell me about all of this?"

I answered with my arms still wrapped around him and my face pressed against his chest. I didn't want to be away from him ever again.

"I did want to tell ye. I tried to the day ye left. 'Tis only that when yer daughter called, I knew if I told ye, 'twould be the most selfish thing I could ever do. I couldna bring myself to do it. Yer family is in America, Malcolm, and I wouldna ever ask ye to leave them. And no matter how much I love ye, ye must know that I canna ever leave my family, either. 'Tis more than just distance that separates us—time does as well."

Malcolm's hands found their way to my shoulders as he pulled me away from him so he could look straight at me.

"Do you love me, Kenna?"

The question surprised me. I thought we'd both made that abundantly clear in Edinburgh.

"Ye know that I do."

"I suspected, I hoped, but I don't believe you've ever said the words before now."

Moving my hands to his face, I stood on my tiptoes and kissed him once more.

"Well, let there be no question about it. I love ye, Malcolm, and I always shall."

Stepping away from him, reality began to set in once more.

"And while I canna tell ye just how glad I am that ye are here and that ye know of Morna's magic, it solves nothing between us. What is it that ye are doing back in Scotland, and how did ye come to know all that ye do? Ye must feel verra out of sorts."

Malcolm laughed and moved to sit on the end of the bed. He looked beyond weary. I knew how exhausting the time travel could be and I'd not experienced it the first time just seconds after learning that something I always thought impossible was very much real. Once he did fall asleep tonight, I expected he would sleep for a whole day, at least.

"I'm not sure that describes the half of it. The flight from Chicago was bad enough. My long legs are not made for eight hours on today's airplanes, and the moment I landed, I rented a car and made the long drive to McMillan Castle. I was so ready to see you, Kenna. But then I arrived only to be told that you weren't there."

"Was it Kamden and Harper that told ye the truth?"

"Yes, and I believe I owe them both an apology. I lost my patience with them. I thought they were simply making an excuse for you. I didn't believe a word until they all but forced me into the tower. Once you actually make the travel, it's rather hard to continue denying it. Kenna, how is this possible?"

I shrugged. There were so many things in life that seemed rather impossible to me.

"I doona know, but 'tis the reality of our lives around here, and if ye wish to be with me, 'twill be one of yers, as well. Do ye wish that ye dinna know?"

He still looked rather dazed. It would take days for him to fully adapt to his new perception of reality, but I was still relieved when he shook his head.

"Not at all. It explains a lot actually—your reaction to my credit card, your fascination with the lights at the symphony. Many things are beginning to click into place. I can't believe I'm in love with someone who was born over three hundred years before I was."

I didn't like the way that sounded at all.

"For the love o'God, Malcolm, doona ever say that again. Ye are older than me, in truth. Doona ye ever forget that."

He laughed then gripped his head.

"Doona worry. We do have some modern medicines here that should help that." I hesitated, but I knew that no matter how much I didn't want to hear his answer, it was a question that had to be asked. "Malcolm, what about yer family?"

"That's the thing, Kenna. It's not the issue you think it is. We're moving to Scotland—all of us. I'm already here, and Madeline and Rosie are coming just after the New Year. They will be living on Skye, which isn't all that far from here, so even with this strange business of time travel, we should be able to see them often. There's only one problem."

"Oh?" If we could be together and still be with our families, there was no other problem that was insurmountable. "What might that be?"

He stood and began to pace nervously in front of me.

"Kenna, I had a very different idea of what I was going to ask you this morning, but now after knowing what I do, I'm not sure it would be appropriate. Will you stand for a minute?"

Completely confused, I did as he asked. The moment he dropped to one knee, I jumped away from him in horror.

"Malcolm, what are ye doing? Stand up this instant."

Brows furrowed, he stood and gripped onto my bedpost for support.

"You...you don't want to marry me?"

I was suddenly getting a headache, as well. I pinched the bridge of my nose as I answered him.

"No. I love ye, Malcolm, but no. Not yet anyway. Why would ye ask that now?"

An expression I'd never seen on him before—one of pure embarrassment—crossed his face. He quickly looked down at the floor to avoid my gaze.

"I...you're right. I wasn't thinking. What I was going to ask you, what I planned to tell you before I learned that you were from the seventeenth century, was that I am currently rather homeless. I was going to ask if I could live with you for a little while. But then..." He started pacing again. "Then, when I learned that you were from the seventeenth century, I got to thinking, and it would hardly be appropriate here, would it?"

Laughing, I walked over and grabbed his hands so he would cease his wandering.

"Malcolm, there is nothing about my family that is customary or appropriate for the times. Even if it were, I've never given much concern to anyone else's opinion of how I live my life. Ye are welcome to live here as long as ye promise not to ask me to marry ye for at least another six months. And even then, I canna promise ye that I will say aye. I might find that living in sin is preferable."

His lips found mine quickly, and his aching head didn't prevent him from loving me in a way that made our night in Edinburgh seem only mediocre. If it was true that some things only got better with age, I couldn't imagine the sort of pleasure we would be able to find with one another in a decade.

It was the happiest holiday season of my whole life.

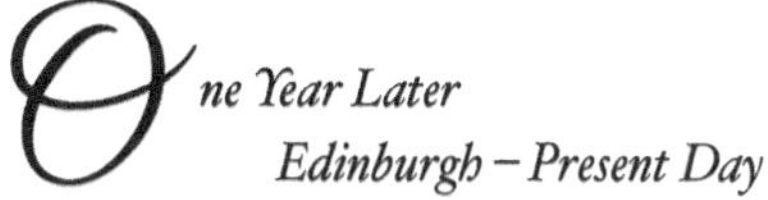

ne Year Later
Edinburgh – Present Day

ix months to the day that Malcolm arrived in the seventeenth century, he risked rejection once again by dropping to one knee. Much to his excitement and everlasting relief, I gave him the answer he hoped for. I very much wanted to be his wife.

We wed in the prettiest little chapel either of us had ever seen, right in the center of Edinburgh. I wore a simple gold gown and Malcolm wore slacks and the sweater I first saw him in. It was intimate, with only those who knew us during our time in Edinburgh in attendance. Cooper stood at my side, while Madeline and Rosie stood at his. Morna, Jerry, Kraig, Emilia, Nel, and the toddler-terror, Robbie, watched on.

It was perfect.

At a certain age, I'd stopped hoping for much more than I had.

But there is so much more magic in the world than we can see. Sometimes, life can surprise you in the very best possible way.

To read all the books in the Morna's Legacy Series, check out the book list on the next page. You can start the series for free with Love Beyond Time.

SUBSCRIBE TO BETHANY'S MAILING LIST

When you sign up for my mailing list, you will be the first to know about new releases, upcoming events, and contests. You will also get sneak peeks into books and have opportunities to participate in special reader groups and occasionally get codes for free books.

Just go to my website (www.bethanyclaire.com) and click the Mailing List link in the header. I can't wait to connect with you there.

Dear Reader,

I hope you enjoyed this special collection of the Christmas novellas in *Morna's Legacy Series*. Christmas is my favorite time of year, so putting these together in a special box set to help you, the reader, save a little money on them was something I really wanted to do. If these are the first books you've read in this series, you are missing out on lots of great love stories. Check the book list to see what titles you've missed.

As an author, I love feedback from readers. You are the reason that I write, and I love hearing from you. If you would like to connect, there are several ways you can do so. You can reach out to me on Facebook or on Twitter or visit my Pinterest boards. If you want to read excerpts from my books, listen to audiobook samples, learn more about me, and find some cool downloadable files related to the books, visit my website.

The best way to stay in touch is to subscribe to my newsletter. Go to my website and click the Mailing List link in the header. If you don't hear from me regularly, please check your spam folder or junk mail to make sure my messages aren't ending up there. Please set up your email to allow my messages through to you so you never miss a new book, a chance to win great prizes or a possible appearance in your area.

Finally, if you enjoyed this book, I would appreciate it so much if you would recommend it to your friends and family. And if you would please take time to review it on Goodreads and/or your favorite retailer site, it would be a great help. Reviews can be tough to come by these days, and you, the reader, have the power to make or break a book.

Thank you so much for reading my stories. I hope you choose to journey with me through the other books in the series.

All my best,

Bethany

ABOUT THE AUTHOR

BETHANY CLAIRE is a USA Today bestselling author of swoon-worthy, Scottish romance and time travel novels. Bethany loves to immerse her readers in worlds filled with lush landscapes, hunky Scots, lots of magic, and happy endings.

She has two ornery fur-babies, plays the piano every day, and loves Disney and yoga pants more than any twenty-something really should. She is most creative after a good night's sleep and the perfect cup of tea. When not writing, Bethany travels as much as she possibly can, and she never leaves home without a good book to keep her company.

If you want to read more about Bethany or if you're curious about when her next book will come out, please visit her website at: www.bethanyclaire.com, where you can sign up to receive email notifications about new releases.